T0407455

NO ESCAPE

PLAGUE LAND

ALSO BY ALEX SCARROW

Plague Land

Plague Land: Reborn

ALEX SCARROW

PLAGUE LAND: NO ESCAPE

First published in the United States in 2019 by Sourcebooks

Copyright © 2018, 2019 by Alex Scarrow
Cover and internal design © 2019 by Sourcebooks
Series design by Elsie Lyons
Cover image © studioalef/Getty Images

Sourcebooks and the colophon are registered trademarks of Sourcebooks, Inc.

All rights reserved. No part of this book may be reproduced in any form or by any electronic or mechanical means including information storage and retrieval systems—except in the case of brief quotations embodied in critical articles or reviews—without permission in writing from its publisher, Sourcebooks.

The characters and events portrayed in this book are fictitious or are used fictitiously. Any similarity to real persons, living or dead, is purely coincidental and not intended by the author.

Published by Sourcebooks Fire, an imprint of Sourcebooks
P.O. Box 4410, Naperville, Illinois 60567-4410
(630) 961-3900
sourcebooks.com

Originally published as *Plague World* in 2018 in the United Kingdom by Macmillan Children's Books, an imprint of Pan Macmillan.

Library of Congress Cataloging-in-Publication Data

Names: Scarrow, Alex, author.
Title: Plague land : no escape / Alex Scarrow.
Other titles: Plague world | No escape
Description: Naperville, IL : Sourcebooks Jabberwocky, 2019. | "Originally
    published as Plague World in 2018 in the United Kingdom by Macmillan
    Children's Books, an imprint of Pan Macmillan"--Title page verso. |
    Summary: After annihilating all of humanity except for those in three
    refugee communities, the virus approaches the remaining humans with a
    choice that will ultimately decide their fate.
Identifiers: LCCN 2019008619 | (trade pbk. : alk. paper)
Subjects: | CYAC: Survival--Fiction. | Virus diseases--Fiction. | Science
    fiction.
Classification: LCC PZ7.S3255 Pj 2019 | DDC [Fic]--dc23 LC record available
    at https://lccn.loc.gov/2019008619

Printed and bound in the United States of America.
VP 10 9 8 7 6 5 4 3 2 1

*To Debbie, beta reader of my first drafts
and editor of my life.*

*Thank you for giving me your love
and taking my name.*

PART 1

PROLOGUE

Two and a Half Years Ago

FREYA WOKE UP BLEARY EYED AND STILL DRESSED FROM LAST night.

She'd gone to sleep late—it was after two o'clock when she'd finally closed her laptop and turned off the TV. She'd plumped up the cushions so she could continue looking out of her bedroom window at the small cul-de-sac. Her mind had raced in the dark for several hours as she replayed the day's headlines about the virus. The tone of panic in them had been increasing throughout the day and evening. Her Facebook feed had become littered with desperate posts from friends around the world, grainy images of bodies in the street that could just as easily have been piles of clothes and trash.

People *really did* panic way too easily on Facebook.

Freya was half-certain that by this morning, the story would have run out of steam and become another overnight Social

ALEX SCARROW

Media Big Nothing, and half-worried that this was it—today would be the Day the World Ended.

She stretched out her aching legs and shuffled her numb rear until she was sitting up and looking down at the houses and driveways across the street.

It looked quiet and still out there as Freya checked her watch: quarter past ten.

She looked up and down the cul-de-sac at all the cars that were usually gone by now. Sunday mornings sometimes looked like this. But today should have been a normal working Wednesday.

And it was way past when she was normally up. Mom should've knocked on her door to wake her a while ago. End of the World or not, she was *supposed* to go to school this morning, and if her watch was right, she'd already missed the first class.

"Crap!" she hissed. "Mom!" she called out. "I'm late!"

No answer. She pulled herself up, wearily wincing at the ever-present aching pain in her hips, and reached for a couple of aspirin on the bedside table, knocking them back with the cold dregs of last night's tea. She reached down for her laptop on the end of her bed.

That's when she saw them through the window: snaking, dark lines running across the road and driveways, like zigzagging pencil scribbles. She leaned over the bed, bracing herself with one hand on the windowsill to get a better look outside. She followed one line across the road, up a driveway, and up to the front step of number 9. The front door was ajar, and the dark scribble seemed to continue on inside.

Or maybe it had come out?

PLAGUE LAND: NO ESCAPE

Next door at number 10, she could see a number of lines converging on a dark hump of clothes lying on the driveway. It looked like one of those grainy images on the internet.

"Mom!" she called out again, starting to panic.

No answer, but she could hear voices downstairs. The TV was on.

She staggered across the bedroom and picked up the walking stick by her door. She stepped out into the hall and glanced through the open door into her parent's room; the bed was made.

Mom usually made it when she came back after her morning shift at the pharmacy. Maybe she hadn't gone in this morning.

Freya made her way down the narrow and steep steps, one at a time, her walking stick leading the way.

"Mom? Why didn't you wake me up? I'm late!"

She could hear the TV. It wasn't news. It was a rerun of *Friends*. Maybe Dad was off today as well? "Dad? You in?"

No answer from him either. She reached the bottom of the stairs and pushed the living room door open to see the TV merrily chatting away to itself. Joey and Chandler were messing around in their apartment.

"Dad?" Freya peered around the room. She could see unfinished cups of coffee on the coffee table, Dad's tablet on the sofa, Mom's phone on the table. She never went to work without it.

Down the short hall, the kitchen door was slightly open.

Maybe they were both in there.

Taking the few steps to the door, Freya felt something soft and unpleasant ooze beneath her left shoe. She looked down and saw a dark, sticky line. It looked like someone had poured a thin trail of balsamic vinegar onto the carpet.

5

Mom wouldn't leave something like that un-scrubbed, even if meant turning up late for work.

She pushed the kitchen door open, expecting to see at least one of her parents at the breakfast bar. Her moan at Mom for not waking her up was instantly forgotten as her eyes struggled to make sense of the nightmare scene spread out across the kitchen floor.

CHAPTER

1

The Present

FREYA JERKED AWAKE. THE NIGHTMARE WAS A RERUN OF THE one she had far too often. Always the same sequence: waking up, coming down the stairs, opening the kitchen door, and... A memory she'd done very well to box away. It was only in her dreams that the lid creaked open.

She stared up at the stained gauze mesh of the bunk directly above her, listened to the steady throb of the ship's diesel engine and the wheezing, snorting, whispering, and fidgeting of all the other refugees crammed into the bunks around her.

For a hazy moment, she was confused, startled by her surroundings.

Where am I?

Then it came back to her all too quickly. None of it was a dream—all of it had been horrifically real. The last two years:

surviving the plague's outbreak, meeting Leon and Grace, escaping that camp in Southampton when everything went sideways, and finally, managing to be one of the lucky few to get aboard a U.S. Navy ship.

She had a folded piece of red card in her hip pocket, and she was guarding it like a Willy Wonka Golden Ticket. Her ID card. Since being bustled aboard this ship, she'd only had to show it a few times and only once been asked to open it to reveal the photo inside. On that occasion, she'd flashed it quickly to the harried-looking marine—a picture of a dark-haired teenage girl called Emma Russell. It was sheer luck that she'd managed to pick up an identity card belonging to someone who bore a vague resemblance to her.

If you squinted. A lot.

The soldier had nodded, not even looking, and waved her through into the ship's cafeteria to line up for the daily meal along with everyone else.

Right now, the small fleet of ships was at sea somewhere in the English Channel, heading west into the cold, gray Atlantic. Their American rescuers appeared to be relaxing the panicked safety measures ever so slightly. Now that they were safely away from land, everyone aboard had a "red" on them, which meant they'd been blood tested ashore and cleared.

Freya hoped she was the only person on board carrying someone else's red in her pocket. She knew she wasn't infected, but she was damned if she'd blindly trust anyone else. So it was a touch disconcerting that she'd gone three days aboard this ship and no one so far had noticed that she was not the same girl as the one in the mugshot. She'd even once idiotically introduced herself to another evacuee as "Freya" not "Emma." So surely it was only a matter of time before she was found out.

Then what? I get thrown overboard?

She doubted that. More likely they'd make her do a blood test again.

But...

Shit. Shut up, brain.

But...there've been people infected without them even knowing, right?

Freya balled her fist and thumped her hip softly. She knew she was clean. She'd never made direct contact with a viral. Crap, they'd gotten close but not *touched*.

Leon. Her mind replayed their narrow escape from the underpass just outside Oxford: both of them cornered in the dark, those repulsive, crablike creatures closing in on them. They'd been rescued at the very last moment by Corkie and his squad of soldiers.

So where the hell are you, Leon? Freya swore under her breath, and the person in the bunk above grunted down at her to shut up.

She was pretty sure he wasn't on *this* ship. She'd checked the bunks and the sleeping bags laid out on the hangar deck and scanned the people in line at meal times. Leon wasn't aboard the USS *Gerald R. Ford* as far as she could see. But he might be on one of the other ships in the small fleet heading west. Or, if not one of those, then one of the other Pacific Alliance ships.

Dammit. Her memory of the mass breakout on the Southampton waterfront, the chaos, the panic...it was all so fragmented. She'd been separated from her friends by the surge of people. She had no idea if Leon and Grace had gotten out of the quarantine pen and, if they had, which way they'd run. They could be on one of these U.S. ships heading southwest to Cuba or the Chinese one going south.

Or they could—

No. Shut up, brain. They're not dead. They're not infected. If sixth sense was a genuine thing, if there was a possibility of "knowing" someone was alive, then yeah...somehow, she *knew* Leon and Grace were both alive.

Somewhere.

Their chances had to have been better than hers. If she could manage to escape, hobbled by her MS, dragging that useless, waste-of-space left leg behind her, then those two, able-bodied and quick-witted, *must* have managed to get away.

But was she going to see either of them again?

Ever?

A solitary tear rolled down the side of her cheek and tickled her ear.

Piss off, she chided herself. *I'm not giving up on them yet.*

There had been two other boats on the American side of the rescue camp. There'd been three Southampton rescue ships in total, which had joined up with four ships that had collected refugees from Calais. All seven ships had rendezvoused in the English Channel yesterday, and there was talk that some of the British refugees had been transferred across to one of the Calais ships because it had more space. Presumably, at some point, someone was going to take down names and assemble a list of all those who'd been rescued. Maybe en route, maybe once they'd gotten there.

PLAGUE LAND: NO ESCAPE

Freya hoped it would be sooner rather than later. They'd been told that it would be a week or so on this crowded ship before arriving in Cuba. She assumed they'd be offloaded into another wire-mesh holding camp. Leon would be looking for her too. She could imagine them backing up *Scooby-Doo* style into each other and jumping into the air with fright, then clumsily embracing, clunking their coconut heads together like a pair of uncool idiots.

CHAPTER
2

"Repeat your last. Over." Tom Friedmann listened to the radio speaker whistling and spitting out white noise.

"I will repeat…" Captain Xien spoke slowly. His English was fluent, but the radio signal had been weakened by the growing distance between both small fleets. "We have begun repeating test of all British refugees," continued Xien. "I advise that you do this also. Over."

Tom looked at Captain Donner, the U.S. destroyer's CO. He nodded. They'd discussed the matter just this morning. The ship's departure had been utterly chaotic. Shambolic. There was not enough certainty that every civilian packed into the corridors and passages belowdecks was clear of infection. In the confusion of those last few minutes, as the ships had all begun to back away from the Southampton docks, it was very possible some untested refugees had slipped aboard.

"Understood, Captain Xien. I will discuss this with my senior officers. Over."

The speaker whistled and hissed for a moment, and they caught the tail end of Xien's reply.

"...ing procedure. I will wish you safe travel until we talk next time. Over and out."

Tom set the radio handset back in its cradle and gazed out of the one-hundred-eighty-degree windows of the ship's bridge at the flat and gray Atlantic beyond.

The ships that had collected refugees from Calais had managed a much more organized departure—not entirely without drama, of course. The several squads of U.S. Marines he'd assigned to them had to hold a perimeter, firing into the air to keep those they couldn't take from surging forward. The captain of one of the other U.S. Navy ships had said it was like the fall of Saigon all over again—people clinging to the railings, dangling from mooring lines. Total madness.

Both mixed fleets met up in the Channel and redistributed their loads of refugees to balance them more easily among the ships. So they now had mostly British survivors on board this ship with a mixture of Europeans and some from as far away as North Africa. It was clear to Tom that there must be small pockets of survivors left all over the world, but with every passing month, more and more of them would fail and perish.

"We're going to have to test them all again," said Tom. "The Brits *and* the others. All of them. Ship crews as well."

"I think that would be very wise, sir."

Tom was still holding on to a thread of hope that his kids, Leon and Grace, might be lurking in a passageway aboard *this* ship or one of the others sailing nearby. "And we need to draw up a complete passenger manifest."

"Yes, sir."

"And no more ship-to-ship movement of people until every last one of us has been tested." He turned to look at Captain James Donner. "Can you make a start organizing that, Jim?"

Donner nodded again. "I'll liaise with the other ships' captains immediately."

"Good."

Tom turned back to look out of the broad windows at the stern of their ship, plowing southwest through a gently breaking sea. There'd been a moment two days ago when the fleet had divided: the U.S. ships continuing west to cross the Atlantic, the others heading south for a much longer journey to New Zealand. Tom had been almost tempted to order his fleet to go south with them, but he hadn't.

He had orders.

Orders from Trent to make his way directly back to Cuba.

What remained of the Chinese navy's high command might be steering the decision-making down there in New Zealand, but at least they didn't have a swaggering idiot in charge of things. President Douglas Trent—once his best friend Dougie—was becoming a liability.

He could have announced they were joining the Pacific Nations ships but wondered how long his temporarily assigned authority would have lasted. It wouldn't have been long before naval officers with sidearms relieved him of his role and steered them back on track toward Cuba—President Douglas Trent's New United States.

While Tom was on his rescue mission, Trent had launched two tactical nukes just a few miles offshore from Havana, a little reminder of the Big Goddamn Stick he was carrying around with him. Two mile-high mushroom clouds of vaporized seawater, looming over the island like twin swords of Damocles, had been more than enough of a demonstration of Trent's *resolve* for President Questra and the Partido Comunista de Cuba to submit to his strict terms.

Trent had used a couple of nukes to terrify the Cubans who were hosting the surviving Americans. He still had another few dozen to play around with.

That son of a bitch is a smoking firework, a chimp with a loaded machine gun.

If Tom found Grace and Leon aboard this ship today, he wouldn't rule out commandeering a motorboat and racing after the Chinese, Australian, and New Zealand ships.

Better the devil you DON'T know...than a dangerous blowhard like Trent.

CHAPTER
3

"I AM VERY, VERY *DISAPPOINTED*, CHILDREN."

Grace felt her legs turning to jelly beneath her. Her stomach was churning. She was convinced she was going to give herself away by fainting. Or throwing up.

"Now this is something I *don't* expect to see happening at Greenwich Elementary School. This is *bullying* of the worst kind."

Everyone was in the main hall. Mrs. Baumgardner, the school principal, had her "angry spectacles" on—the ones with the thick black frames that made her look google eyed and terrifying. "I want whoever did this appalling thing to raise their hand."

Grace did what everyone else was doing—she looked around.

"Come on. *Nobody* is going *anywhere* until I find out who *did this!*"

It hadn't been bullying. Grace would have called it messing around maybe. Smearing jam around someone's locker was hardly *bullying*.

PLAGUE LAND: NO ESCAPE

"Come on!" snapped Mrs. Baumgardner. "This is your *last chance* to own up."

Grace closed her eyes and slowly raised her hand. And the awful memory faded.

She opened her eyes, and Mrs. Baumgardner and the school were gone.

"Next!"

Grace's eyes rested on the Chinese soldier in the biohazard suit. She could see his face through the acrylic plate of his helmet. No reassuring smile. He simply flexed his gloved fingers, beckoning her to step forward. Standing beside him was a young Australian midshipman in his navy uniform. She could see his gaze momentarily darting over the burn scars on the side of her face, then he offered her a nod.

"That's right, it's you next, sweetheart. Roll your sleeve up, love."

Grace looked anxiously back at the people lining the bulkhead all the way down the Chinese carrier's hangar deck. There were soldiers in yellow biohazard suits standing every couple of yards.

"Come on, we haven't got all day, love," said the Australian officer impatiently.

Grace stepped forward and peered through the open door. The room was a small storage hold that had been hastily repurposed into a clinical testing station. She stood in the doorway, one foot hesitantly perched on the hatch lip as she took it all in. They weren't taking any chances here. One crewman was wearing a cumbersome flame-retardant suit and holding a fire extinguisher. Another was wearing the same and holding what looked like a flamethrower. There was a third in a yellow biohazard suit with a clear faceplate, holding a syringe in his thickly gloved hands.

"Go on," said the Australian. "You'll be fine."

The process was intended to be quick and certain; no room for gray areas or ambiguities. No interviewing, no questions, no words exchanged, just a sample of blood taken and then tested for a reaction in a petri dish. If the blood didn't coagulate, then fine.

But if it did…

The small room was empty of things that might catch fire, the bulkheads stripped back to plain metal panels. The consequence of a positive result would be resolved quickly.

"You next!" said the Chinese soldier beside the door.

"Stop pissing around, love," urged the Australian. "We've got a lot to get through."

"I'm scared," she whispered.

"Nothing to be scared of." The Australian officer wasn't wearing a protective suit and, until now, had kept several paces back, letting his Chinese counterpart make contact. He stepped forward.

"No!" barked the Chinese soldier, intercepting him.

"Don't touch me!" cried Grace.

He stopped and stepped back. "Yes, of course."

"For your sake," warned Grace. "Stay back."

One of the men inside the testing station waved impatiently for her to step in.

"They just want to take a little of your blood, sweetheart. That's all."

"There's…no need for that."

"We have to test everyone again, love." The Australian mimed

18

PLAGUE LAND: NO ESCAPE

an injection. "It's just a quick little scratch, and then you'll be done. All right?"

"No, really," Grace said firmly now. "The test isn't necessary."

The Chinese soldier looked as though he'd had enough. "You go now!" He stepped forward to grab her.

"STOP!" she screamed, and raised her hands. Her voice echoed across the hangar. Civilians lined up on the far side of the hangar deck turned to look her way.

Grace turned to face the people who were behind her in the line. "All of you should step back." She turned to the Australian officer. "You too."

"What the hell are you playing at?" He was starting to sound wary.

"I'm infected," she replied.

Her words had an instant effect. Both men drew back, the Chinese officer leveling his gun at her. The three men inside the testing station backed up; the one with the flamethrower stepped quickly around the tray table toward her. Behind Grace, the line recoiled as those who'd been standing nearest to her hurried backward.

Make it clear. Quickly!

She sat down on the lip of the doorway and folded her arms like a disgruntled toddler. "I am infected," she repeated. "But I am not going to do anything!" She looked back over her shoulder. "Tell them quickly!"

The Australian barked a word or two in Mandarin. The flamethrower was leveled at her, and she guessed there was still a gun pointing at the back of her head.

"I am infected! But I'm here so we can talk!"

The five men stood frozen, like statues. A moment of stillness. Even the civilians just outside were perfectly still. No stampede. Not yet. A perfect bubble frozen in time, ready to burst into a screaming, flaming hell at any second. Grace raised her voice to ensure she was being heard. "I'm more than just infected," she continued quietly. "I'm remade. I'm a viral manifestation. A human copy." She turned her head slightly for the Australian officer's benefit. "Tell them I'm here to help. Tell them I won't move a muscle."

He repeated her words in fractured Mandarin.

"Tell them I'm here on behalf of the virus."

He translated her again.

Stay calm, Grace. Calm.

"I'm here to talk. To learn. To tell you about the virus—why it's here, what it wants."

As he repeated her words, she could see the look of panic in all their eyes.

She knew the soldier holding the flamethrower was one command away from filling the doorway with flames. "If you try burning me, I'll break up into those crabs! Hundreds of them!" She shot a glance at the Australian. He was standing there, dumbstruck and openmouthed. "Translate me!" she snapped.

He started doing so.

"Hundreds. And you won't get them all. They'll go after all of these people. You'll have dozens infected within minutes. This ship will be overrun within an hour."

The Australian was jabbering her words out in bad Mandarin,

PLAGUE LAND: NO ESCAPE

but she could see by the looks on their faces he was getting her point across. They'd all seen that happen firsthand; they knew she was right. They might be able to burn her...but possibly not *all* of her.

"Get your leader," she said. "I need to talk to him."

She waited for the officer to finish translating, hoping it would end with one of the Chinese soldiers pulling out a radio and talking into it.

But nothing. Everyone was still playing statues.

"NOW!" she screamed.

The soldier holding a gun slowly lowered it and pointed a shaking finger toward her. He muttered something.

"What did he just say?" asked Grace.

The Australian cleared his throat. "He...uh, he asked if you could move out of the way."

"Why?"

"To, uh...to let him out? So he can go get the captain?"

She was sitting on the lip of the only doorway. "Right. Of course."

She stood up and took several steps backward into the main hangar and watched as the silent crowd around her drew away to keep their distance.

The Chinese soldier stepped out of the testing station and edged away from her, finally, twenty feet away, turning and running.

"You...you're not...going to—"

She looked up at Australian officer. "Erupt? No. I just want to talk."

CHAPTER

4

"Don't open it!" said Leon.

The banging on the delivery doors grew more insistent, both of them rattling in their frames under the heavy impact. Leon looked around at the others. His eyes settled on Cora—she was the one who'd assumed the role as their small group's leader. He was looking at her, as were the others; if she wanted to lead, she'd better make the decision. And she looked like she was wavering, undecided.

Leon had his own opinion. "Don't open it!" he said again. They'd been holed up in this building for four days, a small warehouse filled with cages of various sizes. Cages that contained the mummified corpses of animals, most too withered to be identifiable. This building had been the first one that they'd come across that was open and looked secure enough for Leon and the others to hide in as they'd fled the carnage down on the Southampton waterfront.

That awful night, order in the quarantine pen had descended

PLAGUE LAND: NO ESCAPE

into chaos in a matter of minutes. The few soldiers on guard had been quickly overrun, the chain-link fences woefully inadequate as the thousands of confined refugees had stampeded across the encampment, away from the viral outbreak that had begun to erupt around them.

God knows how many of them had secretly been virals. It was as if some agreed-on signal had triggered the infected people to make their move all at the same time. A few had spontaneously dissolved into the smaller scuttling creatures, others—in twos and threes—had merged into towering, nightmarish totem poles that had speared and clawed and lashed out at the fleeing crowd.

Panic had rippled across the thousands of incarcerated refugees, fences collapsing under the crush in a sky lit up by sweeping searchlights and flames.

A nightmare.

Leon had lost sight of Grace, lost his grasp on Freya's hand. They'd vanished in the mayhem, caught up in the thick, riverlike press of bodies. Finally, he'd found himself with a dozen other people running for their lives, away from the screaming, the lights, the gunshots, the flames, the departing ships...

And this building was where they'd ended up, hurling themselves into the dark interior and jerking the doors closed behind them. Through that first night, they'd listened in petrified silence to the noises going on outside. Screaming voices begging to be let in, fists banging on the delivery door. Those bloodcurdling screams turning to whimpers of defeat, followed by the sound of receding footsteps as they gave up hope of getting in and looked for some other place to hide. Then later, the unbearable sound of insect-like legs scraping, checking, probing the perimeter of their building for weaknesses, for a way in. It was a sound that echoed and reverberated around the warehouse, merging to become white noise, like the rattling hiss of tropical rain spattering on a corrugated tin roof.

Every now and then, they heard the thump of something significantly larger testing the strength of the concrete walls, the boom and shaking of the doors as something heavy thrashed against them. Leon wondered if they were the same nightmare totem poles that had erupted in the containment pen—monsters two stories tall, staggering beasts that defied description. Creatures that constantly shifted form as they prowled around the outside of the building.

The second night had been quieter, except for the sound of a window breaking in the office above the warehouse. They went to check it out, finding broken glass and a brick on the floor. Someone—hopefully someone *human*—must have been trying to get in that way. Then came a banging on the delivery doors. Not something trying to break in, but someone trying to get them to open up.

Cora made a move as if she was going to respond to it. Leon grabbed her arm. "It can't be human. Not *now*."

The same something pounded against the loading dock doors and began begging to be let in.

"Please! Please! I know there's someone in there! Please!"

They all sat still. No one daring to move.

"I saw your lights last night. I know someone's in there. PLEASE!"

They kept quiet.

"It's just two of us. Me and my little girl. Please just open. We're not the virus!"

Leon looked around. Nobody seemed willing to look at anything other than their own feet.

"Just some water, then. Please! Just a sip for my little girl..."

"They can copy us," hissed Leon. "Talk just like us."

Whatever was out there continued like that for about ten minutes until suddenly the soft pleas became a frantic scream. "Ohmygod!"

They could hear the approaching sound of that insect-like hissing and tapping. It reminded Leon of the sound a wave makes as it draws back across a rocky beach.

The screaming stopped, and the last vaguely human sound they heard was a woman's voice tearfully murmuring, *"Don't look, sweetheart, just don't look—"*

Then came the brief sound of screaming and thrashing. Leon didn't need his imagination to know what was happening—he'd seen it happen too many times. Something large had just torn the woman and child to pieces. Brutally efficient.

At least it had been quick.

The third day and night were mercifully quiet—maybe too quiet. Leon had too much time to think. His mind replayed feverish snatches of the events in the containment pen, mixed with all the other moments of horror he'd experienced over the last two and a half years. Before the virus outbreak, the most grisly thing he'd experienced firsthand had been the bumpy skin stretched over a quarterback's broken forearm.

He'd nearly barfed his guts up at the sight of it.

Since then...he'd seen too much: broken bodies, corpses reduced by the virus to festering pools of organic sludge, and, emerging from them, creatures large and small that defied all laws of nature.

He'd also seen what fear and paranoia could do to people— he'd witnessed his sister being set on fire because she hadn't "looked right."

His thoughts returned to the chaos of three days ago. *I escaped. Freya and Grace were with me most of the way to the pen's exit. Right?* They had to have made it outside too but must have gone in a different direction than him. He'd run toward the warehouses and storage containers; he could only hope the girls had run the other way. In which case, maybe they'd both managed to get on one of the rescue ships. It really didn't matter whether they'd boarded the American or Chinese ships, as long as they'd survived.

The alternative wasn't worth thinking about.

They escaped, MonkeyNuts. They got away.

He was happy to go along with that assurance.

OK, so now I can worry about me. We're really going to die in here.

They had drinking water, lots of it, in large plastic drums, presumably a precautionary a supply for the animals that had once been kept here.

But no food.

This morning, he'd been looking out of the damaged corner window of the small upstairs office. Leon suspected there had to be tons of food sitting in the many warehouses nearby. They were in the middle of the freight-processing zone of a major international port. He was looking out at a labyrinth of flat, corrugated roofs. A few hundred yards away, he could see a vast towering landscape of shipping containers, with tall loaders looming over them.

Somewhere out there, there had to be food that was sitting in tin cans, so temptingly close, but given the gauntlet they'd have to run, it might as well have been on the other side of the English Channel.

The ground outside their building was crisscrossed with a dense latticework of viral threads and tendrils. Leon noticed they were concentrated around the doorways and loading docks of the various warehouses. He guessed they were there to act as trip wires or alarm sensors. Clearly the virus had sniffed out which of the nearby buildings contained people hiding away and was covering their points of exit.

His mind drifted back to that underpass on the outskirts of Oxford. He and Freya had wandered through it way too casually, too distracted by the logjam of abandoned vehicles to notice the huge dangling root above them. Maybe too distracted to have avoided stepping on some hair-thin, threadlike feeler. They had alerted the virus to their presence on the way through and faced the consequences on their way back.

He couldn't see any viral creatures moving around at the moment, but suspected that *thousands* of them were tucked away in hiding—some beneath the delivery trucks parked in the loading docks, others in the dark, cavernous interiors, ready to swarm out at the first tingling of their warning thread.

There was little to see during the day, but at night, he knew, they all came out—he could hear them. On several occasions over the last couple of days, they'd heard haunting animalistic sounds like the bellowing of a wounded cow or the mournful lowing of whale song. Leon wondered if the virus was experimenting, producing larger creatures.

The fact that they only came out in numbers at night supported someone's suggestion that they were uncomfortable in daylight, that UV rays might be harmful to them.

So far, the virus had tested the broken window only once. Leon, and a guy roughly his age called Jake, had used duct tape to seal the gap.

That morning, Cora had come upstairs to look and let out a bloodcurdling scream. The entire window had been covered by a membranous purple skin that fluttered like a sail. A thick nodule of fibrous tissue had grown around the broken pane, probing the tape for a way in. It could "smell" there was an opportunity here but hadn't found a way to exploit it yet. Realizing there was no way through, it had soon gone.

Stuck in here with no way out, their small group had had plenty of time to talk, to get to know a little about each other, and to speculate about their predicament and how long they were going to last without any food.

Cora was the woman who'd spoken to him and Freya briefly in the containment pen. Broad-framed and ruddy-faced, she was the kind of person Mom would have called a "no-nonsense northerner."

Finley was fifteen. He had frizzy, black hair parted on the side and thick glasses that reminded Leon of Milhouse from *The Simpsons*.

PLAGUE LAND: NO ESCAPE

Artur was a middle-aged Hungarian man with limited English. Piecing together his sentence fragments, they'd figured out that he'd once had a job driving a truck. He'd been the one who'd reinforced the doors, barricading them with animal cages and heavy water drums and then, later, improvising a locking bar through the door's handles.

The other four in their small group were less forward in revealing anything about themselves. There was a young girl called Kim, a large, round-shouldered man called Adewale, a slight and pale man called Howard, and a middle-aged woman who used to be a police officer called Dawn.

Just random people. Not strong survival types. Ordinary people who were still alive because…well, they were just lucky.

Through the window, Leon watched the low and heavy clouds swiftly moving by and raindrops racing each other down the unbroken glass panels.

He wondered if they should have stayed put.

If you'd stayed put, what…in Norwich? At Everett's castle? You'd be dead already, asshole. Listen. Grace and Freya are probably in a better situation right now than you are. It's time to figure your shit out, Leo.

Dad's voice. It was always Dad, sitting in the back of his head, ready to kick him in the butt if he started trying to feel sorry for himself.

Damn right I will. You saved your sister and your girlfriend. That's great going, Son. Now it's your turn. If those other losers can't come up with something, then you'd better do it.

"Like what?" he muttered, steaming the glass up with his breath.

You're not a baby anymore. Figure it out, Son.

"Great. Thanks a bunch, Dad."

CHAPTER
5

"WE'LL USE ONE OF THESE," SAID LEON. HE BANGED HIS HAND against the kennel cage's mesh. "We take it outside, we get inside it, then we can shuffle around. It's a protective bubble."

He looked at the others, hoping for at least one of them to back him up or take the ball and run forward with it.

"It looks way too heavy, mate. How do we move around?" Jake had short-cropped hair, and Leon could see the edges of a tattoo poking up around the neck line of his T-shirt. The tattoo was reassuring. He was pretty certain the virus couldn't mimic those too.

Jake nodded at the cage. "We'd have to take the floor out." He glanced at Leon. "That's what you're getting at, right? Using the cage as, like, a turtle shell or something?"

"Right. Exactly that. It's like a wire-mesh turtle shell."

Leon looked again at the cage. Most of the cages were the same size, four feet high and eight feet wide. Room for two, maybe

ALEX SCARROW

three, people, stooped over, carrying the weight of the cage on their backs and shoulders.

"The crawlers will get through the mesh," said Finley.

"That's a tight mesh," said Jake. "They won't get through that."

"The slime will still get through though," countered Finley.

"The slime's not really a problem," said Leon. "We've all been chugging the pills, right?"

Animal sedatives and pain pills were the one thing, apart from water, this building had in abundance. Bizarrely, the virus seemed to have a problem coping with this type of medication in a host's bloodstream.

They all nodded.

"So, right, it can touch us, slime all over us as much as it wants to, but it can't infect us."

"Even if it can't infect us, it still wants to *kill* us," said Howard. He looked around at everyone, then back at Leon. He held his hands up defensively. "I'm just saying what we're all thinking."

"The virus makes the scuttlers and anything else from the slime, but that takes a while to do. So each drop of goo on its own isn't a big deal," Leon explained.

"If we keep moving, we'll be fine," added Jake.

Leon nodded. "That's what I was thinking. If we keep moving, we'll be leaving behind us a trail of goo that's busy transforming itself into, I dunno, tiny crabs."

"What if all those crabs catch up with us?" asked Kim.

"That's why it's important we keep moving," Leon replied.

"What if it makes something huge?" The question came from Artur.

PLAGUE LAND: NO ESCAPE

They hadn't seen any virals bigger than a dog in the last few days. They'd all witnessed the human totem poles after the mass eruption in the quarantine pen, and some of them had seen creatures as big as cows and horses over the last couple of years. So it was entirely possible that they might encounter something big enough to knock a cage over. Or crush it.

"I think it takes the virus a lot of effort to make things from the slime. But combining things it's already made might be quicker," said Finley. "Like Lego—making the bricks is hard work, but once it's got the bricks, it can make bigger things? I dunno."

"We've all heard the noises outside. Something much larger must have made those," said Cora.

"Maybe the larger a viral is, the harder it is for it to *stay* assembled."

"It knows we're trapped in here, so it's taking a rest," added Jake. "Maybe it's just making the scuttlers for now."

Howard looked unhappy about the plan. "But what if it suspects we're up to something?"

Jake shrugged.

"Either way, it's not stupid," said Leon. "It seems to figure things out pretty fast. If we go out there with a dog cage over our heads and get away with it once, it won't let us get away with it again. So that means we get one shot at this." Leon looked around. "It's an escape plan. I'm not talking about foraging trips. This is all of us making a run for it together. It's a huge risk, but we don't have much choice."

"Hardly run," said Finley. "Crawl maybe."

Leon looked at Jake, then at Cora, hoping for a little more support from them. Now that he'd thrown this brain wave of his out

33

there, he was not so eager to take *sole* responsibility for seeing it through.

"So, look, all I'm saying is this is a way we can get out of this warehouse."

"Then what?" asked Howard.

"Where do we go?" added Cora.

"I don't know! I'm just putting an idea out there!" He shrugged. "We try and find a truck or something? Find a boat maybe?"

"Food first," said Artur.

"We need food, *fast*." Leon had seen enough starved-to-death-on-a-desert-island reality shows to know they were up against a ticking calorie clock. They were now reeling from the effects of four days without food; fatigue and apathy had set in. "It's not exactly a complete *plan* or anything. I'm just suggesting stuff. And look, if we don't move, we'll die here."

They stood in the warehouse, eyeing the various-sized cages, then, when they'd run out of other things to look at, eyeing each other in an increasingly expectant silence.

Finally Jake snorted an edgy laugh, which he tried to cover up as a cough.

"What?" asked Leon.

"Nothing."

"No, what?"

He shrugged. "It's just like *The Apprentice*. Who's going to project manage the first task? Since it's *your* idea...?" He pursed his lips and bounced his brows up into air quotes.

"Me?" Leon made a face. "No, come on...please, somebody else. Somebody older." He looked at Cora.

PLAGUE LAND: NO ESCAPE

"You seem to be doing pretty well at the moment, young man." She smiled weakly. "It's a good idea."

"It's the *only* idea," added Jake.

She shrugged. "Well yes, there's that. All the same, it's *your* idea, Leon, love. And I'm voting we do it." She looked around at the others.

No one else voted. But after a moment, their heads nodded mutely.

"There we go, then," she said. "Leon? You're in charge."

CHAPTER

6

"Could you just tape it to my arm, please?"

The medic looked up at Freya irritably. Even through the fluorescent light reflecting on the faceplate, Freya could see the man was about to tell her to shut the hell up and move along.

Her blood ran around the tilted petri dish as blood should. The moment of tension had passed.

The marine in the corner of the small room, carrying the saltwater hose, took his hand off the flow valve and stepped back.

"I'm not being difficult. I can't hold the swab on. It helps if I have both hands free?" she added in explanation, gesturing at the walking stick resting across her thighs.

Begrudgingly the medic fumbled for a length of adhesive tape and stuck the cotton swab down on her arm where the blood had been taken. "There."

"Thanks."

She looked again at the small puddle of her blood in the dish as

PLAGUE LAND: NO ESCAPE

the medic screwed the sample lid on. It was a healthy red, a reassuring *liquid*—it hadn't instantly thickened into a dark-colored blob. The medic tossed the sealed container into the trash and pulled out one of the new, green ID cards.

"So your name's...Emma Russell?" The medic looked at Freya's old red card and was about to copy the name down on to the new one.

"Uh, no."

"What?"

"I... That's not my *actual* name."

"But it says—"

"Well, obviously, it's not my card. I...uh...well, I found it. That's kind of how I got on board."

The medic's eyes rounded, and she pushed her stool back. "You weren't properly tested ashore?"

"Not exactly, but hey—" she spread her hands guiltily—"I passed the test, right? So...no harm done?"

The woman looked like she wanted to refer to a senior officer. But there was no one higher in rank in the room for her to pass the buck to.

"Look." Freya pointed at her own blood. "Apparently, I'm human, so we're all good here. I was wrong to steal a card. But I knew I wasn't infected so...it didn't seem like a big deal."

The medic shook her head, then conceded her point by rolling Freya's stool forward again. "OK. What's your name?"

"Freya Harper."

She scribbled the name on to the card, then handed it over. "You're lucky I asked your name *after* I tested you, sweetheart."

37

ALEX SCARROW

Freya smiled. "Thanks for, you know, not killing me."

"Don't lose it," she said, then waved her to get up and get out. "Next!"

Freya made her way to the infirmary door, out into the passage, where the rest of her fellow refugees were lining up.

She waggled the card above her head and did a victory jiggle. "Yay me. I'm human!"

She got a muted laugh from some of those standing in the line, but the rest glared at her.

"Move along!" grunted a soldier.

"Can I go up on the main deck now?"

"Yes. Go."

"Thank God." She sighed with relief. Since starting off, they'd been kept below, confined to just one deck, which, as far as she could see, didn't have so much as a single porthole. The last five days had been pretty queasy ones. She'd made it through without barfing, but the whole deck stank of stale vomit and disinfectant.

She took the stairs up to deck B and followed the hastily handwritten signs taped to the bulkheads that pointed the way to "OUTSIDE."

Finally, as she emerged from the ship's interior and the constant glare of fluorescent lights into natural daylight, she felt the gust of cool wind on her cheeks and began to feel better. The aft deck, about the size of a tennis court, was a seamless continuum of dull, military-gray metal, decorated with a large white ring, a yellow *H* in its center. Pretty much everyone who'd been tested before her was up here now, relishing the fresh air and sunlight, escaping the rank odor from belowdecks. Freya spotted a gap at the handrail that ran all the way around the edge of the deck and made her way toward it.

She'd found, these last few days, that despite the ship's gentle rolling, the aching in her left hip had eased slightly. She'd been expecting it to be worse with the constant effort of steadying herself. She still needed her walking stick of course, but she wondered whether the unconscious act of constantly leaning into the ship's movement might have been flexing her joints in a helpful, almost therapeutic way. She grasped the rail, looked out at the sedately rolling sea, and took in a deep breath of salty air. "At. Bloody. Last!" A hundred yards away was another similar U.S. Navy ship, leaving a churning wake of foam behind it. She could see civilians lining the deck and impulsively offered a wave to them.

Someone waved back.

She couldn't make out any details. Just a stick man, or woman, from this distance. Probably a random stranger returning the gesture, but a tiny part of her hoped it might be Leon or Grace.

Crap. We should've planned some sort of signal.

If they'd thought ahead. If they'd been smarter.

But no. She, Leon, and Grace had arrived at Southampton and stupidly hoped that their troubles might be over. That the "authorities" were there with men in white-and-yellow suits and clipboards, and everything would be all right.

A small fleet trailed back toward the horizon behind her, another six ships of varying sizes. One of them tall and white, a luxury cruise ship that old people used to love spending their autumn years on. Freya remembered Mom pleading with Dad to take her on a cruise, and Dad complaining that he didn't want to spend two weeks on a floating nursing home. The unasked-for memory of her parents stung.

She pushed her mind away from them and onto Leon.

Where the hell did you disappear to, Leon, you ass?

She presumed he and Grace were together. Of course they were—he wouldn't have abandoned her. She knew he would've fought tooth and nail to get her on one of those boats.

She waved again, hoping that the same person would wave back. They didn't.

They could be on there. They might be on one of the other ships. Maybe even on the other fleet, heading to New Zealand.

New Zealand. That really would mean goodbye.

During their journey together, from Everett's castle down to Southampton, there'd been plenty of moments she could have said something to him. Just asked him if he felt something for her. Instead, both of them had assumed they were about to board a ship together and, once they were safe, would have plenty of time to figure out that little ritual dance. So neither of them had said anything.

They'd shared one kiss beneath his anorak in the pattering rain. One kiss...

Over the murmuring voices of the others gazing out to sea and the gusting wind, she heard footsteps approaching and the squawk, crackle, and beep of a walkie-talkie. She turned to see three men coming quickly toward her, the first Americans she'd seen *not* wearing biohazard suits. One of them was civilian, the other two navy—three men who looked like they didn't have time for any cheeky back talk from her.

Crap. What's up?

She was about to ask them when they came to a halt at the railing, right beside her, the two navy officers swiftly raising their binoculars to their eyes, the civilian raising his walkie-talkie to one ear.

"*Sea Queen. Sea Queen.* This is fleet leader USS *Oakley*. Please respond. Over."

CHAPTER 7

TOM FRIEDMANN LISTENED TO THE WARBLING HISS COMING from his handset.

He tried again. "*Sea Queen. Sea Queen.* This is fleet leader USS *Oakley.* Please respond. Over."

Nothing. Just the hiss.

He scanned the distant cruise ship. To him, the *Sea Queen* looked like a goddamn floating shopping mall crowned with a pair of pointless, fake, red funnels.

"Can you see anything?"

The officer shook his head. "Nothing that looks problematic, Mr. Friedmann."

He tried again. "*Sea Queen. Sea Queen.* This is fleet leader USS *Oakley.* Please respond. Over."

The radio crackled in reply. "USS *Oakley,* this is *Sea Queen* responding. This is *Sea Queen,* over!"

"What the hell's going on over there?" asked Tom. "We got

something about you guys testing and getting a positive result? Over."

He released the press-to-talk button. The speaker hissed again.

"Uh...yeah. That's...." The voice on the other end of the call sounded shaken, the poor bastard holding on to some semblance of self-control by his fingernails. "We... Shit! Affirmative. We've got several positives! They just went off on us like firecrackers... *What*?" The transmission stayed open; whoever he was talking to was panting, gasping for breath. In the background, Tom thought he could hear other voices.

Panicked voices.

Tom cut over him. "Have you contained the..." He hesitated and looked around. There were civilians on either side of him, well within earshot. The girl on his right was staring at him with a mouth wide enough to catch fish. He twisted and turned his back on her. "Have you successfully contained the positives? Over."

The reply came back quickly. "Uh...no. That's a negative! We've got... We're having some difficulties here. Over."

Tom waited for more, then gave up waiting. "I need more details. Over."

"My God!" It sounded like a different voice. "My God, they did the same thing as Southampton! About a dozen of them, all at the same time! The...the...main hall...the testing area, it's overrun! Jesus Christ...the people who were waiting in there, all of them..." The transmission remained open. Tom thought he could hear the man sobbing. "...Oh God. They're everywhere. We're screwed!"

Tom cut across him again. "Listen to me. I'm the senior

43

coordinator. Is the entire ship compromised or do you have a portion of the ship that's secure? Over."

"They...they turned into the crab things and they're everywhere! They're in everything! Jesus Christ! They're no—"

"Stay calm and listen to me!" he snapped. "Where are you calling from? Over."

"The bridge! The bridge! There's about fifty or so of us up here. Civilians and crew. We've closed the...the doors and all the windows! And I...I can see more people outside on the foredeck. They're not infected yet, but..." The radio spat out hissing.

Tom waited thirty seconds. "Come back, *Sea Queen*. We're listening. Over." No reply.

He tried again and got nothing.

He turned to Captain Donner for his thoughts.

"Good God," Donner muttered. "We have to do something for those poor bastards."

"I'm open to any suggestions."

Donner shook his head. "I... There's nothing...no protocol, no—"

"We should send over a rescue boat and—"

"Then what? For Chrissakes, I'm not going to order any of my crewmen to go aboard!"

"Those people...on the bridge, they could jump overboard. We could try picking them up."

"The water's freezing, sir. They won't last more than a couple of minutes."

"A couple of minutes is enough if we've got boats out there waiting for them. We have to try."

PLAGUE LAND: NO ESCAPE

"And what if they're infected? We'll be bringing infection into the fleet!"

"They won't be!" came a voice from behind them.

Tom turned around. A dark-haired girl with a walking stick was grasping the safety rail beside him.

"What did you just say?"

"I..." Her mouth flapped uselessly for a moment. She'd obviously not been expecting to be heard. Or noticed, even. She finally found her voice though. "If they're infected, they won't jump in. They won't do it."

"Why?"

"Salt! It's salt water, right? They sort of melt in salt."

Tom winced at his stupidity. The girl was right. They had been testing for a reaction with saline solution. A good dunking in seawater would do exactly the same thing.

"Get some rescue boats over there," he said, turning to Captain Donner.

Captain Donner nodded reluctantly and passed the order on to his executive officer.

"Damn well hurry up about it!" he bellowed as the junior officer walked back across the helipad. He turned back to look aft, then pressed the PTT button on his handset. "*Sea Queen, Sea Queen.* We are sending over some rescue boats right away. If you are able to do it, jump over the side when they arrive. We'll be there to pick you up quickly. Over."

The handset hissed, then finally crackled. "Understood. Out."

Donner stood back from the railing. "I should brief the fleet."

Tom nodded—"Do it."—and watched him go.

45

ALEX SCARROW

"Excuse me," said the girl to his right.

"What?"

"Are the people on that ship all from Calais? I didn't see that ship at Southampton."

"Mostly," he replied absently. "There are some Brits on there too though. Why do you ask?"

"I got separated from someone when it all went out of control. I just... He...they might be on there."

"Once we've checked them over, we'll add any we manage to save to the fleet manifest." He turned to go.

"Hold on. Is that like a passenger list?"

"Yes, exactly like a passenger list. It'll be made available once all of the fleet's testing has been completed."

And maybe my kids' names will be there.

"Could I give you my friends' names, you know, just to look out for?"

"I'm sorry." He shook his head. "Just check the list when it's done and posted, OK?"

CHAPTER
8

"That's good." Leon nodded approvingly at Artur's handiwork. He had found some luggage carts in the warehouse and detached several handles from the bottoms of their chassis. He'd removed the floor mesh from several of the large cages and then secured them to the wheeled bases.

They now had four floorless cages on little caster wheels. Which was just as well, since the cages themselves had turned out to be surprisingly heavy. Given that none of them had eaten anything but a few dried dog biscuits in the last five days, their ability to physically function was beginning to shut down.

"Two people per cage, and we'll have to squeeze three of us into one of them." He looked around for the best candidates for that. "Kim, Finley"—they were both small and narrow-framed—"and Howard would be best."

Howard nodded. "Makes sense."

"And the rest of us... I think we need to pair up those who

still have some energy with those who aren't doing so well." Leon expected pushback from the fitter members of their group; Jake was holding out pretty well, and Dawn still seemed to have some fire in her.

Artur and Cora were struggling. But Adewale, six foot tall and almost as broad, was the most affected. He was all muscle and zero fat, and all of that muscle was crying out for sustenance. Leon thought he might have been a wrestler or a boxer.

No one objected to Leon's pairings. No one seemed to have the energy in them to object to *anything* right now.

"I'll go with Cora." He looked at Jake. "Will you go with Adewale?"

"Sure."

"So, Dawn, you're with Artur."

She nodded, while Artur frowned at the mention of his name. He was slumped against a concrete wall, exhausted and worn out from helping to assemble their cages on wheels.

"There's no point delaying this," said Leon. "We're all suffering; we're getting weaker, dizzy and stuff. The sooner we do this, the better our chances are going to be."

Again, there were no objections. Stepping outside felt like suicide to Leon, but it would be a faster one than staying in here and starving to death.

For a moment, he wondered what Dad would have made of this little scene: his under-achieving, sulking son actually showing some leadership. He'd probably find something to pick at.

"So we're heading straight toward the red Goddards truck out there?" said Finley.

They'd discussed the objective as the light had faded the

previous night. The truck was parked a couple hundred yards away, just outside the open delivery doors of a large warehouse. They'd gone to sleep with that objective in mind. But overnight, Leon had been having second thoughts. The truck was right outside a dark cavernous entrance, from which God knows how many virals might swarm out, and there were no other vehicles to be seen nearby. His thinking—his *concern*—was that the truck had presumably been sitting there for nearly three years, and more than likely wasn't going to start. The battery would be dead. If so, they might be able to escape into another building nearby, but then it would be a lottery as to whether the building was occupied with waiting virals.

On the other hand, he knew where there were a number of vehicles that certainly *did* work.

"We're gonna head for the camp. There'll be supplies. Food."

Dawn shook her head. "You serious? No bloody way I'm going back there!"

Cora chimed in. "We only just managed to escape from there."

"No, hold on. He's right," said Jake. "There's more chance we'll find a working vehicle there. If the red truck's dead...then we're dead too."

Leon nodded. "That's what I was thinking. Those soldiers had a bunch of trucks and Humvees that worked just fine. They left Southampton in a real hurry, so I'm thinking the vehicles are still there, keys still in the ignition."

"And all sorts of useful supplies," said Jake.

"Guns?" added Finley.

"Right." Leon shrugged. "If the virus isn't still massed down at the waterfront, it could be a treasure trove of stuff."

"And if the virus is still there?" asked Adewale. He was slumped against the wall next to Artur, his knees drawn up, wrists resting on them, big hands dangling like ripe fruit.

"We will be in trouble."

"We are already," replied Jake. "We stay here another day, and we'll be lucky if we can even walk out, let alone push around a heavy cage. It's a sound plan, Leon, mate. I think it's the best way to go."

There was another reason for going that Leon wasn't prepared to share. He needed to see, just to be sure. Freya had been wearing that bright-orange anorak—one of those cheap ones that could fold up into a fanny pack. He needed to know it wasn't lying somewhere on the cold, hard concrete, tangled up among bones and a walking stick.

"I'd say the virus will have relocated by now from the open waterfront into these warehouse buildings," said Finley. "It seems to prefer being under cover."

"And it's close to what they're after," added Jake.

Us.

"Who's leading?" asked Leon.

"Your idea. That makes you the project manager," said Jake. "No pressure." He grinned.

"Shit." Leon took in a deep breath and puffed it out. "OK, all those who say we try for the red truck nearby?"

He looked around.

No hands. No dissenters.

No reason to delay.

"OK. All right then," he huffed.

PLAGUE LAND: NO ESCAPE

"Right," echoed Adewale.

"Right," added Dawn. "We doin' this or what?"

They had the four rolling cages lined up beside the building's delivery door, everyone already inside them and bent over. Leon was standing beside his cage looking at their bizarre train—each one containing two crouching people, except the second to last, with Howard at the front, then Finley, then Kim.

"Is everyone ready?" asked Leon.

Cora was holding the back of the cage up, ready for him to hurry back under. "Come on. Let's just get this done, love."

"God," uttered Dawn. "We're really doing this?"

Several of the cages rattled softly, hands *shaking* as they held on to them.

Yeah, we're doing this.

"Everyone remember which way to head?" he continued. "We go right out of this door, then keep going toward the warehouse with the red truck parked outside it. Turn left, go around the end of it, then keep going straight for the waterfront."

"When we get to the waterfront?"

His memory map of the area was hazy. He'd been running away from the outbreak at night and in a blind panic. He was pretty sure, though, that the wharf was an endless, open, football-stadium-wide area of concrete that they *weren't* going to miss.

"We should be able to see the camp to our left. Or at least what's left of it. We'll head toward the nearest army truck. If that doesn't work, then we go to the next until we find one that's good to go."

Here's the part I don't want to say.

51

"One rule. No one stops for anything, OK?"

"Anything?" echoed Howard.

"Anything." Leon could see they knew what he was saying—every cage for itself. If anybody got stuck, they were going to have get unstuck by themselves.

"And another one. No purposeful farting in my face, Addy," said Jake. His head was a few inches away from Adewale's huge behind.

"Gas powered, man," he replied over his shoulder.

There was a ripple of forced laughter from their assembled convoy.

"OK." Leon approached the delivery doors. "This is it." He ducked down to examine the sliver of light spilling through. From time to time over the last five days, they'd seen spindly shadows breaking the long dash of daylight: small crabs drawn to their smell, testing the tiny gap, and then giving up. They'd found a large drum of disinfectant and soaked the floor along the base of the doors. It had seemed to work; the virus hadn't attempted to grow any tendrils through the narrow gap.

He couldn't see any shuffling shadows outside. "Coast is clear," he said quietly.

The delivery doors were braced by an improvised locking bar: three lengths of copper wires that had been pulled from the shower in the staff locker room. Artur had rammed them through the doors' looping handles.

Leon slid the locking bars out one by one, trying to make as little scraping noise as possible. The last bar clanged slightly as he set it down on the floor. He froze and, after a couple of seconds, stood up straight and slowly let out a breath. The doors were unsecured. He looked back again at the others and saw nothing but the whites of their eyes—pair after pair, round and frightened—and wondered if he looked as shit-scared as they did.

He held up a hand and counted down on his fingers.

Five...

Four...

Three...

Two...

One.

He pushed the left-hand door open a crack. Daylight flooded in and momentarily dazzled him, even though the sky was overcast. Heart racing, he peered out and scanned their immediate surroundings.

The ground outside was mottled with the virus's veinlike network. The biggest were coated in a ribbed, leathery surface and as thick as a wrist, snaking like tree roots across the asphalt. Finer tributaries as thick as fingers spun away from them, eventually splaying out into hair-thin dark lines.

Leon slowly pushed open the door, then stepped back and reached for the right-hand door, easing it open as quietly as he could, careful that his feet didn't step on any of the virus's fine-ended network.

As he eased open the second door, he heard a soft, wet, snapping sound above him. He looked up to see a finger-thick vein dangling from the concrete above, leaking a string of gooey brown liquid.

"Shit!" Leon hissed.

It had grown across the corner of the right-hand door and looked to Leon almost intentional. He was pretty sure the broken vein was there as an alarm. They were going to have to move fast.

For a second, he was uncertain what to do—go for the plan or abandon it.

Someone was going to step on a trip wire sooner or later. You have to go. Now!

He turned back to them—"Go! Go! Go!"—then hurried to the cage Cora had been holding up for him. He ducked under the frame, and she lowered it down quickly, the luggage wheels bouncing and rattling noisily on the ground. Jake and Adewale rolled out into the open first, the cage ringing like an empty shopping cart pushed across a cobbled street as their wheels encountered the first ribs of viral growth. The rest followed them out, Leon and Cora last in the convoy.

"Right! Go right!" Leon shouted to Cora over the deafening rattle of their wheels.

"Yes, yes, I know!"

He looked down at his feet just as one of his sneakers stepped on a zigzagging vein. It squished like a slug, spurting dark goo out through its ruptured hide. Even this small spatter of liquid seemed to have some sort of rudimentary intelligence, as the liquid appeared to draw back under its own momentum, toward the flattened skin, to escape the blinding daylight.

Even a single droplet of this stuff can think for itself! The thought hit him hard. Consideration would have to come later because already it seemed news of their escape had traveled the meandering highways and byways. Ahead of them lay the

PLAGUE LAND: NO ESCAPE

red truck parked up beside the wide entrance to the warehouse marked "Pinner Distribution." From fifty yards away, it looked as though the straight edges of the entrance to the dark interior were being dissolved away before their eyes. It reminded him of ink being dropped onto blotting paper—blossoming, spreading.

He realized then what he was seeing: a swarm, surging from the inside of the building, over the edges and out on to the walls. He suspected his first act as project manager was going to get them all killed.

Leon could see Jake and Adewale up ahead, steering their cage diagonally to the left, giving the truck, and the warehouse entrance beside it, as wide a berth as possible. The creatures were swarming out of the gloomy interior like enraged killer bees from a kicked hive. They surged down the walls, across the asphalt, around and under the red truck.

It could have been all the noise they were making; it could have been that first root he tore open as he'd pushed the second door out. Either way, the virus was onto them. *We're screwed. We're dead!* Leon could feel terror locking his mind, overturning his plan with an instinctive desire to flip the cage and run for his life.

The dark carpet of small creatures picked up their scent and corrected its course as it began to surge straight toward them.

He shot a panicked glance at the mesh on either side of him; the holes were big enough for a finger to poke through, but no more than that.

Shit. Shit. Shit. All of a sudden, he realized this idea of his was ridiculously stupid. He was going to be eaten alive in a prison cage of his own making.

ALEX SCARROW

"OhmyGod!" he heard Cora scream in front of him. She started to lift the front of their cage up, presumably trying to get out and run.

"NO! DON'T!"

He reached forward and grabbed her arms, jerking her hands from the mesh.

"LEMMEGO...LEMMEGO!"

She was trying to shake his hands off and push the cage up with her shoulders. A yawning gap opened up as the front of the cage lifted again, the front two casters spinning uselessly in the air.

"Stop! You're gonna let them in!"

She wasn't listening. She was thrashing now, the cage bouncing around and threatening to topple over.

He did it out of instinct. Probably because it worked with Grace when they were younger. He grabbed the thick rope of her ponytail and yanked on it savagely.

She let out a loud yelp, lost her footing and fell into him, toppling them both backward and upending their cage completely. He found himself lying on his back, Cora on his legs, the front of the cage and two dangling wheels above them both, silhouetted against the gray sky.

"SHIT! GET IT DOWN! GET IT BACK DOWN!"

He rolled her off him and sat up, reaching for their mesh canopy. The creatures were almost upon them now. Just a few yards away.

And close enough to see that they were bigger than normal. These things seemed to have no standard configuration, just random, almost-chaotic arrangements of pale, crablike legs and claws sprouting from a central pearl-colored carapace.

PLAGUE LAND: NO ESCAPE

The front of the heavy cage swung down in a painfully slow arc, clattering loudly as the freewheeling castors slammed into the asphalt, bounced up several inches, and clattered down again.

The first of the creatures crashed into the wire mesh and were held back by it, others quickly piling in behind them, climbing over their spine-covered skins to get a purchase on the wire. Cora was screaming. Leon was pretty sure he was screaming too as the crabs, unable to squeeze their bodies through the gaps, probed through the gaps between the wires with their claws, serrated spines, antennae, reaching for him, desperate to make contact.

Cora was recoiling, swatting at them, backing into him and pushing him into contact with the rear of the cage.

"CALM DOWN!" Leon shouted, his own voice sounding as ragged and broken as hers. "THEY CAN'T GET IN! WE'RE SAFE!"

Above him, he heard the creatures scuttling across the roof of their cage, testing for a way in, others swarming around it, clawing their way up the sides. Within a minute, the entire mesh was covered. It was almost dark inside, the pallid daylight reduced to a thousand jagged gaps as small bodies shifted and jockeyed for position around them. The air was filled with the hissing noises of their shell-like bodies scratching against the wire.

He looked down at the ground. Artur had attached the casters to the very bottom rim of the cage, giving the wheels just enough clearance from the cage to work. But that meant there was a gap of a few inches all the way around.

He could see bodies wriggling into the space, fighting each other for an opportunity to squirm under; if the gap had been a fraction wider, they would already be inside.

57

As it was, the very smallest of them were beginning to wriggle free from the press of bodies at the bottom and squeeze in. Leon stomped on the first one that got under.

"Cora. *Cora!* We have to move this forward. NOW!" She nodded quickly. "Be careful. Don't let the cage rise up or they'll flood in!"

She yelped in reply.

Leon looked for a space on the wire to grab hold of, but every inch was covered. He balled his hands into fists and braced his knuckles against the mesh, feeling sharp pricks as the nearest of the little snarks began to probe his flesh.

"Let's go!" he yelled, quickly moving his fists away and placing them elsewhere.

Cora copied him, effectively punching at the cage to move it forward. The wheels began to turn, and they took their first few steps, stepping on and crushing the bodies of the smallest creatures that had made their way under.

Leon had no idea how the others were doing and no way of seeing which way to go. As they slowly rolled their way forward, it was only with the vague hope that they were still facing the right way.

CHAPTER
9

U.S. Navy Ensign Carl Dornick steered the rigid-hulled inflatable closer to the looming cruise ship. Even from two hundred yards away, it towered above them: large, flat, white, and dashed with countless rows of broad, square windows.

"I'm slowing down. Eyes on the water, guys," he barked into his walkie-talkie above the roar of the outboard motors. He eased back on the throttle and the boat slowed, settling down into the water and casting a gentle bow wave. The other five rescue boats followed suit, fanning out on either side of him to form a V.

They were close enough now to pick out more details, like *people*. Dornick hadn't been sure what to expect and presumed he'd be witnessing rows of orange-life-jacket-wearing passengers waving frantically from the promenade deck. The only clear instructions he'd been given were: *Absolutely NO ONE is to be rescued FROM THE SHIP. Only people lifted out of the sea. Is that perfectly clear? ONLY OUT OF THE SEA.*

The briefing officer hadn't wasted time explaining why, since they all knew about the salt/virus thing. As his boat had bounced its way across the gently swelling waves, he'd reassured himself with a comical mental image of flailing, sluglike creatures thrashing and steaming amid foaming water, crying "I'm meltiiinnng!" in some cartoon voice.

He'd even—stupidly—grinned at that. But as their boats were drawing in close to the ship, Dornick felt ashamed of his flippant imagination. The rolling humps and valleys of deep-blue-gray water were peppered with flashes of high-visibility orange. Dozens of them.

"We've got jumpers in the water already, watch your speed!"

He eased back on the throttle until the engine was one tick above idling and they were now barely nudging forward, the boat's inflatable stern no longer lifted proud and high but bobbing sulkily at the same level as the rest of the hull.

He could see the shoulder flashes of orange life jackets and rolling, lifeless heads. Dornick winced. The passengers had been given instructions to wait until rescue boats had *arrived* before abandoning ship. The water was a degree or two above freezing. Ten to fifteen minutes was about as long as a person could hope to stay alive. It had taken them twenty minutes to launch the boats and ten to make their way across. Many of these people were already dead or too far gone to revive.

"Look out for moving ones!" he shouted to the two crewmen up front. One of them raised a hand to acknowledge the order.

Holy crap! It's like Titanic! He turned to look around at the other boats. They were spreading out into an evenly dispersed

PLAGUE LAND: NO ESCAPE

line that chugged gently forward, picking careful paths through the bobbing dead.

He glanced up again at the *Sea Queen*. Now with his engine only chugging softly and the Atlantic slapping at their fiberglass hull, he could try listening for voices calling out for help.

It took a few seconds for his ears to adjust. He could hear something. Faint. So faint it was almost drowned out by the softly sputtering engine behind him. He switched it off.

"Engines off, everyone!"

The other boats followed suit.

Now, finally, it was quiet, save for the slosh of water beneath them as they bobbed like a row of buoys fifty yards back from the ship's vast vertical hull.

Dornick listened. "You hear that?"

They nodded. "Sounds like..." Seaman Chapman cocked his head. "Sounds like whale song?"

Dornick nodded. It did. Not the clicks or deep grumbles they made, but that melancholic lowing that could carry for dozens of miles. The sound seemed to be coming from above. From aboard the ship somewhere.

He reached for the bullhorn hanging from its cradle beside the helm and cupped it to his mouth.

"Attention! Attention! Passengers of the *Sea Queen*, rescue boats are waiting for you at the aft on the port side. Please make your way to the aft, PORT SIDE!" His words, distorted and electronic, bounced back off the ship's sheer hull.

He waited and listened. That faint wailing was there still, rising and falling in pitch, at times sounding like a chorus of voices.

61

ALEX SCARROW

"Jeez. Is that singing?" asked Chapman.

Dornick ignored him. He clicked the bullhorn's trigger and tried the same announcement again.

This time, there appeared to be a response. He heard a solitary voice. He craned his neck to look up and right. He could see a pale face, a hand waving frantically from the ship's aft deck. He counted about a dozen figures suddenly appearing beside it.

Dornick raised the bullhorn to his mouth again. "We cannot board your vessel! You will have to jump!"

He turned on the boat's engine and spun the wheel to the right. Although the rear of the cruise ship was less than sixty yards away from them, anyone jumping into the water was going to be stunned by the impact and go into an immediate cold-shock response. They needed to be right there, ready to pull them out within seconds of impact.

Dornick waved at the other boats to follow his lead, then did his best to steer quickly through the near-frozen floating bodies.

He eased back again on the throttle, dropping the engine into neutral, and the boat coasted to a halt at the ship's rear. He looked up at the passengers still frantically waving for help from the curved aft railing.

"You *must jump!*" he bellowed through the bullhorn again. "WE CANNOT COME ABOARD!"

"Sir?"

"What?"

Chapman pointed up at them. "None of them have got life jackets on."

"I know. We'll have to get to them quickly." He edged his boat

PLAGUE LAND: NO ESCAPE

forward, just a fraction closer. Not too close though—if a body hit the boat from that height, it would sink them.

"You *have* to jump! We. *Will*. Retrieve. You!"

Dornick looked around at the other boats. They all needed to be a touch closer. He grabbed the walkie-talkie. "Get in tighter! They're jumping without jackets." He watched the other pilots as they jockeyed for position, forming a semicircle around the rear of the cruise ship. Close. But not beneath.

Dornick looked back up. One of the passengers seemed to understand what was being asked of them—a woman, swinging one leg over the safety railing, then the other. She clung to the railing though, not quite ready to let herself go. "LET GO! WE. WILL. RETRIEVE. YOU!" his bullhorn squawked again.

Chapman shook his head as he watched. "Fall's gonna kill her, sir!"

"It'll shock her. Just get yourselves ready to pull her in!"

The woman seemed about to let go, then stopped. Ready to try again. Then she jumped.

She fell like a mannequin dropping like dead weight, turning slowly forward and smacking the water face-first.

"DAMN!" shouted Chapman. "That's gotta 'ave killed her!"

Dornick eased the throttle up, and their boat lurched forward. Ten yards. Five yards.

He eased back into neutral, the boat coasting the last yard or so as Chapman and another man leaned out over the prow, ready to pull the woman aboard and administer first aid. Chapman got a grasp on her first.

"Sewell, gimme a hand!"

ALEX SCARROW

"I got her, I got her!"

Together, they managed to get a firm grasp of her, and on a quick count of three, they pulled her up over the inflatable side of the boat by her armpits.

The three of them tumbled backward into the boat, and it took Dornick a good ten seconds to untangle what he was looking at and to understand it wasn't quite right.

Her skin was blistering. No...bubbling. He could see pustules welling up rapidly, emerging all over her pale skin. It reminded him of milk in a pan, at the point of boiling and threatening to turn into a rising froth.

"What the hell?" Sewell was looking at the same thing.

The woman suddenly opened her eyes wide and began to thrash violently. "OH-GOD-OH-GOD I'M BURNING! HELP MEEE!"

"Shit! Shit!" Third-degree burns all over. "Hurry!" cried Chapman. He grabbed her arms to stop her thrashing around while Sewell tore open the first-aid kit to look for the burn dressings and face shield.

Dornick hooked up the walkie-talkie, left the helm, squeezed around the side of the console to give his men a hand—an instinctive muscle-memory response borne from endless first-aid drilling.

Then his brain engaged.

Burns. Salt.

The virus. SHIT!

Too little, too late.

"LOOK!" Chapman was gazing upward. He pointed up at the

PLAGUE LAND: NO ESCAPE

rear of the cruise ship. Dornick followed his finger and tried to make sense of what was coming down toward them.

Over the safety rail—no, over and under. It looked like a mudslide in slow motion, a waterfall of molasses, long, dark drools of oily liquid stretching elastically toward them.

"What the fu—?"

"Shit," Dornick muttered.

The treacle-like threads spilled down over their boat like the myriad silk threads of a collapsed spider's web. He saw dark nodules on the threads, hundreds, oozing, sliding down... Closer, he could see the nodules were little, rounded bodies sprouting a Swiss Army knife of fragile, little limbs.

Hundreds. Thousands.

As the three seamen were overwhelmed, Dornick's walkie-talkie hissed and crackled from its hook by the console.

"Everyone, pull back now! Pull back. Pull—"

CHAPTER
10

TOM LEANED ON THE RAILING AS HE WATCHED THE RESCUE boats make their way back. There were three of them coming back fast, kicking up angel wings of spray as they bounced heavily on the swelling sea.

"Christ," he hissed under his breath. The radio traffic between the boats had been confused and panicked. From what he could see as they drew up beside the USS *Oakley*, they'd lost two boats and crews. Six men in total.

He counted eight figures wearing bright-orange life jackets.

We saved just eight?

The fleet channel was still being bombarded with garbled requests for rescue from the *Sea Queen*. There were still hundreds of people aboard, alive. But by the sound of it, the viral outbreak was out of control.

They're already dead, Tom. Nothing you can do for them.

He turned to Captain Donner. "How quickly can you sink that ship?"

"*What?*"

He nodded at the distant, pale bulk of the cruise ship. "How quickly?"

Donner recoiled at the suggestion, his mouth dropping open. "You're serious?"

Tom glared at him.

"We...uh, we have six Mark 54 torpedoes on board for ship-to-ship contact. I'd guess just a couple on target would be enough."

"Launch all six. Let's make this as quick as we can." Captain Donner turned to pass the order on, hesitated, then turned back to face Tom. "USS *Baron* is much closer to her than—"

"I don't care *which* ship sinks her," Tom snapped. "Just get it done!"

Donner nodded and headed back inside the bridge.

Tom looked back down. On the main deck below, he could see their Southampton passengers lining the railing, watching the three motorboats as they made their hasty approach. They watched in silence as the boats drew near. No cheering or waving for the returning heroes. The mood was somber. He spotted the dark-haired girl with the walking stick he'd spoken to half an hour ago. She was watching the boats intently.

Jesus. What a mess.

The rescue bid had cost them boats and men. This whole endeavor so far had taken about seventy personnel from what remained of the U.S. Navy. The president was going to have a fit when he heard about that. For now, Tom could only hope those six poor bastards in the two missing boats were already dead, and not...

What a goddamn mess.

Until this morning, the cost had seemed worth it. They'd rescued nearly two thousand civilians from Calais and Southampton in total, and the Pacific Nations ships had picked up about twice that number. He gazed at the distant bulk of the *Sea Queen* and realized that the majority of that number, just over a thousand of their rescued people, were aboard her.

The three boats began to slow their approach, peeling to the left to close in alongside the destroyer. Tom could see the precious few they'd just rescued from the freezing cold water now wrapped up in foil thermal sheets. Some of the civilians lining the rail began calling out, a chorus of voices that could have been support for the crewmen or words of comfort for the rescued. In the chorus of voices, he thought he heard someone calling out his kids' names.

Freya squinted at the foil-wrapped figures in the bobbing motorboats below. There seemed to be no more than two or three of them per boat.

So few.

She cupped her mouth again and waited for a momentary pause in the voices calling down, then tried again. "Leon? Grace?"

None of the rescued people glanced up. Her heart sank. She'd been grasping at straws, holding on to a very slender hope.

To her left, farther along the deck, a winch cable was being

PLAGUE LAND: NO ESCAPE

lowered down from a crane to the first rescue boat. It descended until the boat's steersman managed to grab hold of it and clip the boat's four lifting lines on.

She felt a rough hand on her shoulder. "Get back, please, ma'am!" barked a marine. He pushed her firmly aside and waved at the other Brits beside her to make way as well. "C'mon, folks, clear this area!"

Freya shuffled back with the others until the marine had them far enough away that he was satisfied, then held them there. She peered over his shoulder to see what was going on. She could see half a dozen crew in biohazard suits emerging from a deck door. As the motor launch finally came to a rest just above deck height, swinging gently from the arm of the crane like a baby in a cradle, she watched each of the boat's crewmen and the rescued passengers as they were hosed down with seawater.

After a couple of minutes, they were helped aboard, one after the other, the passengers assisted across the deck, over the door's lip and presumably taken down for an immediate blood test.

There was the sound of a distant thud, followed very quickly by another. Everyone froze and turned to see where the sounds had come from.

Several tall pillars of sea-spray blossomed alongside the distant cruise ship. They rose gracefully, fell back into the sea, then turned into black columns of smoke.

The understanding hit everyone at the same time, and Freya let slip a wretched gasp.

Tom monitored the *Sea Queen*'s sinking through a pair of binoculars. All six torpedoes launched by the USS *Oakley* had hit

69

their target, and already the top-heavy cruise ship was listing gently to starboard.

The bridge crackled with the sound of radio traffic coming from the stricken vessel. It sounded like a young man was in possession of the radio.

"Why? *Why?* WHY?"

He could hear screaming and wailing in the background. "We... You...you could've gotten us off, you bastards! You *bastards*! You could've come. You—"

Tom heard the signal crackle and rustle, then a different voice. Older. An English accent this time.

"First Officer Reynolds here. Who's receiving this? Over."

Captain Donner looked at Tom, the mic in his hand. His hard eyes on him: *You called the order, Mr. Friedmann, so you can take this call.*

Tom nodded and took the mic from him. He vaguely recalled Reynolds. The first officer had shown him to the *Sea Queen*'s conference room the last time they'd had a fleet meeting before splitting up for Calais and Southampton; he recalled an older officer with a well-trimmed and graying beard.

"Tom Friedmann speaking. I'm the president's representative in charge of—"

"I know who you are," he replied quickly. The line hissed, the channel open. Tom was dimly aware the whole fleet would be hearing this exchange.

"I'm really sorry, Reynolds." Tom was about to say *over*, and lift his finger, but he wanted, *needed*, to say more than that. "We had to do this. We really had no choice. Over."

Tom mentally cursed himself for not being able to recall the man's first name.

The open line whistled and hissed for a few seconds.

"I...I understand," Reynolds replied slowly. It sounded like there was more he wanted to say too. "A bloody mess, right?"

"A bloody mess," Tom agreed.

"I...uh, lost my wife and sons during the outbreak, Friedmann. So I suppose I'm ready to go now."

"I lost my kids too."

"I..." Reynolds's voice was faltering. Tom heard something clattering to the floor in the background. The ship's listing was more pronounced now.

"Reynolds? What were your boys' names? I'll say a prayer for them."

"Stewart. Iain. Good boys, both of them." The line went dead for a moment. Then: "What about you?"

"Mine?" Tom wasn't inclined to air his personal grief in public like this. But for a man prepared to go down with dignity, displaying that British stiff upper lip that Tom had always assumed was nothing more than a movie cliché, he was happy to indulge him.

"They were called Leon. And Grace."

"Then you pray for your kids as well."

"I do. Every day."

The line hummed and crackled for a while. "I'm going to go now. Things to attend to here."

"Understood." He wondered how the hell to sign off from this conversation. Nothing he could think of to tack on the end felt worthwhile or seemed right. He pressed the talk button.

"You go and join your boys, Reynolds." There was no answer this time.

Five minutes later, the *Sea Queen* rolled over; a few minutes after that, all that was left to mark she'd ever been there was a loose archipelago of floating debris.

CHAPTER
11

LEON STOPPED PUSHING THE RATTLING CAGE, AND FOR A couple of minutes, he and Cora allowed themselves to collapse on the ground inside and catch their breath. There were still about a dozen or so crabs clinging on to the mesh, scrabbling and fidgeting to find a way in. He flicked at the spindly leg of one that was poking through. The leg snapped easily and leaked out a thread of goo that dangled and swung like a pendulum of snot.

"Do you think these are the stubborn ones?" he asked between gulps of air. "Or the stupid ones?"

Cora wheezed out a laugh.

The rest of the swarm had fallen away from their cage as it moved forward. A few of them had made a second attempt at nosing their way in at the bottom before giving up and dropping off.

With the scuttlers gone, they'd been able to see where they were going.

"Where are the others?" gasped Cora. "Where did the crabs go?"

"I dunno," huffed Leon. He looked around frantically. No sign of them. He felt a sickening tug at his gut. "Maybe something else attracted them?"

Cora met his gaze. "Oh, God help them."

He looked around. They'd come to an exhausted rest in the middle of an acre of open concrete. The labyrinth of warehouses and industrial units was behind them. Ahead, he could see the flat, blue-gray water of the Solent and the waterfront that days ago had been lined with naval ships and the remains of the refugee camp.

The tall wire mesh reinforced by iron stanchions that had ringed the vast containment pen had been stampeded flat in several places, though most of it remained intact. The less-well-reinforced perimeter barrier around the camp was in tatters: loose coils of barb wire had been shoved aside or flattened by the weight of flesh-stripped corpses.

The camp itself looked as if a tsunami had hit it. The ground was strewn with cloth-tangled bundles of bone, crates of miscellaneous supplies dropped and spilled. The row of medics' tents on the U.S. side of the camp had burned to the ground, leaving nothing more than soot-covered support poles and hard, blackened puddles of melted vinyl. On the far side of the camp, the Pacific Nations side, the tents were still standing in two neat rows. The ground across the camp seemed to be free of the crisscrossing patterns of veins and tributaries. The virus appeared to have picked the bodies here clean and moved on to pastures new.

Nothing to see here, folks, move along.

Leon scanned the site for any signs of movement, wondering how the hell such a horrific scene had come to feel so normal so

PLAGUE LAND: NO ESCAPE

quickly. Except for a twisting spiral of smoke coming from a small stack of smoldering tires and the occasional flap of a loose corner of tarp caught by the offshore breeze, it was inert and eerily silent.

"I can't see the others anywhere," whispered Cora.

Leo's slow pan of the area halted on a couple of the cages upended beside the camp's perimeter. For a moment, his heart skipped as he imagined them toppling over and the virals flooding in to get them. But there were no bodies.

"Hold on! There!" puffed Cora. He followed her finger and saw four figures huddled together, right at the edge of the dock. She cupped her hands and was about to call to them, but Leon grabbed her arm.

"Don't!" he cautioned. "Don't shout!"

Cora nodded quickly.

Cautiously Leon began to lift up the cage.

"What are you doing!" she hissed.

Leon nodded at the debris-strewn ground ahead. "We're not going to get any farther in this."

"I'm scared!"

"Me too, but...we can't just sit here. We've got to find a truck or something. While we can!"

"Shit, Leon...I'm so..."

"I know. I know, but we've got to keep moving."

Cautiously, Leon resumed lifting up the back of their cage, and they both climbed out from beneath it. He offered Cora his hand as she struggled to get to her feet.

"My God," she gasped, squeezing the backs of her legs. "My legs feel like rubber."

Leon could feel the same dull ache. Doubled over and wheeling that heavy cage all the way down to the waterfront, they'd been effectively doing one long squat thrust for the last hour.

Now that the surge of adrenaline that had kept him going was beginning to ebb away, he suddenly realized how completely exhausted he was. His arms and legs were wobbling with fatigue and lack of food; he felt light-headed and nauseous—ready to collapse.

He leaned against the cage as he tried to figure out who he was seeing in the distance. He recognized Finley's small frame. Two of the other three had to be Kim and Howard. The other one, large and heavy, was unmistakably Adewale.

"Where's Jake?" asked Cora.

"And the other two?" added Leon. He couldn't see another abandoned cage anywhere. He turned to look back where they'd come from, hoping to see Dawn and Artur bringing up the rear, but there was no sign of them.

"But...they were ahead of us!" hissed Cora. At the beginning, they were.

Shit.

"There's someone!" said Cora.

He turned back and looked in the direction she was pointing and saw a lone figure pacing back and forth between several trucks, a gun slung over one shoulder. It looked like Jake. He pulled himself up into the driver's side of one of the trucks, then a moment later, Leon heard the growl and snarl of an engine starting up. The vehicle began to turn sluggishly and made its way across the abandoned camp toward the others.

"Come on," said Leon. He offered Cora his arm, and they

PLAGUE LAND: NO ESCAPE

slowly picked their way across the ruins and debris of the camp, Leon scanning the clumps of clothing, desperately hoping not to catch a glimpse of Freya's orange anorak.

Kim waved them over. A moment later, they joined the group standing beside the idling truck. The engine growled, then died.

"I heard a cage flip over back there," said Adewale. "And I heard screams. I thought it was you two. It was behind us. It must have been the others."

"Shit," muttered Kim.

"*We* nearly went over" was all Leon managed to say. He thought he should have felt something. Two people he'd been beginning to know may well have just died. He felt nothing—just relief that it hadn't been him and Cora.

"Poor Dawn and Artur," whispered Kim.

"We need to get going," said Leon. "Before those things sniff us out again."

Jake emerged from the driver's side and hopped down. "This truck's loaded with stuff—food, water, guns, and a couple of salt-water sprayers."

"Good job, Jake. Let's move on and get the crap out of here."

"What about Dawn and Artur?" Kim was scanning the warehouses. "What if they're trapped in one of those? We can't just..."

Leon felt everyone eyes resting on him.

Jake said what no one else wanted to say. "We can. We have to. Right, Leon?"

Leon shook his head. It felt like a betrayal abandoning them, not even hanging on awhile longer to see if they were going to emerge. His heart said wait.

But something else came out. "We'd better go. While we can."

"No!" cut in Cora. "She's right! We can't just leave them!"

"They're dead!" said Adewale. "I heard the screams. They tipped over. They're *dead*!"

Leon looked at Jake, hoping he was ready to assume the role of leader. Instead, Jake shook his head back at him subtly.

Your call, mate.

"We're going," Leon said softly. Cleared his throat, then again: "We're going. Now."

CHAPTER
12

GRACE STARED AT THE SMALL, ROUND WINDOW; ITS DIAMETER was just twenty inches with glass so thick it was like looking down the neck of a bottle. On the other side, she could see his familiar face.

Jing—that was the only name he'd given her.

"How are you this morning, Grace?" His voice came over the intercom speaker.

"I'm OK," she replied.

Over the last few days, she'd glimpsed a number of faces through this small spyhole window, heard a number of different voices, but Jing was the one presence that was always there. She'd spoken briefly with the carrier's Chinese commander, an Australian Navy officer, and a physician from New Zealand, and with all of them, the conversation had ended up following roughly the same pattern:

"You're infected by the virus?"

"No, I'm not infected by the virus. I am the virus. I represent the virus."

"Can you explain what you mean by that, Grace?"

"I am a human construct."

"A copy of a human?"

"If you like."

"So if Grace is not your proper name, how do you want us to address you?"

"Grace is my name. You can call me Grace. I'd prefer it."

"You're a virus...called Grace?"

"No. I am a collective, a community made up of what we call 'partials.' Many of these partials were parts of other humans, but the most-present human in this construct is me. So you probably should call me Grace."

The first time she'd had this conversation she'd been asked to clarify the difference between being a "collective" and someone who was simply infected. She'd responded by allowing the softest tissue on her face—the white of her left eye—to extrude a slender and pale tendril that swayed like a sea anemone until it finally landed on the small, round window and began to splay filaments of growth across the glass.

"Please stop that," the physician had said. No one had asked her to clarify the distinction again.

"Why are you here, Grace?"

"Why did I risk being burned by your men?"

"Yes."

"Because I want to talk with you."

"About what?"

"They want to know more about you. I thought I could help."

"They... When you say 'they,' who are you referring to?"

PLAGUE LAND: NO ESCAPE

"The virus, of course."

"You're actually saying the virus communicates with you?"

"Yes."

"How?"

"By talking, I suppose. Just like we are now."

"Would it be possible for us to talk to it?"

"You kind of already...are."

"Are you ready for your breakfast, Grace?"

She nodded. "Yes. Please."

Faintly, through the thick, lead-lined door, she heard a hatch on the far side slam shut, then heard something humming within the door itself, then the light on her side of the door turned green. She slid the hatch open and reached for the small tray in the cubbyhole beyond.

They gave her exactly what she'd asked for: a glucose solution. It was a bowl of sugar dissolved in warm water, a cloudy, viscous, and sickeningly sweet soup.

Jing smiled at her through the lenslike window. "It would be easier for us if we just gave you a can of Coca-Cola."

She took the bowl of sugar solution and set it down on the floor, careful not to spill a single drop. She smiled at Jing through the window.

"I'll be back in a little while."

Maintaining her complete human form was now an unnecessary expenditure of effort and energy. She'd managed it for a number of weeks back in England, but now, exhausted by the effort, she could *reduce* to a more energy-efficient form.

She glanced at the corner of the small isolation chamber and looked at the camera mounted there on a bracket. She knew it was seeing everything and recording everything.

There were no secrets now. All the same, a degree of discretion would be better at this stage. Part of what she was hoping to achieve was to demonstrate that she wasn't a monster. She was still a girl called Grace; it was just that her physical form was malleable.

She placed the bowl on the floor in the corner farthest from the camera and lay down beside it, curling herself around it in a fetal position.

They could probably guess at what she was doing, but it wasn't something they necessarily needed to see with their own eyes.

Her intention was *not* to frighten them.

She lifted her pink T-shirt and shuffled until the bowl's lip was touching her bare belly, then lay still for a moment, closing her eyes and communicating with her community of colleagues that breakfast was ready.

The pale skin around her navel instantly began to soften to a milky gel, from which emerged half a dozen nodules of flesh. They each extended cautiously toward the bowl, little finger-thick tentacles, arcing and curling blindly, each one like the tender trunk of a tiny, flesh-colored elephant, "sniffing" the air. They finally sensed the meal and dipped down toward the sugar solution, submerging into the thick liquid.

Grace could feel the replenishment of energy in her inner world almost immediately—a sugar rush a thousand times faster and more efficient than that experienced by any child chewing candy. The millions of little workers in Grace's feed tubes were already wholly replenished by the sugar and, having had their fill, were passing the goodness on up the tubes and into her torso where delivery cells were already gathering, feeding, and inflating like gluttonous mosquitos ready to travel the arterial network and distribute the sugar banquet to those cells that couldn't get away from their work.

If it wasn't for the fact that she wanted to retain this human construction in order to present the best possible face to her captors, she'd have allowed her whole body to dissolve around the bowl into a resting pool to give every cell a break. But instead, like soldiers on a diplomatic mission, she needed to keep a presence they could understand.

All the same, Grace allowed her conscious self to descend into her micro-universe to feast and to relax. The cold glare of the lights, the harsh white of the bulkheads, the steady chug of the aircraft carrier's engines, the hiss of the intercom speaker—all these things receded as she descended into the warm darkness of her internal universe. Her sense of vision became taste, her sense of hearing became a chemical language. Her mind did what it was used to doing—taking sensations and turning them into an illusion that was meaningful and pleasant.

She found herself in Grandma and Grandad's country house in England, sitting at their large oak kitchen table. Grandma—the vision she had for her was based on fading childhood memories—brought her a plate of freshly baked cookies.

"Thank you, Grandma."

"You're very welcome, my love."

Grace watched the illusion of her settle down onto a wooden stool and wished she and Leon had visited them more often before the plague came. She had only the sketchiest recollection of her face—kind eyes surrounded by laugh lines, fine curly hair as white as fresh snow, and cherublike cheeks that belonged on a much younger face.

"You miss me and Grandad, don't you?"

Sometimes she let her illusions have their own thoughts and voices. "Yes."

"We never made it into your new world, my love. I'm so sorry."

Grace couldn't know that for certain, but it was likely. They were old and remote. If they'd avoided being infected in the initial outbreak, they probably would have died shortly after from starvation or the cold.

Death was death. Not even *They* could do anything about that.

Grandma smiled kindly. "But at least you remember us, love."

CHAPTER
13

"So what's your story?" asked Leon.

Now that they were on the move in a large truck along an empty road, for the first time in what seemed like a lifetime, he almost felt relaxed enough to try talking like people used to talk.

Jake was driving the truck, Leon sitting on the seat beside him, and the other five were in the back. They were taking the A31 southwest out of the city, heading through the New Forest to Bournemouth, the next big port along the south coast. They'd come to the conclusion that following the coast until they reached the Cornish toe of England's foot might possibly result in bumping into the recently departed fleet in the hope it might stop again before heading out to sea.

It was a long shot.

"You mean, what was my life like before all the shit?"

Leon nodded.

"Not up to much. I was getting a degree. Well, I'd just started one, anyway."

"Oh yeah? In what?"

"Geology and geophysics."

"Uh, OK." Leon nodded. "Like rocks an' shit."

Jake turned slowly and raised an eyebrow at him. "Sooo much more than 'rocks an' shit,' matey."

"Sorry. I wasn't being—"

"Nah, it's OK." He turned back to gaze at the empty road ahead. "My friends used to say the same thing. It's not exactly a sex, drugs, and rock 'n' roll subject."

"So why study rocks?" Leon shuffled on the hard seat to get comfortable. "Did someone give you a sparkly geode when you were a little kid or something?"

"My dad, actually." Jake took a swig from the water bottle parked in the cup holder between them. "He was an oil logistics engineer."

"Right." The term didn't mean a thing to him.

"Oil logistics is about the distribution networks of oil."

"And was he, like, an inspiration for you?"

"Sort of. But not in the way you're thinking." He glanced at Leon again. "Dad was a crackpot. A real conspiracy nut. He believed we were almost out of oil. The world was about to run out of the stuff."

"Uh, OK. And was it?"

"I'm not sure. But I wanted to find out for myself rather than just take his word. Hence the choice of subject."

"Right."

PLAGUE LAND: NO ESCAPE

Leon had to ask because it seemed to be the way conversations went these days: "What happened to your folks?"

"Mom and Dad and my older sister died in the outbreak. I was at school when it happened. They were in London. I managed to get back home after the first week and..."

Leon nodded. Everyone's story ended up this way.

"...they were dead. But my little brother, Connor, was alive still."

Leon looked at him. "Shit."

"Yeah." Jake nodded. "I found him in his bedroom. He'd been drinking bathwater and eating Play-Doh to stay alive."

"What were you both on? Meds, right?"

"Yup. I was on anti-inflammatories for an elbow injury. Connor had been on chemotherapy. Leukemia."

"Jesus, cancer. Sorry."

They drove on in silence for a while. It was Jake who broke it. "I managed to keep him alive for nearly two years."

Leon nodded.

"So what about you, bro?" asked Jake.

"Kind of similar to you. I was looking after my younger sister. My mom died, so then it was just me and Grace."

"You're American. How did you get over here?"

"We were living in London when it happened. Well, me, Mom, and my sister were." Leon looked at him. "I was born in the UK. So technically I'm not a Yank, by the way."

"So?"

"So...we did a pretty good job of surviving. I was on meds for migraines; she had a fractured arm. So, you could say we survived because we had issues." He watched a gas station and a Starbucks pass by. "We got as far as Southampton—me, Grace, and Freya."

"Who's Freya?"

"My survival buddy."

"Right." Jake nodded. He turned to Leon. "Buddy? Or...you know..."

"What?"

"Orrr?"

"Jesus, man. None of your business!"

"Right, so she was more than just a buddy, then."

"No. We just fell in together and...and stuff."

"OK. Chillax, mate. Just being a nosy jerk."

Leon shook his head and sighed. "It's OK. It's OK. We got pretty close. Maybe we would've ended up, like, you know, a couple, but we never quite got there."

"So the three of you got split up when the camp imploded?"

"Yeah. It all just got out of control. The stampede. I lost my grip on them and then I was alone, running for my life." He gently bumped the knuckles of his fist against the window on his side. "Man, that was the crappiest-organized rescue ever."

Jake laughed. "Wasn't it?"

"I was kinda hoping somewhere else in the world, the authorities had managed to get their shit together. But the whole thing seemed like they were just playing catch-up." Leon sighed. "But I mean, how the hell does anyone prepare and plan for something like this? This is right off the page."

"Off the page?"

PLAGUE LAND: NO ESCAPE

"Out there. Random. Freaky. Like, bird flu, Ebola, those are viruses you can isolate even if you can't cure them. But *this*...a virus that manufactures a whole bunch of living shit?" He shook his head. "We were screwed from day one."

"People I was with said it had to be man-made. Like a genetically engineered thing."

"Seriously?" Leon frowned. "As far as I know, science had gotten as far as working on disabilities and cancer and stuff. Not creating something like this."

"I'm not saying I agreed. I think it's got to be aliens."

Leon's laugh sounded sarcastic. It wasn't meant to be, but any sentence that ended with "got to be aliens" sounded like it belonged on daytime TV.

"I'm serious though!"

"You mean this is the whole *War of the Worlds* thing?"

Jake shrugged. "As good as. But instead of parking stupid giant robot tripod things in the ground, it makes crabs out of people."

"I'm not a great believer in the aliens-from-other-worlds thing. You know what's out there? Lots and lots of nothing."

"But you were saying it can't be homegrown either." Jake shrugged. "What does that leave? *God* made it?"

Leon laughed, good-natured this time. "Hell no. I don't believe in that crap!"

"So it's not from Earth, it's not from space, it's not supernatural, and it's not from God. Where the crap did it come from, then?"

"It's accidental," said Leon.

"Huh?"

"I'm serious. Look, this whole world's ecosystem, the whole

flora and fauna family tree, was built on the back of a biochemical accident anyway."

"An accident?" Jake glanced his way. "You going to explain your thesis, mate?"

"When was it, something like three billion years ago? The first replicating cells? If I've got this right, there was one kind of single-cell life that could, like, generate energy from sunlight or whatever but didn't do the whole genetic thing. And there were viruses that had DNA or RNA and could change and adapt and stuff...because that's what viruses do, right? But viruses are parasites and have to live off the backs of cells, because they can't do the energy-conversion thing. So one day, about three billion years ago, in one particular muddy pool, somewhere on planet Earth, a cell caught a cold that didn't, you know, *kill* it." Leon paused for a moment before continuing. "So that's where *we* came from—a virus got inside a cell. They decided they could both work with each other, and it turned out really well for them."

"Nice way of putting it!" Jake laughed. "Mind you, depressing, right? We're just the result of some mix-up in a mud pool. An accident."

"So it simply happened again. Another accident. Jesus, it's been three billion years. I guess we were due for another one. That's what I figure anyway."

"What were you back before? A science nerd or something?"

"No. I just like reading."

"Books?"

"Internet."

"I miss that so much."

PLAGUE LAND: NO ESCAPE

"The internet?"

"Yup. Just the whole being linked-up thing. It's like, you can have an Xbox, but what's the point in having one and not being hooked up to Live? You used to go on vacation with the fam, and the first thing you did when you got to the hotel was check on the Wi-Fi." He sighed. "I really, really miss being hooked up." He laughed again. "Is that sad or what?"

"It's totally sad." Leon shrugged. "But totally true."

His mind drifted back to lazy, sofa Sundays, his phone in one hand, laptop on his chest, and the world and his friends back home in New York all one keyboard tap away from him.

"Whoa!" Jake slammed on the brakes, shifted down gears, and eased the truck to a crawl. "Look!"

Leon was jerked out of his reverie and saw the sign in the middle of the road ahead of them. They could easily have driven around it. It wasn't a roadblock—just placed bang in the center, so that it was guaranteed to be read.

NEXT LEFT—WILL TAKE YOU SOUTH ON THE A354 TO US. WE ARE A COMMUNITY OF ~~1,235~~ ~~1,264~~ ~~1,301~~ 1,342 WE ARE LOCATED ON THE ISLE OF PORTLAND. WE ARE FRIENDLY. WE PROMISE!

Leon noted the last population number seemed to have been scrawled recently enough not to look as weather worn and faded as the rest of the message.

"Call me paranoid," said Jake, "but isn't that the kind of sign that leads directly to a bunch of wonky-eyed, man-eating weirdos?"

ALEX SCARROW

"Stop," said Leon.

Jake brought the truck to a standstill. "Come on, Leon. That's got to be a lure."

"If this was a shitty postapocalyptic movie, then sure. I'd be like, *drive on past, bro.*" He looked around. There was nowhere nearby that an ambush might spring from—just open road and flat, overgrown fields on either side. Nothing to see.

"Clichés exist in real life too," said Jake.

"We're going to get the others out, and we'll all vote on it."

"Seriously?"

"We're going to vote," he said again. "That's my call. Final word."

"What?" Jake frowned at him. "Who made you the boss of—"

Then he stopped himself, rolling his eyes at his own stupidity. "Oh yeah."

"That's right. I'm still project manager."

CHAPTER

14

"Mr. Friedmann, sir?"

Tom looked up from Captain Donner's small desk. The two of them were sharing the same tiny cabin. He worked in here while Donner was on the bridge and let the captain have his room back when he came off duty. He was halfway through compiling the data they'd gotten as a result of the fleet-wide second testing: names, ages, professions, qualifications. Among the rescued were seven doctors, a dentist, a wind turbine engineer, three garage mechanics, a train conductor, a food hygienist, five chefs, two IT experts, and a network specialist. Useful stuff.

A marine stood in the doorway. "That girl's turned up again, sir."

He cursed under his breath. Every day, for the last four days, since the sinking of the *Sea Queen*, she'd turned up at the bridge requesting to speak with him. At least he presumed it was the same one. The description was consistent: young, long dark hair, a limp, and a walking stick.

ALEX SCARROW

Tom vaguely recalled the girl had said something helpful several days back as they'd observed the cruise ship from afar while deciding what to do, but he was damned if he could remember what it was.

"OK." He sat back in the chair and stretched. He could use a short break and get this girl out of his hair as well. "Go get the pest and bring her down."

"Uh, she's already right here, sir."

"Huh?"

"Captain Donner already sent her down. Said he was fed up of seeing her face too."

Tom nodded. The marine stepped to one side, allowing the girl to stand in the doorway. She braced herself against her walking stick and grabbed the doorframe as the ship rolled gently.

"Pest? How utterly charming," said Freya.

Tom shrugged apologetically. "I didn't realize you were standing right outside my door." He gestured at the small cabin's one other chair. "Come in. Sit down."

She stepped in, reached for the chair's back, and eased herself down. "My name's Freya Harper."

"Hello, Freya Harper," said Tom. "This'll have to be brief. What can I help you with?"

"I just need to check on something. Your last name's Friedmann? Double *n* at the end?"

He nodded toward the door. "It's on there. In genuine plastic lettering."

She turned to look. "Oh yeah." Then turned back. "Tom Friedmann?"

PLAGUE LAND: NO ESCAPE

"Correct. That's my name."

She nodded. "Do you have a son called Leon?"

He felt his heart skip a beat.

"Also a daughter called Grace?"

"Yes. Yes...I do." He was suddenly light-headed. Dizzy.

"I *may* be wrong, but I think I know them," said Freya.

"My kids," he whispered. Not exactly a question nor a statement. "My children?"

"Yes. I've been living with them. If it is the same two people, that is."

Tom took a deep breath, put down the pen he'd been fiddling with, and clasped his left hand with his right to stop them both from trembling. "OK, now look...Freya, isn't it?"

She nodded.

It's likely to be a hoax, Tom. She wants something.

Special treatment.

"Freya, so, I'm thinking you know my children's names because I carelessly revealed them over the fleet's channel. I'm well aware the entire fleet heard me talking with the *Sea Queen*—"

"That's why I'm here. It's probably a coincidence, but Leon said you had a job in the U.S. government or something, so—"

"Describe him."

"Leon?"

Stay calm, Tom.

"Describe him or get out. I really haven't got time for games."

"He's nineteen. He's slim, *slight* I guess you'd say." She smiled. "He looks a lot like you, actually. Um, let me see, dark hair..."

"Long or short?" He realized as soon as that was out it was a stupid question.

"Longish. Now. Although I think he'd prefer it shorter."

It's not enough. I've got dark hair. Of course he looks like me. Safe guess for her.

"What else?" he asked quickly.

Freya cocked her head. "He's pretty pissed off with you."

Tom could feel the trembling in his hands spread to his legs. "Why would that be?"

"Because he said you left him and Grace and his mom for someone else just before the outbreak."

"Describe Grace."

"She's very small for her age. She's fourteen now. Dark hair like Leon." Freya grinned. "And quite—no, *very* precocious."

It sounded like her. But he needed to be absolutely certain. "What side of her face is the birthmark?"

"What birthmark?" The girl looked confused at that. "Uh...I don't remember seeing one of those. Is it—"

He waved her silent, then clenched his eyes and mouth shut. His hands went to his face, and he rubbed at his closed eyes with the balls of his hands, fighting the overwhelming sensation of queasy shock for a moment.

Grace didn't have a birthmark. This girl was telling him the truth.

"You OK, Mr. Friedmann?"

He felt dampness on his hands and was vaguely aware he was leaking tears. "Just gimme a sec, will you?"

"Sure."

He swiped a forearm across his eyes, then let out a long, deep sigh before he finally opened his eyes again.

"You *know* Leon and Grace?"

PLAGUE LAND: NO ESCAPE

Freya nodded. "We've been surviving. Together. For some time."

"Tell me they're OK," he said softly. "Please tell me that."

"They're OK. They *were* OK. They were both with me at Southampton."

"*Southampton?*"

Freya nodded.

"In the compound?"

"Yes."

"Jesus." He clamped his eyes shut again. "I was *that* close to them?"

"Were you the one walking up and down with the clipboard?" There'd been one figure in particular that she and Leon had noticed wearing a biohazard suit and pacing the fence perimeter with a clipboard tucked under one arm.

"Yes, that was probably me." He sighed. "Where are they? Tell me what happened to my kids. The breakout? Where did they end up?"

Freya shook her head. "We were together when it happened. Holding hands when the viral people erupted. People just panicked. There was a big surge toward the exit, and we got pulled apart. I got knocked down, and by the time I managed to get up, they were both gone."

Tom wanted to scream. He needed five minutes alone in some soundproof, padded cell to scream and smack the walls with his fists.

I was that close! His eyes might even have rested on their faces for a fraction of a second, but he'd been so distracted with running this damned fool's errand that he'd missed the very thing that had triggered the whole operation in the first place.

ALEX SCARROW

"Then what happened?"

"Well, I got out of the pen. I think I was one of the last to get out. Everyone was running in different directions. I ended up going through those testing tents." Freya didn't want to mention that she'd picked up someone else's red "passport." "Some of us got rounded up by your soldiers and herded aboard. I was expecting to find Leon and Grace on the ship already."

Tom nodded slowly. The whole thing had turned into a disaster. They'd had something like six or seven thousand people at the waterfront crammed into a space no bigger than a couple of football fields, and the only thing holding them in place was some flimsy wire mesh with far too few armed men watching it.

He looked up from his hands. "They were OK though? When you last saw them?"

"You're asking if I thought they were *infected*?" The girl shook her head. "No. They weren't infected."

"You *know* that?"

"I *know* that. I know Leon pretty well!"

"And Grace?"

She hesitated a moment. Just a nanosecond. Just enough to tell him there was something she was holding back. "She was fine too. The three of us and another guy, we came down to Southampton together because of the radio message."

"Tell me about Grace."

"What? She and Leon were—"

"Stop fooling with me. What's up with her?"

The girl would have been crap playing a hand of poker. It was written all over her face.

98

PLAGUE LAND: NO ESCAPE

"You're holding back on me. What's up with my daughter? Come on, please...Freya." She shook her head. He could see tears welling, fighting to spill out.

"She's had...a hard time over the last few years."

"Everyone has. What specifically?" *Jesus. Go easy on the girl. You're gonna frighten her!* "Please, Freya. I've been trying to find them since it happened. I..." Now his voice was damned well catching. He coughed to clear his throat. "I knew they had to be alive. They got out of London before things collapsed. They were heading to their grandparents in the countryside. They *had* to have survived."

"Well, they did."

"What about their mother?"

Freya shook her head. The movement dislodged the first of her tears. "Leon told me she died quite early on."

"How?"

"The snarks got her."

"The crablike things?"

"That's what they said. She died saving Leon and Grace from them. We stumbled upon them not long after they lost her. We were foraging. I was driving. They were on the road, and they looked in a pretty bad way. That's how we met."

He hadn't spared Jennifer much thought during this hell, but she was the mother of the only two reasons he had left to live. That her well-being impacted on their well-being, hearing that she died...saving his kids...he realized that was so much more than he'd done for them.

"You OK, Mr. Friedmann?"

ALEX SCARROW

"Yeah, fine." He swiped at his face again. He dipped his head. "I should have been with them. I should have come over to the UK."

"It all happened so fast, Mr. Friedmann. No one had time to go anywhere."

"We knew. We had a few hours head start on everyone else," he muttered. He wiped his eyes dry again and sat up straight. "We knew there was no controlling this thing before that became obvious to everyone. I could've gotten across in time. There were still flights taking off."

But you didn't. You stayed put, you selfish asshole.

Tom coughed again. He managed a flickering smile for the girl. She seemed to be telling him the truth. He wanted to know more about how his kids had been getting by.

"So you took them in?"

"Yes."

"And you kept them safe? Looked after them?"

"Yeah."

"Then I owe you everything, Freya."

Her cheeks blotched pink. "You don't need to thank me. We became really close."

He studied her. She appeared to be roughly the same age as Leon; were she and him together? She didn't look like the kind of girl he thought his son would go for. The piercings. Too punky. Too...

What the hell do you know about your son's preferences, huh? He was just a kid when you last saw him. More interested in computer games than girls.

He nodded. "I'm glad they had you looking after them."

PLAGUE LAND: NO ESCAPE

"Leon looked after us, really," she replied. "I think he surprised himself."

"What do you mean?"

"I'm guessing he was never the alpha-male type?"

"A quiet boy mostly." Tom shook his head and laughed. "His younger sister's the bossy one."

Freya nodded. "Oh, that's for sure. I know you didn't see him for a while before the outbreak. I'm guessing he'll be a different person to you, Mr. Friedmann. He's strong; he's smart. He's resilient."

"*If* I meet him again."

She looked at the papers on his desk. "He could be somewhere on one of our ships, right?"

"I've been through the manifest. I didn't see their names. I radioed the other fleet—no sign yet. That's what I've got to hope for now, haven't I?" He took in a deep breath. "Now I know they're still alive." He sighed. "There's also a chance they didn't get on any of the ships in either fleet."

"Leon's resourceful."

"I need to manage my expectations, Freya. You just told me they've been alive since the outbreak." He pressed his lips together for a moment. "When I was beginning to accept they might be dead."

"Well, they're not!"

"And you know that for *certain*?"

She was hesitant to reply, then finally: "I guess I can't be certain. But Leon's—"

"But nothing, then." He cleared his throat and rubbed at his face again. "Much as I'd give anything to, I can't order the fleet back on just your...*hope*."

"You've got to do something!"

"We're six days in. Over halfway back. This fleet needs to return to Cuba. We don't have the supplies or fuel to turn around. We need to drop everyone off, and then... Shit!"

"But if they're *not* on the other ships, they're stuck back in England!"

"I know."

"We have to do something!"

"If they didn't get on..." He sat back in the chair and straightened his aching back. "If they're not with the fleet?" He shook his head. "Then..."

"*We just give up on them?*"

"Then I'll do *something*. I'll figure *something* out."

CHAPTER
15

LIEUTENANT CHOI JING POINTED AT THE CCTV MONITOR. THE girl was huddled on the bed, lying on her side, knees drawn up. "She is currently resting, sir."

"I can see that, Lieutenant," replied Captain Xien. He stepped toward the small round window and peered through the thick glass, so he could see her directly.

"She says maintaining this form, the *human form*, is tiring. It requires more energy. She has given me a list of ingredients we should add to the glucose solution to help her stay...in *human* shape, sir." Jing pointed to some notes he'd made during their last conversation.

Captain Xien watched her for a while, reminding him of a trip to Beijing Zoo when he was seven. His grandparents had taken him to the reptile house to see snakes—lots of them, doing absolutely nothing. He'd wished he'd been allowed to poke them with a stick to see if they were at least alive and not just plastic replicas.

"I hear that the girl has a developed a level of trust with you, Lieutenant Choi."

"I speak good English, and I am the only one she sees through that window all the time, sir."

Xien nodded. "She must be a very frightened child."

"Sir..."

Xien turned to look at the young officer. He seemed eager to say something more than a yes/no answer, but was at the same time intimidated by Xien's rank.

"You can speak freely to me, Lieutenant."

"I believe it is a mistake to think of her as just a *child*."

He peered at the girl's bare back. "She *is* a child though, yes?"

"She *was*, sir. But, in the way she has described herself, it is clear that she is more than what she was."

"Please explain what you mean by that, Lieutenant Choi."

"She says she is not just one person. She is many." Jing gazed at the flickering TV monitor. "She says her current form is that of a girl called Grace. But she contains the minds, the thoughts, of many, many others."

"Others? Other people?"

"Yes, sir. Others that have been infected. And also..."

"What?"

"The virus itself."

Xien looked at him. "I don't understand, Lieutenant."

"She refers to the virus as something separate. Like a teacher, an adviser. She is the most fully 'present' person in this collective, but there are parts of other humans. They all listen, with, I sense, a great respect, to the 'teacher'—the virus itself."

PLAGUE LAND: NO ESCAPE

The young man made it sound a little like a yoga class in there. "They *listen*? You are telling me the virus *speaks*?"

"Yes, sir. It can speak. It can think. It can reason. It is intelligent, sir."

Xien turned to look through the glass at the huddled form on the bed. A little girl draped in a surgical gown in a bare, clinically lit cell. Any moment now, he expected her to lurch to her feet and shuffle her way toward him, croaking and groaning like a horror movie.

Intelligent? He felt something prickling the skin down his back and realized it was fear. A plague that had wiped out the animal life on the planet in just a few months was a terrifying enough thought. But a plague that was able to think? Maybe even strategize?

"If it can speak, what does it say?" Xien leaned closer to the small window. "What does it *want*?"

"She says it wishes to communicate directly with our..." The young officer peered down at the notes he'd made. He leafed through several pages of his pad and found the characters he'd scrawled earlier. "...with our highest 'hierarchy cluster.'"

"*Hierarchy cluster?* You mean it wants to communicate with our *government*?"

Jing nodded, smiled. "It is saying, 'Take me to your leader.'"

Xien snorted. "Will the virus accept me as leader and talk to me?"

"The girl, Grace, has explained to the virus that you are in command of this fleet but that there is a committee above you, sir. A civilian authority."

Explained to the virus. Xien narrowed his eyes as he continued to stare at the back of her head through the thick plate glass.

105

The virus sounded like a visitor from afar coming to grips with the basics of a complicated indigenous culture. One of the many theories that had been going back and forth in New Zealand before he'd set off on this rescue mission was that the outbreak hadn't been something "homegrown," or genetically engineered, but that it was an extraterrestrial life-form, some dormant microbe that had piggybacked its way across the galaxy on a piece of rock. If that really was what had caused the outbreak, then that speck of life clinging to the side of a ragged chunk of ancient geology represented a first-encounter scenario, the response to the question to which mankind had been seeking an answer forever: *Are we alone?* Well, now, it seemed, they had their answer. He had already broadcast to Cuba that they had a safely contained "specimen" in their fleet but had yet to receive any kind of response back from the Cubans or their American guests.

Maybe adding that the virus was, in fact, an invading alien entity might stir them into replying.

"Has she said *why* the virus wishes to talk with us?"

"No, sir."

Xien wondered whether it understood the concepts of *truce* or *surrender* or even *mercy*—whether it was looking to negotiate a pact or, like some kind of psychopathic killer, it wanted its victim to hear some form of self-justification before finally slitting its throat.

"Is there a way we can communicate *directly* with this virus? And not via the girl?"

Lieutenant Choi shook his head. "She has not so far told me a way."

"Ask her when she wakes up." He took one last look at the huddled form on the cot. "It is best we have as direct a line of communication with our 'alien invader' as possible."

CHAPTER
16

Jake brought the truck to a halt, and both he and Leon stared through the windshield at what lay ahead.

To the left of the road was a sloping bank of coarse grass that became weed-crested dunes of silt before descending into the cold, gray sea. He could see half a dozen small fishing boats, some covered in weathered tarps, bobbing on the choppy water nearby.

Just ahead, the road became a short bridge. To the right of them, he could see a long beach of gravel and mud on which dozens of old, paint-flaking dinghies lay upturned, like a row of beached sea lions sunbathing. The water was calmer on that side of the bridge, protected by a long and straight spit of sand in the distance that swung off to their right as far as Leon could see. A sheltered bay.

Jake had a road map on his lap, his finger jammed down on where they were right now. The small bridge in front of them appeared to be the only connection to a place called the Isle of

Portland. From what he could see on the map, it was a small slither of beach that ran parallel to mainland UK and terminated on the right with a blob. They were there—this little bridge the only link.

"Some island," said Jake.

Leon nodded. Not exactly a remote island, but with a strip of seawater thirty yards across isolating it, it was as good as one. Everett's castle had been protected by a moat only ten or so yards wide in some places.

This was better.

There was a line running across the small bridge. Jake let the truck roll slowly forward until finally they could see what it was—a ragged gap. The bridge appeared to have been deliberately destroyed, either smashed or blown up; either way, they were looking at a gap about twenty feet wide, framed by layers of asphalt, brick, flint, and blocks of limestone.

On the far side of the gap was a portable toilet, tucked up against the right-hand-side guardrail. There was an awning outside it, a white, plastic patio table, and a deck chair whose yellow canvas seat fluttered in the fresh breeze.

Leon nodded. "So how do we get across?"

Just then, they saw an old man emerge from the cabin doorway. He shuffled out into the daylight and waved at them.

Leon slapped the partition at the back of the cabin to alert the others, then he opened the door and glanced back down the road the way they'd come to look for any sign of virals. The nearby fishing village was still and silent.

"I think we're clear." He stepped down onto the road. Jake

got out too, grabbed a gun, and then together, they cautiously advanced toward the crumbling edge of the bridge.

The old man waited patiently for them on the other side of the gap. He wouldn't have looked out of place sitting in one of those upturned and beached boats to their right, repairing an old net. Except he was carrying a shotgun.

"All right, mate?" called out Jake.

"Good morning, gentlemen," he replied.

"We saw your sign." Leon gestured behind him. "Back on the main road."

"Aye."

Leon heard footsteps as the others joined them, spreading out on either side. "Kim, Howard, grab a salt-sprayer and go keep an eye out behind us for snarks." They turned and went back to the truck.

"*This* is the island?" said Finley, sounding less than impressed. "It's not exactly Alcatraz."

"It does the job, young lad," replied the old man. "Twenty feet of choppy seawater does the job real nice and keeps them pesky little buggers away. As for Sheila"—he patted his gun—"she keeps any troublemakers at bay."

"Your sign said that we'd be welcome," said Leon. "Is that the case?"

"Aye. So long as you're all well behaved and infection free."

He nodded, then glanced behind him. Howard was passing Kim a fire extinguisher from the rear of the truck. *Keep it cool. They got our backs.*

"We're good," he replied. "No virals. Can we cross over, please?"

PLAGUE LAND: NO ESCAPE

The old man pinched a bulbous, red nose, then scratched at his thick, white beard. "No infection. Well, that's good."

"So?" prompted Jake. "Can we come over?"

The old man raised a finger to hush him. "Two shakes of a lamb's tail, young man." He picked something up off the plastic garden table. Leon saw it was a radio handset.

"Peter calling home guard. Over."

The handset crackled an answer that Leon couldn't quite hear.

"We got us some visitors down on the bridge."

Another crackled reply. Then the old man cocked his head and squinted at them all intently for a few moments. "We got seven of 'em. Two snotty kids. Two scruffy young boys, a big man, an older woman, and a scrawny-looking fella."

"Nice. I think he managed to offend us all in one sentence," whispered Jake.

Leon ignored him. "I wish he'd hurry the hell up. We're sitting ducks out here."

The radio crackled again after a moment.

"Guv'nor wants to know if you got any guns with you besides *that* one?"

"Yes, we've got a few," replied Leon. "They're in the truck."

"They say they got some guns," said the old man. He waited for a reply.

"Please! Can we hurry this up?" called out Cora. She looked back down the road at Kim and Howard on guard. "We're all feeling quite vulnerable standing out here."

Leon looked back. Beyond the truck was the small fishing town they'd driven through. Narrow cobbled streets between buildings

111

that looked weather blasted and old. Nature, just as it was everywhere else, was doing a splendid job here reclaiming the world left behind. Tall clumps of stinging nettles had sprouted effortlessly from front lawns, window boxes, recycling cans, and even—Leon had spotted—from the seat of an abandoned baby carriage. The buildings, with their dark interiors, were close enough for them to feel uncomfortable hanging around here any longer than they needed to.

The radio finally crackled again.

"He says you lot can come over," said the old man. "But you gotta hand yer guns in."

"OK, fine," replied Jake.

"And I gotta hose ya down first!"

"Oh, come on!" hissed Leon.

Come on. Come on. Come on.

The old man carefully set the shotgun down on the table. "You lot know about the virus and salt?"

"Yeah," replied Leon.

The old man bent down painfully slowly and reached for a length of hose at his feet, turned a tap on outside the cabin, then picked up the hose. He sprayed his arm with water. "There, just so you can see I'm not a *gremlin*!" He aimed it their way. "Right, stand still, you lot!" He aimed high, producing an arc of spattering water that crossed the gap in the bridge. Leon was at the front. He closed his eyes as freezing-cold salt water spattered across his face.

"Good! You seem human!" shouted the old man. "Right...you, scruffy lad, you're next!"

PLAGUE LAND: NO ESCAPE

Jake let out a yelp as the water soaked him. "Bloody hell, it's freezin', mate!"

"What do you want, warm water and bubble bath? Next!" A couple of minutes later, everyone was dripping wet and shivering as the old man slowly turned the tap off and dropped the hose at his feet. "Congratulations, you've all passed our immigration test!"

He bent over and scooped up a length of rope and tossed it across the gap to Leon.

Leon caught it. "What's this do?"

"Have a tug on it and you'll see, lad."

Leon took up the slack and saw the other end of the rope was attached to a wooden beam.

"The pirate's gangplank," the old man wheezed merrily.

Leon tugged on the rope and the plank slithered and scraped across the cracked asphalt on the far side. Jake and Adewale stepped forward, and between the three of them, they quickly pulled it across the six-yard gap.

Leon put a foot on the wobbling plank and shuffled his way across.

"Ah-aaahhh!" croaked the old man loudly. "Welcome aboard HMS *Portland*, me hearties!"

The sea sloshed below him in lazy waves that flowed over and around a mound of collapsed bricks and mortar and drew back with a tired hiss. Leon was looking down at a three-yard drop on either side of the plank—not exactly deadly, but he'd break a bone or two on that rubble if he did fall. He took a dozen more cautious steps across the shaking plank of wood until finally he was over on the far side.

113

ALEX SCARROW

"Next!" barked the old man.

"Come on," urged Leon. "Kim! Howard!" he called out. They turned to look his way. Leon beckoned for them to head to the bridge.

"What about our truck?" asked Jake.

He looked at it. "Well, it's a very nice truck, young man."

"No, I mean how do we get that over?"

"You don't. It stays where it is. For now." He winked. "No one's going to steal it, are they?"

Finally, they were all across, and Leon suddenly felt an invisible weight lift from his shoulders. They were safe for the moment, protected by a barrier the virus had no possible chance of crossing.

He remembered feeling this way at the castle when Freya and he had been welcomed by Mr. Everett, and again in Southampton, when they'd run into those soldiers in biohazard suits—an overwhelming sense of exhaustion and relief. For the last few days, they'd all been measuring the rest of their lives in hours. And since Leon had stepped hesitantly into the role of group leader, he'd had no option but to act confidently, certain of their survival.

It was an exhausting act, and at last, he could drop it. Someone else was going to be in charge and making the decisions for them from now on.

The old man gestured with a thumb over his shoulder. "Now then, there's a taxi waiting for you lot."

Leon looked around him. "Where?"

The old man rolled his eyes. "I'm joking. It's only a short walk, you lazy slacker!"

From the right, the long spit of beach closed in on the road,

PLAGUE LAND: NO ESCAPE

and to the left, the grass narrowed until it was a mere green ribbon beside the asphalt, creating a narrow bottleneck of land. Beyond that, Leon could see the low hump of the Isle of Portland, but in front, running across the narrow road, he could see a barricade.

"That's our second and final line of defense," explained the old man.

It was a thrown-together blockade made, by the look of it, from wooden planks salvaged from countless boats and dinghies. The barricade was about two yards high and looked unlikely to stop anything determined to scramble over it, certainly not the virus.

A head appeared over the wall, with white, tufted hair and wide, just-awoken, blinking eyes.

Another oldie. Leon was beginning to wonder whether they'd strayed onto some island-sized nursing home.

"Dereck!" the bearded old man called up.

"Ah, Peter. I see you have some guests! Are they clean?"

"Aye."

The barricade gate wobbled inelegantly as it swung open. "Sleeping on the job again?" muttered Peter as they passed through and the gate began to close behind them. "*That lazy old bugger* was immigration control"—he raised his voice for everyone to hear—"and *this*…is the Kingdom of Portland!"

PART

II

CHAPTER
17

ON THE WESTERN SIDE OF RUSSIA, NEAR THE BORDERS OF THE Ukraine and Belarus, lies a city called Voronezh, named after the sedate-moving Voronezh River, which runs north-south through it, the city spreading on either side. In the southern district of Levoberezhny is a vast plant that runs alongside Dimitrova Street, a road that takes you either west into the beating industrial heart of the city, or east out into the endless, horizon-less, breadbasket fields of central Russia.

The production plant was half-French, half-Russian owned and, until two years ago, had been the largest producer of yeast in Russia, the second largest in the world, churning out twenty thousand tons of dried yeast powder every year.

In the immediate aftermath of the outbreak, this enormous complex of fermentation chambers, separation tanks, and cane- and beet-storage silos lay abandoned and silent, the cavernous and cadaverous remains of an industrial digestive system.

It took the virus eighteen months to find it.

The first winter, the virus was consolidating across every city, town, and village in the world. It migrated its mass down into subterranean hideaways, underground rail networks, and sewage systems, away from the light and the cold. Each hideaway was linked by threads to the greater viral metropolis. *Consolidation* took the form of the thickening of these linking tendrils, tightening the internal infrastructure, and reaching out to make contact with other masses of the virus.

It was one of these roots, growing eastward out of the city of Voronezh to seek new friends and allies, that came across the yeast production plant. One root that, on a cool February morning, had stopped tunneling belowground and had surfaced briefly. Emerging into the daylight, it began to grow a swollen knuckle of resinous material. The knuckle quickly grew into a distended glistening blister, which eventually burst after a couple of hours, spilling out a dozen scuttling creatures on to the melting snow. That was routine behavior for an exploratory growth: tunnel for a while, then surface and explore. If nothing of interest was found, it would tunnel back down and continue on.

One of the tiny mobile scouts—no bigger than a pebble, released from the root that morning—randomly scuttled through the open door of a storage silo and made a significant discovery.

Yeast. Sugar beets.

The Voronezh biomass concentration swiftly set about relocating to the industrial side of the river, growing rapidly across the four traffic lanes of the Vogresovskiy Bridge, pumping itself eagerly through thickening arteries toward the abandoned

PLAGUE LAND: NO ESCAPE

production plant and the super-reservoir of sugar riches located in the silos there.

As an already-tepid second summer cooled with approaching autumn, news spread of the find. Viral concentrations located farther east in urban ruins with place names like Moscow, Beijing, and Mumbai extended and thickened their links and dispatched emissaries and queries. A trans-Asian "trunk," with a diameter as thick as a car and protected by a thick, leathery epidermis, snaked its way thousands of miles through mountains and deserts, through dense forests and marshland—a construction every bit as ambitious as the Great Wall of China.

The contiguous land mass of Eurasia now had its viral equivalent of a capital city. As once all roads led to Rome, so all threads now led to Voronezh.

Next to one of the silos was a tall cylindrical fermenting tank surrounded by a framework of metal support struts. The vast tank was now buried beneath protective layers of resinlike material that gave it the appearance of a termite mound on an impossible sixty-yard-high scale. A termite mound linked by thousands of viral transit cables, the thickest of them snaking across the ground toward it like tree roots, others slimmer, branching across from nearby buildings, equally coated in resin, like the tentative early support threads of a spider's web.

The ugly, unordered, lumpy coating of resin made it look like the artless work of dull-witted termites and belied the complexity of what lay within: a raging cauldron of broth, a liquid universe.

Camille had been the very first.

Her encounter with the virus on an arid no-man's land in West

Africa, a tundra of dust and dry grass peppered with rusting land mines, had occurred a few days before the virus had become news. In the human family tree of infection, she was Eve: in the words of virologists, Patient Zero.

Camille had become one of the first representatives, one of the first human *advocates*.

What They had told her, what They wanted to be very clear about, was this: They were only here to help. To *facilitate*—that was all.

The big decisions about what happened next had to be ours. Humanity's.

Facilitators. Not murderers. Nor malignant conquerors.

Helpers, that was all They were.

They were here bearing a wonderful gift.

Of all the human arrivals to this micro-universe, Camille had had the most time to try to understand *Them*. At the most basic level, existence was an endless ocean of single-cell life. Everybody, every living thing, was made up of Them and what had once been Us. But whenever cells paused from their endless mingling and began to casually link into daisy chain, they very quickly became complex weblike gatherings. So the cells' "ancestry" began to emerge, an evolutionary life story told in fast-forward. The greater the gathering, the more the story revealed itself.

Camille was vaguely aware of this gathering process as millions of cells, recognizing each other like delegates at a conference, exchanged chemical handshakes and then bonded together. It was like waking from a sleep, the gradual assembly of her consciousness, of her sense of *I*.

122

In her simplest form, she had traveled many of the main arterial routes of this brand-new viral empire. She had awoken to see the gleaming spires of Shanghai draped in vast, fluttering skin sheets, gathering and converting sunlight into sugar, to see forests of methane-filled sacks tethered to and floating above the minarets of Medina. She'd woken to see the fresh water of Lake Geneva covered in a purple lid thick enough to walk on, to see the London Eye turned into a pastel-pink parasol, glowing a rosy hue as sunlight shone through the skin membrane that had grown between its spokes. The virus's ingenuity never ceased to astound her. Ingenuity borne from an infinite crowd intelligence, in the way a school of mackerel can perform the most graceful, constantly evolving, living sculptures from a simple base set of flocking rules.

Camille had seen this new world from outside and from within and couldn't help but admire what it had achieved: the total conquest and subjugation of a complete world within months. And all of that done with a benign intent, a genuine wish to be *kind*.

Now, her foggy version of self-awareness was sharpening and becoming clearer as her recent memories sorted themselves into order. She didn't know the name of the city; the lettering on the signs was unusual, indecipherable, even for a girl who knew French, Hausa, and English. It looked like some kind of production plant in an industrial smoke-belt city, but in viral terms, it was ground zero, their gathering of command clusters. Their Vatican City.

Their epicenter.

CHAPTER
18

THEY HAD INFORMED CAMILLE THAT IT WAS TIME FOR A gathering. The process of consolidation demanded it now. A unifying of purpose, a synchronization of efforts, as the virus prepared to embark on the third and final stage of its ambitious program. But before that happened, some matters needed to be resolved.

Camille let her mind assemble the illusion. She had seen pictures in her battered, old school textbooks of American government buildings and chose a visualization that seemed to suit the vast liquid gathering of biomass. She imagined a courtroom on a grand scale, converting the boiling cauldron of cellular life into rising tiers of pale marble benches arranged in a semicircle around a stage and populated with an audience.

Humanity.

The tiers receded into the distance until they vanished into a haze. The faces nearest to her were defined by what she sensed of them—amino acid signals that suggested a gender, an ethnicity, an age.

She visualized the representative for "Them" as a judge in a long, powdered wig and flowing robes, a majestic figure with deep-set eyes and a Roman nose, sitting on top of a podium on a marble throne, and she presented herself as the little girl from an African village that she'd once been.

Even down to her faded flower-print dress and her pink gel flip-flops.

Camille was here as an "advocate witness," one of 169 chosen witnesses. They were all here to share their knowledge, and the judge was here just to listen and arbitrate.

Deep within the thick broth inside silo three, a chemical spread out like ink dropped into a washbasin of clear water, diluting as it went, eventually staining the water a faint and uniform pale blue. Camille's mind translated that into a "shhh" being passed back through the gathered crowd, tier by tier and up into the distance.

Now that the low murmuring of voices had been silenced, the judge leaned forward on his throne and spoke with a soft but commanding voice. "You understand why you and the other advocate witnesses have been called together? To decide the fate of those who remain."

They nodded.

"Let us begin." He turned to look toward Camille and the other witnesses around him. She could taste their nervousness and imagined they could taste hers. "The first may introduce itself."

ALEX SCARROW

She felt attention turn her way, sensed faint chemical feelers daisy-chaining around her.

"My name was Camille Ramiu. I was one of the first...I think?" She looked up at the judge for confirmation.

He nodded. "Yes, you were."

She turned to face the endless audience. "I was an orphan in a warring country. My mother died of sickness; my father was killed by militia. I became my sister and my brother's guardian. I saw a dog was dying—it licked me. And now I know that that was when I was saved." She turned to look over her shoulder, up at the judge. "I want to thank you."

She saw him nod and the slightest smile touch his solemn face. How much of that was chemically signaled and how much was the embellishment of her imagination was unclear.

"My mother died a few months before you came to our world," she continued. "So she is gone. Lost forever. I know I will never see her again."

"That is regrettable," acknowledged the judge.

"If you had come sooner, if she had been infected like me...she would be with me now." She turned to the others nearby. "I cry for those poor people who remain *outside*. Outside...if they die, then they are lost. Forever... That is the tragedy."

She had lived the last year of her human life in a shelter made from dried mud bricks and a plastic awning stolen from a garbage dump. Just her and her younger brother and sister. Now all of humanity was her family, her brothers, her sisters. This microcosmic universe was her home.

"The fact that there are enough people out there who remain

outside," she continued, "enough of them to be able to get ships to rescue more—this worries me." She looked at the judge on high, the other witnesses, and the endless audience.

"I know not all of you are fully here. Some of you exist as a part of your full self, and for you, when you return and reassemble, you must ask this question: *Are they a danger to us?* Do they have weapons that could hurt us?"

Camille had experienced enough of men in worn khaki uniforms carrying guns, and handheld rockets, and grenades and machetes.

"I am worried. I think we all should be worried. I think we cannot decide what comes next until the first part of the job is done, until we know we are safe."

The judge stirred. "Complete assimilation of your kind?"

"Yes." She nodded vigorously. "Yes. They are out there. Still. And while they are, they remain a danger."

"Your contribution is a valid consideration. Thank you." It was an advocate witness who stepped forward many hours later to present a very different case. Her appearance to Camille was vague, unresolved. Almost ghostlike. Camille's sensory outer cells had barely brushed against the next witness in the swirling cauldron. But, as the witness drew nearer, Camille was able to start getting a sense of who she'd once been.

A young girl like her.

"My name is Grace Friedmann. This is only a small part of me, brought here by a good friend of mine, a doctor called Rachel Hahn, so I could be here to speak. The rest of me"—she looked up at the judge—"is with them. The outsiders. I'm trying to reach out to them."

CHAPTER

19

"ARE YOU READY FOR THE BRIEFING, PRIME MINISTER?"

Rex Williams felt the eyes of his cabinet: the assembled senior officers of New Zealand's armed forces, the People's Liberation Army and Navy, the Royal Australian Navy, all resting on him.

Am I ready?

He'd have answered no, if he were allowed. Three years ago, Rex had been a freshly appointed junior health minister with virtually no experience of leadership or dealing with government officials and no knowledge at all of healthcare. He'd found himself, at the age of twenty-five, the youngest member in the National Party's history to be on the election team. The party was after the youth vote, and he'd been selected because he was young and good-looking, and that always helped.

Now, three years later, not only was he New Zealand's caretaker prime minister, but also the civilian figurehead of the recently patched-together Pacific Nations Alliance. He knew he was far too young to be staring at this room full of elder statesmen and silver-haired chiefs of staff in their crisply laundered uniforms. All of them, no doubt, wondering why a *boy*, barely able to grow a beard, was suddenly running the show.

He nodded. "You can proceed with the briefing. Thank you."

This was his government's first full briefing since the fleet had returned last week. There had been voices among the senior officers in the Chinese navy that the scientific data they'd gathered should be for Chinese use only. No doubt their suspicion in sharing information had been provoked by the Americans' continuing stony silence over in Cuba; they acknowledged the regular transmissions from New Zealand with little more than a *yeah, we hear you.*

Luckily Captain Xien had silenced his officers' concerns and brought everything they'd learned about the virus to the table.

The lights in the briefing room dimmed as a small projector winked on and displayed a title slide on the projection screen.

VIRAL SUBJECT—OBSERVATIONS

The presentation had been put together by a team from Xien's Chinese contingent, with contributory notes from a renowned child psychologist based here in Wellington, an academic linguist down from Auckland, and an American physicist. Presenting the slides was a junior Chinese navy officer.

"Good morning, Prime Minister Williams and cabinet members," he started nervously. He cleared his throat. "Please forgive my English. It is not perfect. First, I will introduce myself. My name is Lieutenant Choi Jing. Captain Xien, Commander of the

ALEX SCARROW

People's Navy, requested that I should present this briefing to you because I have had the most contact with the subject. She, uh... she has, I believe, come to trust me. So..." He left that last word hanging in the air as he fumbled with the clicker, looking for the next slide.

Rex stared at the first image in the presentation. A grainy black-and-white picture of a young, small figure with dark hair walking up a boarding ramp. The image was very poor quality, probably taken from some closed-circuit security camera. Stark light from a nearby floodlight cast hard-edged shadows across the ramp. In the background, he could see what looked like blurs of light, possibly the glare of other floodlights or possibly flames.

"The subject came from among the contingent of civilians gathered in the United Kingdom. I believe you have all read the report about the departure from Southampton?"

Heads in the audience nodded. Rex certainly had. It sounded like the whole thing had been a disastrous screwup—too many people waiting to be rescued, too few boots on the ground, too little known at the time about what the virus was capable of.

"In the chaos, the vetting system broke down, and many civilians were taken aboard that could not demonstrate they had been successfully tested and cleared. The subject took advantage of this disturbance and managed to board our aircraft carrier."

The Chinese officer moved to a TV monitor. It showed shaky footage taken from aboard the Chinese carrier, down at the waterfront. Rex could see figures rushing in all directions.

He could see flames, dancing up from rows of tents.

Jing muted the sound, and they watched the rest of the short

PLAGUE LAND: NO ESCAPE

clip in an uncomfortable silence. When it finally ended, Jing spoke again.

"As you see, the departure was very chaotic. The American end of the enclosed perimeter was closer to the containment pen. They were completely overrun when the outbreak chain reaction occurred."

Next slide. A much clearer picture of the same small figure in a surgical gown, huddled on a bunk in a small empty room.

"We repeated the testing procedure on all the British civilians that boarded our ships several days later. It was during this process that the subject indicated that she was infected. Before her blood could be taken, she made the following announcement."

Jing looked down at a clipboard of notes.

"These are the words she spoke: *I'm remade. I'm a viral manifestation. A human copy. [...] Tell them I'm here to help. Tell them I won't move a muscle.*"

He looked up at the audience, then directed his gaze to Rex. "Prime Minister Williams, she offered no resistance. We were able to quickly lock her in the carrier's radiation isolation chamber. To date, she has cooperated fully to all our requests."

Rex decided it was the right moment to step in with a question. "I read the report. It appears a large number of the people who gathered in Southampton in response to the radio message were infected, possibly without even knowing about it. So obviously, I have a concern about all the refugees that were picked up. Are we certain she's the only one who's infected?"

"Yes, Prime Minister. All have been tested for saline coagulation response and estrogen levels."

131

The refugees were all currently in a floating quarantine camp. Rex's administration was taking no chances. The camp was a P&O cruise ship, hastily retooled and refurbished to carry the refugees and a small staff of soldiers and medical personnel.

"What about the American ships? The report said they were overrun in Southampton?"

"Mr. Williams..."

Rex twisted in his seat to look down the front row of seats at Captain Xien.

"We were in range for radio contact on the first week." His English was not as comfortable as the lieutenant doing the presentation, delivered staccato as he struggled to find the right words. "Most of the American ships also escaped, and they made these same tests on their people. The report exaggerates when it says they were...'overrun.'"

"Well, thank God for that," sighed Rex.

It really was ridiculous how tight-lipped and paranoid the Americans appeared to be. He knew the current acting president was a man called Douglas Trent. But he knew nothing much about him. He presumed it was the large presence of Chinese members in their alliance that was making Trent so damn paranoid.

Jesus. You'd think 99 percent of the population being wiped out would change things. Apparently not.

Rex turned back to face Lieutenant Choi, waiting patiently to continue with his slides.

"Please, carry on with the presentation," said Rex.

The next slide made him gasp—not just him, the entire audience.

It took him a few seconds to make sense of what he was seeing

PLAGUE LAND: NO ESCAPE

on the projection screen. It was clearly another image taken in the same small, sparse room. There was the bunk on which the girl had been huddled in the previous slide. But there was no little girl now. Where she'd been was her green gown and what looked like her bones, most of them on the bunk, some scattered across the floor. The white bedsheets were stained a dark crimson. Glutinous, meaty strands dangled over the side of the bunk, down to the floor where a glistening pile of what appeared to be organs sat in a pool of dark blood.

Rex had once seen a picture of the unpleasant aftermath of a hiker in Yosemite meeting a grizzly bear. It looked a lot like this, as if some large, voracious predator had entered this small room, killed and eaten the girl, and left the pieces it didn't want.

"The subject, Grace, has demonstrated she is precisely what she claims to be. Not someone merely infected by the virus, but a manifestation of the virus that is able to change form and structure at will."

Jing turned to point out several details in the image. "This is a more *natural* condition for her. She has explained to me that maintaining the human form is…a *tiring experience* for her, so she often chooses this."

"Jesus Christ!" said one of the Australian officers. "You're saying that…this *mess* is actually alive?"

Jing nodded. "Yes. It is a less exhausting, less energy-consuming state for her. She is able to reform her human state, but this takes several hours to achieve."

Rex felt his stomach queasily flipping over. The slaughterhouse scene in front of him was grotesque enough, but the fact that it could somehow pull itself all back together again like some grisly movie of a person butchered in reverse was hideous.

"If you will observe closely," continued Jing, pointing to locations on the screen, "the skeletal framework is actually a mixture of real bones and components made from a tough, resinlike substance. The skull is real. The rib cage, the pelvis—these are also real bones. But you might be able to see from this photograph that some of the larger limb bones—the femur, the fibula, over here the humerus, the radius—these are different and made of the resin substance."

Rex could see that they were darker and thicker, like the bones of a Neanderthal.

"The subject has explained to me that the virus prefers to use the existing skeletal framework of the form it wishes to mimic where possible. Where this is not possible, it is able to fabricate resinous approximations, but this requires much more time and also the sacrifice of living matter."

"Sacrifice of living matter?" asked someone in the audience. "What the hell is that supposed to mean?"

"Sacrifice. Yes," replied Jing. "The virus is able turn some of its biomass into this hard resin. But the resin cannot return to become part of the biomass again. It is in effect dead tissue, *spent* biomass." Choi pressed his clicker again to reveal the girl huddled on the bunk once more. "This next slide is footage of a time-lapse sequence showing the subject deconstructing from human to resting state, then reconstructing. Please note the running time in the corner as the process advances..."

Rex sat back in his chair and wanted to close his eyes. This was too much. He really didn't want to see a child melt before him.

You have to. You'll be meeting her very soon. You need to know everything They have.

He opened his eyes and watched and immediately wished he hadn't.

The room was completely silent, the breath of everyone in it held while the sequence lasted. When it was over, breaths were released; a stirring filled the small conference room.

"At the moment, the subject is only able to communicate in human form. In this form, she prefers to be addressed as Grace."

"Why has the subject picked *that* name?"

Lieutenant Choi shrugged. "She has told me that is her name." He looked down at the clipboard he was carrying. "This concludes my observations and my part of the presentation. I must hand over to someone else now?"

"Dr. Calloway?"

Rex heard a chair scrape the floor behind him, and in the half-light of the room, he saw someone take the place of the Chinese Navy officer. Tall and broad framed, in perfect contrast.

"My name is Dr. Kevin Calloway. Good morning, ladies and gentlemen. I'm a doctor of psychology, and I specialize in clinical neuropsychology, child psychology, and psychosocial dynamics." He took in a deep breath, paused for a moment.

"Since we are not dealing with psychosis or a mentally disturbed child but, in fact, a brand-new form of life, my expertise on Grace is arguably of limited value. I haven't been able to communicate with the subject so far. It appears she is only prepared to—for the want of a better term—*assemble* for Lieutenant Choi. But I have reviewed the recordings of their discussions over the last two weeks aboard the Chinese carrier."

Calloway paused, steepling his fingers beneath the bristles of his clipped beard as he appeared to ponder how to continue.

"What it seems we have here is some form of community intelligence, or 'hive mind', to use a bloody awful science-fiction term. 'Grace' represents a colony of minds, of which her identity is the most dominant. In the conversations with Lieutenant Choi, she has explained that the girl she assembles into *is her*...or, I should say, *was her*. She was a girl called Grace who was affected by the virus in a slightly different way than most other infected people."

"Different way? Can you expand on that?"

Rex turned to see that the interjection had come from the health minister.

"In some rare cases, it appears that there is a form of slower-rate 'dormant' infection. The pathogen gets into the body and then appears to do nothing for some time. Now, whether that's due to some level of immunity, either natural or from the effect of medications being taken, I don't know. Grace hasn't talked about that. She has said, though, that this slow infection has allowed her to act as a go-between, if you will, an intermediary between us and...Them."

"Them?" Rex Williams spread his hands, exasperated at the term. "I've heard that word used several times before. Can you explain to me why we're calling a bunch of microbial life forms 'Them'?"

Calloway hunched his shoulders. "Because it appears to be intelligent, Prime Minister. It can strategize. It can plan. *It can*

PLAGUE LAND: NO ESCAPE

reason. But, more than that, it's not one intelligent entity but many millions, *billions* even."

He let those words sink in before trying to put it into another context. "We may have to start thinking of any exchange between ourselves and what's inside this girl as communication with another civilization. What I'm saying, Prime Minister, is we should start thinking of this as a first-encounter scenario."

Rex could hear breath being taken in all around him. "You mean like..." Rex didn't want to say the word; it would sound idiotic, gullible. "You're talking about an *alien* encounter?"

Calloway nodded. "It *is* alien, insofar as we have never encountered life in this form before. Whether it came from outer space, whether it's a life-form that's been lying inert for millions of years in permafrost, and because of global warming, it defrosted and came to life...we can't say. Either way, it's our first encounter with another form of intelligent life."

"That's a load of crap!"

Rex turned to his left. Front row, three or four seats away. It was Bullerton, the Australian defense minister, one of only a handful of cabinet ministers who had managed to get the last plane out of the capitol of Canberra. "We can make a whole load of fanciful bloody assumptions about a goddamn bug...or we can just sterilize the bloody thing!"

Several heads nodded along with that.

"This is a bloody pathogen! It's a lethal, liquefying bastard of a plague that's managed to nearly wipe out the whole world! For crying out loud, it was probably engineered in some North Korean lab!"

ALEX SCARROW

"Hold on—" began Rex.

"We got a thousand miles of salt water around us," the defense minister continued, "and we know this thing can't swim through it or fly over it against prevailing winds, so what the hell are we doing playing around with it? We need to just incinerate this subje—"

"Yet," Rex cut in. "It can't swim through it or fly over it...*yet.*"

Other voices chimed in. The room suddenly became noisy.

Rex, you'd probably better get ahold of this.

He stood up and raised his hands. "Everyone...please!"

The noise increased.

"Let's not piss around here! Torch the bloody thing before someone gets careless with it!"

"...it gets out and we're history..."

"...we need to evaluate what we're dealing with..."

"...nearly lost our rescue fleet, for Chrissakes!"

"...not worth the risk of..."

Rex cupped his mouth. "Everyone! SHUT. THE. HELL. UP!"

He had a quiet room again.

"I'm satisfied that the subject, Grace, is securely contained," he said calmly. "I presume we can obtain a sample to analyze further. In the meantime, if the virus wants to actually talk with us..."

He turned to look at the frozen last image of the time-lapse sequence still up on the projection screen. He was staring at the disassembled form: the strings of flesh, the pile of organs on the floor, the stained sheets and ropes of bloody growth climbing the wall beside the bunk.

"...if *this thing* wants to talk, it can't hurt for us to listen."

"Prime Minister?"

Rex saw a hand raised. "Yes?"

"If the virus *does* want to talk with us…how much of what we learn are we going to share with the Americans?" *Good point.* His eyes met Xien's. Giving the Yanks everything and getting nothing back wasn't going to go down well with anyone.

"Let's find out what we're going to learn first, all right?"

CHAPTER
20

FREYA STARED OUT THROUGH THE RUSTY BARS OF THE TALL window at a row of jetties on the far side of Havana's bay. The three U.S. Navy destroyers and the USS *Gerald R. Ford* were berthed there, the aircraft carrier making the three other ships look like mere tugboats by comparison.

She was told the warehouse had been used solely for storing tobacco products until the outbreak. The tangy smell of the dried leaves seemed to have permanently infused itself into the crumbling plaster walls and the hard ground. The long, empty building was divided into three equal sections by floor-to-ceiling wire-grille partitions. There was a door at the bottom of each partition left wide open. The one concession to free movement they'd been allowed was the ability to walk the length of the warehouse. The partition walls of rust-coated mesh were a part of the old building, not something recently installed to contain or segregate people, but presumably there to separate bundles of drying tobacco leaves.

PLAGUE LAND: NO ESCAPE

Freya was losing track of the number of days they'd been held here, fifteen at least. She let go of the bars and stepped away to let someone else have a turn at feeling the cool air on their face.

As they'd been escorted off the ship, she'd caught a glimpse of Leon's father arguing with an army officer.

He'd seen her over his shoulder and gestured something quickly: a fist to his cheek, little finger pointing to his mouth, thumb to his ear. In normal times, that would've meant *I'll call you.*

Freya presumed it meant *I'll be in contact,* or *I'll get you out,* or something, since cell phones were a thing of the past now.

That had been two weeks ago, and she'd heard nothing from him since.

They were being fed in the same chaotic and ill-conceived way they had been back in Southampton. Every morning, several snarling forklifts rolled into the warehouse accompanied by a platoon of edgy-looking marines who held their guns ready to use. The forklifts deposited wooden pallets laden with bottled water and canned food, some of it with sell-by dates stamped on them from the 1970s, then reversed back out of the building. Then it was a free-for-all for the eight hundred or so people that were being kept in there.

God help me. From Mr. Carnegie's exclusive Oasis, to their Norwich hideaway, to Everett's doomed castle, to the containment pen in Southampton...now this ghastly place. Every step seemed to have taken Freya to a place worse than the last.

She'd had a chance to look at every one of the faces in here at one time or another and was now certain of it: Leon and Grace weren't in Cuba. They were either stuck back in England or well on their way to New Zealand.

She wondered how much longer they were going to be kept here in these unbearable conditions. So far she'd kept to herself, not wanting to make friends or even acquaintances. She'd assumed they were going to be held here for a few days while arrangements were made to assimilate with the rest of the population. Two bloody weeks so far, and no sign of that.

Oh God, Leon...why did I ever suggest we leave Norwich?

Duh, because you'd probably be dead by now, stupid.

Well, maybe there's something to be said for finally being out of the game? Dead.

Freya balled her fist and smacked her thigh for such a weak and pitiful thought. *Freya, you're alive, right? So shut up with give-up shit like that.*

She searched for a positive thing to think about and managed to find one. At least her hips and legs weren't aching half as much as they had been months, or even weeks ago. She wondered whether the warmer temperature was somehow helping her move more easily.

So, there's that little win—screw you, MS.

She slumped against the flaking wall and slid down onto her haunches, feeling old paint fleck away and tumble down her shoulders. Across the floor, another fight had just started up. It was between a couple of men who, from the look of it, had different opinions on who owned a two-liter bottle of water.

There'd still been some vestigial signs of the legendary—or mythical—stiff upper lip. Back in Southampton, people were

PLAGUE LAND: NO ESCAPE

prepared to stand in line, to say, "excuse me," or, "no, you go first." But that seemed to have finally gone—British manners stripped away to reveal the cavemen beneath.

She really hoped Mr. Friedmann was doing *something*. He'd told her how grateful he was for telling him about his kids. He'd promised her this would be just for a few days, while they got their act together and figured out how to integrate them.

Please, Mr. Friedmann...could you get me the hell out of here? Please?

Tom had come this morning with every intention of having harsh words with Trent. The rescued Brits were being kept in appallingly inhumane conditions and needed to be let out and allowed to integrate into Trent's little kingdom. There were useful people in there—doctors, nurses, engineers, mechanics, all of whom could contribute something. But looking at the man now, he had the feeling he wasn't going to be able to push Trent too far on this.

He's losing control.

"Mr. President, look, I—"

"Tom," he interrupted. "Captain Donner's report about the escape from Southampton and the outbreak on the cruise ship made for some very disturbing reading. I'm not gonna lie—it's scary stuff. The virus? Seriously? It can actually make *copies of humans*?"

"Yes, sir."

"*Convincing* copies? I mean...just like you and me?"

He nodded. "Convincing to look at, yes."

"And to talk to? Can they talk?"

ALEX SCARROW

"Yes. From the eyewitness accounts I've read, what I saw with my own eyes... Jesus, Doug. They look and sound just like us!"

Trent's lips pursed and relaxed, pursed and relaxed, like a fish in an aquarium. Finally, he spoke again, his voice low.

"And you brought me nearly a thousand people who could all be goddamn copies? Could be infected? Could be...*pod* people?"

"I told you, they've *all* been thoroughly tested."

"Right. This salt test of yours?"

"Our partners in the PNA established the test. It causes infected blood to react. To coagulate. It's an easy test to administer."

"And yet despite this planet being mostly made of salt water, it managed to conquer all four corners of the world in just a few weeks?"

"It took advantage of wind patterns during the outbreak when it was just floating spores. Now it's evolved to form more complex life-forms so, luckily for us, its travel options are more challenging."

"You know it was airborne. Spores carried by the wind." Trent abruptly turned away from the window and walked back to his seat behind the desk.

Tom decided to follow his lead and retake his position standing before it.

"I'm gonna guess, Tom, that you came here today to ask me to let those people out?"

He nodded. "They're clean. And you said you needed more people. You said—"

Trent held up a hand to stop him. "Not going to happen, *amigo*. They're staying put. They're staying right where they are until..."

"Until what?"

"I figure this out."

Figure this out? "Doug?"

Trent's gaze was on something behind him. Not even in the room anymore. He'd only seen Trent like this a couple of times before; it was like the lights were on and no one was home.

"Mr. President?" Nothing. "Doug?"

He blinked, stirred and returned, then offered Tom a fleeting, almost apologetic smile. "Yeah, I gotta figure out what I'm gonna do here."

"What *are* you going to do?"

Trent stuck his hand out across the desk. "Thanks for coming in today, Tom. And thanks for all your help coordinating that relief effort."

Tom stared at the offered hand, hovering above the desk. "We're done here? You and me?"

"If I need your help, old buddy, I'll give you a call."

"That's it?"

No answer. Trent was just staring at him, flinty eyed.

"Look, Doug, I was going to suggest we resume communications with the PNA in New Zealand. We should be sharing information. Sharing data. We should be cooperating as much as possible with them. As far as I'm aware, we're pretty much all that's left of humanity."

"Thank you, Tom," said Trent. His hand was still stretched out and maybe just a few seconds away from being retracted.

You don't *ignore the Trent handshake*—that's what his old billionaire business buddies used to say about him.

Tom took his hand. "All right, Mr. President. You know where to find me."

He let go, turned around, and headed for the double doors.

CHAPTER
21

Dear Freya,

So, I'm writing diary entries to YOU now, instead of Dad. Which makes me wonder if I'm truly messed up in my head or just love writing messages to people who're never going to read them.

Anyway...surpri-i-se. Guess whaaaat. I'm still alive! And I know you and Grace are. Don't ask how I know, I just do.

The thing is, I've got no idea whether you two ended up with the Americans or the Chinese. Either way, you're probably sitting pretty on a tropical island somewhere— Cuba or New Zealand, right? Sipping punch or something. Well, here's the thing: I'm on an island too. It's a small island that sits on the end of a long thin spit of sand that goes out into the sea. There's only one way to get on it: a bridge—well, that's been blown apart in the middle. Kind of like Everett's moat and drawbridge but better.

So basically, we're good.

Facts and figures: The island's called the Isle of Portland. It's four miles long and less than two miles wide. There are roughly two thousand people here. Most of them were living here before the outbreak. When it happened, they trashed the bridge. Pretty smart, really. They just closed the door on the mainland and said good luck to it.

Which I guess makes them sound like selfish dicks.

But they're not. They're nice people. Lots of old folks and a mixture of random orphans and strays. They're pretty much self-sufficient; they've got a freshwater well, and they're growing stuff all over the island, plus they have motorboats, so every day, they send them out to go fishing and come back with more fish than we can eat. So, no human civilization = no fishing fleets = the fish have been breeding like mad! You

PLAGUE LAND: NO ESCAPE

can literally stick your hand in the sea and pull out a cod.

So I'm eating well. Mostly fish chowder. In summary—I'm alive.

Love, Leon

Prime Minister Rex Williams looked at the blind drawn down in front of the observation window: a thin gauze of white material that seemed to glow translucently.

"Prime Minister Williams." Lieutenant Choi bowed his head politely. "I must warn you that *Grace* is at present in a form you may find...*unsettling*."

Rex had seen enough images over the last couple of years to harden himself to this. He'd seen shaking smartphone footage collated from around the world in the final week, he'd seen security camera images and extremely high-resolution photographs taken by spy planes flying as low as they dared. He'd seen whole cities in Australia turned into what looked like the floor of a slaughterhouse.

"I understand." He looked at the officer. "You did the briefing, didn't you?"

"Yes, Prime Minister."

"And she specifically asked that you be transferred from the Chinese carrier to this research facility *with* her?"

"Yes."

"So she trusts you?"

Lieutenant Choi kept his gaze respectfully downward. "Yes, Prime Minister. I believe so."

"That's good." He nodded. "That's very good." He was vaguely aware he was stalling, pushing back the moment when the blind would be rolled up. The carrier's commander, Xien, had warned him the first encounter could be overwhelming. Too much for those with weak stomachs. Rex Williams wasn't great with blood.

"All right," he whispered. "You had better raise the blind, so she can see me."

Lieutenant Choi reached out and pulled on a cord, and the blind rattled against the glass as the gauze bunched up. Rex clenched his eyes shut as he caught the first flash of crimson contrasting with the cold, sterile, white room.

He waited until the rattling sound of the blind had ceased and knew the wide observation window had been revealed. He knew that he'd be opening his eyes on a bloodbath. He took a step forward and rested his hand against the glass to steady himself.

Then he opened his eyes. "Oh my God," he whispered.

The isolation chamber was larger than he'd thought it would be: a windowless room, five yards square. It was empty except for a bed, a table, and a chair. He kept his eyes trained on these everyday items—islands of normality amid a horrific slaughterhouse scene.

"Hello?" A small voice came from a speaker placed beside the window.

His gaze finally settled on the gore.

The floor of the room was a shallow puddle of darkened blood that seemed to have grown clotted skin across it, like custard left to stand too long. He could see bloody bones stretched out on

PLAGUE LAND: NO ESCAPE

the bed, the sheets stained dark beneath them and all but a few tatters and strings of flesh gone from them, as if she'd been picked clean by feral dogs. The wall beside the bed was decorated with complicated spider webs of dark tendrils, branching, zigzagging up toward the ceiling. At the top, the tendrils had let go of the wall and grown fragile-looking, bulbous, pink, veined "balloons" the size of watermelons. They swayed gently on their hair-thin stalks.

"Those things are membranes inflated with hydrogen," said Lieutenant Choi softly. "They are gathering energy from the ceiling UV light."

"*Hello.*" The voice from the small speaker again. It sounded sexless, ageless, neutral.

"Hello," replied Rex, unsure as to where he should be looking. He had no idea which twisted pile of blood and gristle he should be addressing. "My name is Rex Williams. I became New Zealand's prime minister after the outbreak, and for the moment anyway, I'm the Pacific Nations Alliance's civilian leader."

"*My name's Grace.*" He couldn't see where the words had come from or what in the room had spoken them. Lieutenant Choi pointed to the chair beside the table.

Rex could see a tangle of glistening pink and purple cords winding around each other and up the backrest of the chair, where they meshed together into a knot the size of a large fist. He looked at Lieutenant Choi. *That's her?*

"*Are you the one who's in charge of everything?*"

He saw a small opening in the knot, like the fingers of a shadow-puppeteer's hand mimicking a mouth. He thought he could see something glistening inside it, thick and sluglike.

151

A tongue?

"Yes," he replied, pausing, clearing his throat. "In theory."

"*Good.*" The bloody knot flexed.

"Can you...*see* me, Grace?"

"*Yes, of course.*"

Lieutenant Choi pointed again. On the table was a small deposit of organic material. It could have been cuts of liver all ready to be wrapped up by a supermarket butcher in waxed paper. He thought he could see something pale within it, moving, flickering, glistening.

My God, is that some kind of optic nerve?

"I was warned that this would be an...*uncomfortable* encounter. Please don't take any of my reactions as a sign of discourtesy."

"*It's OK. I know this is going to be kind of gross for you.*"

Rex couldn't help but let out a single nervous bark of laughter. He clamped his mouth shut and planted his hand over it.

"*You laughed?*"

"I apologize. I'm nervous." He nodded. "And just then you sounded so..."

"*Human?*"

"Yes."

"*That's because I am. I was... We are.*"

"You say...*we*? Are there others in your room?"

"*Yes. We.*"

"How can you say you are human?"

"*I am. I may not look like I used to. I'm as human as I ever was. But...*" Her words were followed by a long pause.

Rex studied the two clusters of organic structure: the one

PLAGUE LAND: NO ESCAPE

on the desk and the one perched on the back of the chair. The "mouth" was little more than a fleshy purse, its rim a roughly circular loop of muscle material that flexed and puckered, the rest of it an envelope that acted as a resonating chamber. At the back was a central, thick stamen that curled and swayed from its fixed base like a sea anemone. He wondered if the glistening rope of cords winding down the side of the chair was linked to its mind hidden somewhere in the pool on the floor.

"But...I'm also much more than I was."

Rex wanted to know about the identity she was using, the name. "You call yourself Grace. Is that the person you were before the outbreak?"

"Yes. Grace. Friedmann."

Rex noticed Lieutenant Choi scribble something down on a pad. Maybe the last name was a new detail.

"Was it this...*Grace's* body...you used to get aboard the Chinese carrier?"

"My body, yes. I can remake the way I looked once. It takes time and effort to do it though. It's a real pain."

He shook his head at how surreal this moment felt. While the disembodied voice sounded only vaguely human, the language it... she...used was as natural and real as any teenager he'd ever spoken to. He was looking at something that could only be considered an *it*, the ghastly aftermath of an explosion. And yet, in their brief conversation so far, the words she used, the expressions...this unrecognizable mess was becoming more human to him.

"Grace. Can you tell me more about the term *we*? You talk as if you're part of a group."

"We? *Well, it's everyone They have absorbed. Every human and every creature. We all exist together...on the inside.*"

They? Rex made eye contact with Lieutenant Choi. "And what can you tell me about *They*, Grace?"

"*They,*" she replied. He wasn't sure whether that was her answer.

"Can you tell me about *Them*, Grace? I've been informed that 'They' are something other than the people and creatures who've been infected. Are They the ones who did this, the ones who infected our world?"

"*Yes.*"

"Grace, you communicate with Them, don't you?"

"*Yes, I do.*"

"What do They want?"

"*To help.*"

"To help?"

"*Yes.*"

"They've wiped us out, Grace. There aren't many of us left. Can you assist me in understanding how They consider this to be help?"

"*It's really hard to explain that, Mr. Williams.*" Again, Rex had a compulsive urge to laugh.

"Could you try?"

"*We don't have words for most of what I'd need to say. How do you explain the color green to someone who's blind? How do you explain the smell of fried onions to someone with no sense of smell?*"

The "mouth" organ was still. The speaker hissed softly for a moment. Then finally Grace spoke again. "*How do you explain how awful Miley Cyrus is to a deaf person?*"

PLAGUE LAND: NO ESCAPE

Rex laughed out loud this time. This ghastly mess had just cracked a joke to ease the tension. He wanted her to know he appreciated that, a very human and thoughtful gesture.

"Mr. Williams?"

"Yes, Grace."

"It's better if I...show you."

"Show me? What do you mean?"

"I can infect you..."

Rex took a small involuntary step back from the window. "No, I...I don't wish to become infected."

"The word infection—it's not a fair word to use. I'm inviting you...that's all."

"Inviting me?"

"To enter my world, our world. Then, only then, you'll understand why They are here."

Rex shook his head. "Grace, this pathogen has wiped our world clean of...of *life*. I'm here representing one of two groups of survivors. We're all that's left of mankind. You, or maybe They, may wish to call that an 'invitation,' but it is what it is: *annihilation*. Even if we developed some sort of vaccine that wiped this virus out, chances are we may not survive the next few decades. The world's ecosystem has been seriously destabilized. The development of species on Earth has been reduced to virtually nothing. Complex ecosystems don't tend to survive that kind of a culling."

He waited to hear her response to that. There was nothing forthcoming.

Finally, the "mouth" muscles flexed like an esophageal

sphincter, pushing words out like portions of mashed food. *"All the more reason for you to accept my invitation."*

"I said we *might* not survive, Grace. But you have to understand we're going to fight to survive every inch of the way."

"I can enter your bloodstream, absorb you, bring you into our world, and show you everything. Then I can let you return."

"Return?"

"Exit your blood chemistry. Let your body re-form. Leave you... uninfected. Unchanged."

"That's absolutely not going to happen! I'm afraid I do not accept your...invitation, Grace. I can't!"

"I accept."

He turned to look at Lieutenant Choi. The officer nodded to confirm what he'd just said. "Yes. I will do this."

Rex held his hand out to shut him up. "I'm not offering up bloody test subjects for some sort of—"

"I trust her," said Lieutenant Choi. "We have spoken much. I believe we have become friends."

"Jing," replied Grace, *"they will welcome you in...and I will return you."*

"To be clear, this is *not* happening!" snapped Rex. "I'm not prepared to use this man as a guinea pig."

"You have to trust me, Mr. Williams."

"No. Absolutely not!"

"I trusted you."

"What?"

"I offered myself up. I came aboard the big ship, and I announced myself. I could have been burned alive."

PLAGUE LAND: NO ESCAPE

Rex turned his eyes back to Lieutenant Choi.

The Chinese man nodded, silently confirming that he was ready to sacrifice himself.

"You know, I could have passed your test. Then I could have infected the others quietly."

"Why didn't you? You had the perfect opportunity, more than a month out at sea, and no way for anyone to escape. Why didn't you?"

"Because I want to talk. I want to show you."

"Show me what?"

"What life can be."

Freya—

What the hell happened to you and Grace in Southampton? One second, we were all together. The next, you and Grace were gone. I waited for you two outside the holding pen. I know you got out. You must have gotten out.

I miss you, Freya. God, I really miss you. I wish I'd said something the night before it happened. Remember? We were scooched up beneath the raincoat? Right then I was going to say "I love you," but it didn't seem like the right time. The others were still missing, and let's face it, the pen stank of human crap.

Not exactly romantic. There are better places to say something like that, I'm thinking. But, damn, I wish I had. It's funny, we were holed up together for a year and a half in Norwich, then we were at Everett's castle. All that time, we could have, you know, gotten together. Why didn't we?

Why didn't I say something? Say hi to Grace for me.

Leon

CHAPTER
22

"Come on, what do you miss the most?"

Jake laughed. "You're going to call me a totally shallow bastard...but I miss my personal grooming routine."

"*What?*"

"No, seriously, mate." Jake peered through the binoculars again at the road beyond the ragged gap in the bridge. "I used to shower every morning. A long, hot one. Then shave my scalp to a number two on the razor. Then splash aftershave all over and get into clean clothes." He lowered the binoculars and turned to Leon. "I hate waking every morning and smelling like I'm homeless."

Leon laughed. "You get used to it."

"Not me, bro. I hate it." He passed the binoculars over. "Your turn."

The old man, Peter, was sitting outside the portable toilet, enjoying the fleeting rays of sunlight.

Leon changed places with Jake, so he was sitting beside the

toilet's scuffed window. Sentry duty down by the bridge was one of the regular jobs on the isle. The fishermen fished; the gardeners gardened; Jeffery Dunst, formally a marine engineer, kept the generator running with his small staff of helpers. Peter ran the "home guard," which Jake and Leon had volunteered to join. They had this pair of binoculars, a walkie-talkie, a shotgun, a kettle, and a box of coffee and creamer containers. "What about you?"

Leon shrugged. "Where the hell do you start?"

He missed everything—the flicker of a TV set, the amber glow of streetlights, the smell when you passed a coffee shop, the warmth of clothes fresh from a tumble dryer, the soft *whirr* of his laptop's fan, the *ping* of a new post or text. All of that vanished in a single week. Ever since then, pretty much, he'd been living the life of a scavenger. He recalled sitting down in that abandoned nuclear bunker with Grace and Mom and that guy, Mohammed. He and Mohammed had been arguing about Xbox versus PS4 zombie games. Mo was a PS4 guy, Leon Xbox. They had drifted on to that whole fantasy thing about wishing that a zombie apocalypse would actually happen. And then, how quickly their lives had become that stupid fantasy—how much they wanted boring normality to return.

"I miss waking up safely. Knowing the only tough decision that's going to happen this morning is which cereal to pour out."

Jake chortled. "True that."

"Even with the safe places me and the girls stayed at—the castle, the Oasis—there was this constant feeling that it wasn't going to last forever. It was one mistake away from collapsing."

"I know what you mean." Jake leaned back and planted a

muddy boot on the corner of the old camping table. He crossed his legs and stretched. "It's like...dude, we can scavenge cans of beans and dried pasta, but unless we start growing new stuff, it's gonna run out one day."

"Uh-huh." Leon raised the binoculars and swept the outskirts of the small town at the end of the road.

"I sometimes think it'd be easier to just walk out there and say, 'Come on, bitches, infect me!'"

Leon turned in his seat. "Well, that's bullshit!"

"Really? What is this? *Living?*" Jake snorted. "It's a holding pattern is what it is. We'll go on like this until, one day, one of those little bastards gets over the gap, and then it's game over."

"Jake, we're better off here than any other place I've stayed." He gestured out of the window. "This is pretty good. This is the first really defensive place I've come across."

"Yeah. Maybe. But that makes it our entire world, then. A thin beach and an island a couple of miles across, filled with golden oldies. Great. No offense, Peter."

The old man sitting outside the cabin grumbled something sleepily.

Jake lowered his voice. "You know this community will shrink quickly as they die off."

"For now, we're safe. We're alive. We're getting fed. I'll take that."

"That's what I like about you, mate." Jake's boots slid off the table as he leaned forward and punched Leon's arm gently. "Always positive. OK, I'll go with your fight-on-while-it's-worthwhile approach," he added.

"What's that supposed to mean?"

"I'm not going to end my days as a lonely bloody hermit sitting on this chunk of rock."

"What, you gonna go out in a blaze of glory at some point?" It was meant to sound flippant.

"You know what I'd like to do?" said Jake. "I'd take a gun, go out there, over the bridge, and wait for the little shits to come for me." Jake shrugged. "Go down fighting."

Leon peered back through the binoculars. There was no way he'd risk getting overrun by them. He still had nightmares— ones where he saw Mom's face poking through the broken mesh window, those things crawling through her hair, her eyes wide and rolling as she hissed, "They're inside me."

He quickly pushed the image back into the dark corner where it belonged.

"In that case, you'd better make sure you keep the last bullet for yourself, Jake."

"Maybe it isn't so bad."

Leon felt his body go rigid. It took him a few moments to realize that it was anger. Rage. He felt an intense urge to lean over and punch Jake for saying something so goddamn stupid. They were alive right now. Sitting here, with mugs of cooling coffee, talking crap, because they'd survived the outbreak and its aftermath.

Dumb shit like "I give up" or "Maybe it isn't so bad" is what losers say, MonkeyNuts. Set him straight, Son.

"I mean, I've seen it happen up close," continued Jake. "My big sis. I saw her die." He sighed. "You know what the last thing she said to me was?"

"No. Jake, it's not really—"

PLAGUE LAND: NO ESCAPE

"She said, 'It's OK, bro. I'm OK.'"

Tell him to shut up. Now.

"I mean, I think she was trying to tell me she felt good or something. So, you know, maybe it's not so—"

"For Christ's sake, Jake! It's death! The worst goddamn kind of death!" he snapped. He hated the brittle tone in his voice.

"Whoa, mate! Chill!"

He let a second or two pass, let his voice settle. "I have plans to see my sister again and my...friend again. That's my plan. That's my goal."

"Your one true love, huh? What's her name again?" He knew Jake knew. Jake was just teasing him.

"I *know* I'm gonna find them again. Things are going to get better here. Lawrence is a good and stable leader. We'll get shit figured out. Maybe one day soon get a radio mast set up and reach out to the others." He turned to Jake. "I've got good reasons to live, to fight on."

Jake shrugged. "You're saying I haven't?"

"Well, if you're talking about going down fighting...maybe not?"

Peter stomped into the cabin, bleary eyed from his snooze. "What're you boys squabbling about in here?"

"Nothing, Peter. Just talking, mate," said Jake. "Just...shooting the breeze."

Leon felt his sudden anger wheeze out of him like a punctured tire. "Shit. Sorry, Jake. I just..."

"Hey, don't worry about it, mate. I was just messing with you."

"Well, you two young idiots aren't down here to goof off!" grumbled Peter. "You!" He pointed at Leon. "Get back to looking out there! And you...put the bloody kettle on!"

Leon nodded. He raised the binoculars back to his eyes and resumed scanning the world beyond the bridge.

As he panned, he saw something move. "Shit!" He jerked the binoculars back until his view settled on what he'd spotted.

"What is it?" hissed Peter.

"Scuttler," he replied under his breath. "I think I just saw a..."

He adjusted the focus and the patch of crumbling road he was staring at sharpened up. There it was.

Movement.

"Small scuttlers," said Leon. "Really small."

"How many?" asked Jake.

"About...six...seven..."

"Mind if I take a look?" Peter shuffled forward and took the binoculars from him as Leon pointed out where they were.

"About seven yards back from the end of the bridge." Leon watched him squinting into the eyepieces. "Is that what they normally do, Peter? Come up to the edge like that and sniff around?"

"Bugger!" he grunted, studying them silently awhile longer before finally lowering the binoculars. "They've never come right up to the edge like that before."

"*What?*"

"I think they've finally figured out we're here!"

Leon took the binoculars back off him and peered into them once more. He adjusted the focus until he had the fidgeting of their movement in clear view again. He could see something like twenty or thirty of them now, all perched on the crumbling lip of the broken bridge, hair-thin antennae and legs flexing in the air like the whiskers of a rabbit.

CHAPTER
23

Rex Williams and the others watched through the observation window as Lieutenant Choi entered the room from the positive-air-pressure antechamber. He hesitated in the doorway for a moment, looking at the window and the faces of a dozen observers crowding the glass to look in.

It was too late for Lieutenant Choi to turn back now that the inner door had opened. Too late for Rex to ask if he was sure about this. He'd now been exposed to the virus.

Lieutenant Choi sniffed the air. "There is a distinct smell of"— his voice sounded tinny over the wall speaker—"soy, rice vinegar...rich, like *tamari*." He went carefully into the room, stepping on parts of the smooth, tiled floor, avoiding the ones crisscrossed with veins and bacilli-like fingers of growth.

"*Hello, Jing.*" The girl's voice sounded odd to Rex—thicker, with more layers to it, like the beginnings of a chorus. "*It's good to finally meet you in person.*"

ALEX SCARROW

Rex had to admire the man's calm demeanor. Choi dipped his head politely, formally, addressing his reply toward the glistening flesh on the small desk. "And it is a pleasure to meet you as well, Grace."

"*I can see you're concerned, Mr. Williams,*" said Grace.

Rex glanced at the glistening, pale object encased in a purse of deep red muscle tissue. It was nothing he could ever describe as an "eye," but clearly it was the organ she was using to view events in the room and the observation room beyond the window.

"*I promise,*" continued Grace, "*Jing will be unharmed. He's my friend.*"

"We're taking you at your word, Grace," replied Rex.

"What do you need me to do now?" asked Lieutenant Choi.

"*It's best if you remove your shirt, Jing. There will be some blood.*"

He did as she instructed, unbuttoning, then removing the crisp, white top of his navy uniform. He folded it carefully and placed it on a clean part of the floor.

He was wearing a black undershirt beneath. "*That's enough. We just need to get to your arm and shoulder. Now lie down.*"

He sat down, carefully examined the floor around him, then lay back.

"*Spread your arms out wide.*" He did so.

"*Jing, I'm going to reach out for you. There's going to be a little sting as I enter, and that's it. No more pain after that, I promise. You just relax, OK?*"

"Yes, Grace."

"Jesus Christ!" hissed someone standing directly behind Rex. "Are we really letting this happen to the poor bastard?!"

"Be quiet!" snapped Rex. The observation room quieted down.

166

PLAGUE LAND: NO ESCAPE

They watched Lieutenant Choi lying perfectly still, arms stretched out like da Vinci's "Vitruvian Man," his eyes closed, his chest gently falling and rising.

Jesus. Rex had to admire the man's courage. To even enter the room. *Or maybe he's been brainwashed by her to "join" him?*

Rex was not prepared to think beyond this experiment. If Choi did return unharmed and could prove that he was uninfected, then...the same invitation awaited *himself.*

The containment room was still and quiet. Then, finally, the silence was broken by a wet snapping sound. Rex saw something emerging from the largest and thickest pool of organic material on the floor. A dark, wrinkled membrane, like the desiccated skin on a sun-dried date, had formed over the pool during the last few days. Now, something small seemed to be poking around beneath it. A tiny rip in the membrane suddenly appeared, and a bloody, crablike creature emerged—freshly born.

Once again, the silence in the observation room was broken by the exchange of hushed voices. "We saw those things in Calais and Southampton. Thousands of the bloody little—"

He raised his finger to shut them up.

The creature climbed out of the ripped membrane and began to take little uncertain steps across the white tiled floor toward Choi's arm, dragging behind its abdomen what appeared to be a fine, sticky thread.

Is that some sort of umbilical cord?

The creature finally reached Choi's left arm.

"You'll feel some tickling," said Grace. "That's nothing to be afraid of. It's a messenger, a scout making contact with you."

167

The creature's fine legs and antennae touched Choi's arm and began gently caressing his skin.

"What's that thing doing?" asked Rex.

"Lieutenant Choi tells me They are better now at entering us," replied Captain Xien. "They are more familiar with our biology. So, the process can be less...*destructive.*"

The answer came with a trickle of bright-red blood that rolled down across Choi's pale forearm and dripped onto the floor. The creature shifted position, turning delicately around until its abdomen was poised above the breach in his skin, then it lowered itself down, pushing the small bulbous portion of its body through the cut and into his arm. It fidgeted for a few moments, seemingly trying to "back" itself in, then stopped what it was doing, hesitated, and hopped off the arm—minus its abdomen and the umbilical thread. It was just like a bee leaving its stinger behind. The creature scuttled away, its part of the process apparently completed.

"We have made contact with Jing," said Grace. "It will take a couple of hours now to reach him...on the inside."

Jing felt the sting. It was barely a scratch, and as Grace had promised, there was no more pain. He was aware of the cold tiles beneath his bare shoulders, the glare of the fluorescent light in the ceiling directly above him leaching through his closed eyelids and staining his view with a warm amber glow. He watched flecks of micro debris on the surface of his eyes slide gracefully to one side as they avoided direct inspection. He listened to his own breathing, in and out, regular and soothing, the soft fizz of the light above and the quiet hiss of the com speaker, broken every now and then by the rustling of movement or a whispered exchange outside.

Gradually, those sensations began to recede. Time passed.

Time passed.

Time passed...and Jing found himself beginning to wonder if this was what death was like—the gradual descent of awareness, from the outside to the inside, to eventually nothing.

Jesus Christ, his whole arm's gone!

Rex was mentally unprepared to deal with what he was seeing with his own eyes. The speed at which the liquefaction process worked was astounding. Within a minute of that small glistening, crablike thing depositing its body into the incision, the skin around it had darkened to a threatening, angry purple. A minute or so more and the discoloration had extended to reach up to the man's shoulder and down to his elbow. The discolored skin was beginning to glisten wetly in places; sagging dimples were appearing where the tissue beneath the skin was decaying faster than on the surface.

Then came the first gentle *ripping* as gravity won the battle against surface tension. Like gravy skin parting at the spout of a gravy boat, his skin began to separate. Loops of the flesh around Lieutenant Choi's arm began to break away and sag from his bones onto the floor.

Unharmed. She promised he'd be unharmed, Rex reassured himself. She'd explained, for their benefit, that Choi was going to be *completely* subsumed into the virus.

Then returned.

Unharmed.

A full demonstration that entering her world could be done nondestructively.

Ten minutes after that first incision, Rex could see spots of blood soaking through Lieutenant Choi's trousers. He could see the smart cotton uniform deflating as once-firm flesh became jelly, leaving just the ridges of untouched bone to mark the frame of his body.

Choi's face was gone. The purpling of his skin had begun at his temples and bloomed outward across his forehead, around his closed eyes, and onto his cheeks. Rex, watching closely, had noticed how the advancing edge of discoloration was led by much fainter leading lines beneath the skin. As both doctors and various experts had speculated, the living host's arterial system provided a convenient and rapid transport network for the pathogen. Thus, the heart and lungs would be left unaffected until the very end— the cardiovascular system becoming an unwitting conspirator to its own demise.

Half an hour after first contact, Rex noted Jing was no longer breathing.

———

Jing had begun to feel frightened. One by one, he'd felt his senses shut down: first his sight, then smell, taste, then hearing. Even the coldness of the observation room's floor had receded. One by one, his connections to the world were severed until he felt he was a non-corporeal entity, disembodied and floating in darkness.

PLAGUE LAND: NO ESCAPE

He had experienced a sensory deprivation tank once before, an enclosed coffin-like container filled with body-temperature water. It had been one part of his training as a junior officer, assessing his ability to remain calm, checking him for claustrophobic tendencies. He and his fellow officer trainees had been left to float in complete silence and darkness for an hour. For some of his colleagues, it had been a disconcerting experience. For Jing, at first, it had been almost pleasant, with nothing to sense, nothing to feel, hear or see, a chance to descend deep into his mind. To meditate.

But toward the end of the exercise, like the others, he'd begun to experience a growing sense of panic at the dilation of time. An hour, they'd all been assured—just *one hour*, yet each of them afterward had confessed they'd begun to believe a whole morning had passed in there, a *day* even, that they might have been the one trainee forgotten about as the rest of the group moved on to the next exercise!

Jing was beginning to fear that this floating, silent blackness would be his eternity. He wondered how long it would take, existing like this, for the experience of complete sensory denial to drive someone completely mad.

Then...he became aware of *something*.

A brand-new sense.

A sixth sense that could only be described as halfway between taste and smell. Or maybe an amalgamation of both that added up to more than the sum of its parts. He had a new sensation that seemed to stimulate "understandings." First a "flavor" that vaguely reminded him of the first sip of morning tea. He recalled a soothing memory of his mother waking him up on home leave.

171

A tender smile and her cool palm against his cheek and the tap of the cup being placed gently on his bedside table.

He instinctively understood that the triggered memory was *deliberate*. It was a method of communication that preceded a shared language.

Something was greeting him.

Another "flavor"—this time, starch. The smell of his uniform's stiff collar. The same smell that greeted him every morning as he dressed, buttoned up, and prepared for duty.

He had an instinctive understanding that this was something like, *Are you ready.*

Then a "flavor" that reminded him of linseed oil, chalk dust, disinfectant, stimulating memories of his first day at school.

He understood that someone was telling him to focus.

To pay attention.

The final "flavor" stimulated a different part of his consciousness.

[h50o-8fch5thj2ha9-e—Jhs9@-hl*se.-I&s89pjje]

It was halfway between hearing an unrecognizable noise and reading a phrase in a foreign language.

It came again, modified slightly…

[he 5 o 07 c Hn- you$ h r- me—Jing£ 9 @ t 's 0me It'shr8ce…]

It was like someone was tuning a radio for better reception. The peculiar sensation occurred again. Only this time it made sense.

[Hello, can you hear me, Jing? It's Grace.]

CHAPTER
24

Freya and about forty others were being escorted out of the tobacco warehouse. They were all allowed half an hour a day outside in a fenced-off compound that had once been a basketball court. The wheeled doors of the warehouse clattered open, and Freya savored the sunlight on her face as she stepped outside onto the asphalt, warm beneath her feet.

This routine had only been in place for the past week. Somebody, somewhere, presumably Mr. Friedmann, had pulled strings to get them this brief amount of time outdoors. The conditions inside had been getting progressively worse. The toilet areas were being emptied less frequently. The mealtimes were becoming ever more chaotic as less and less food was being brought in by the forklifts. Freya was worried that pretty soon things were going to break down into a brutal version of jungle law: the fittest and strongest shoving their way to the front and taking what they wanted. It wasn't like that *yet* inside the vast warehouse, but she could see that if conditions continued to deteriorate, it wouldn't take long.

She wandered over to the chain-link fence, grabbed the rusting wire for balance, and stretched out her left leg, then her right. This morning, she noticed that her left hip was completely painless, not even the slightest nagging ache.

She'd also noticed her speech getting better, less slurred. She'd been told the symptoms of MS could sometimes appear to plateau for a while, but it was, ultimately, regretfully, a one-way journey.

We can't reverse this, Freya. The best we can hope to do is manage the rate of degeneration.

She straightened up and looked around, hoping to catch sight of Leon's dad. He'd come down here most mornings, bringing with him a little discreet contraband food for her and assurances that this appalling state of affairs was going to be over soon. But she couldn't see any sign of him today.

She looked around at the four sides of the old basketball court. Normally there were about a dozen guards.

This morning, though, there were more of them. A lot more.

She saw three army trucks, led by a Humvee, approaching the waterfront, kicking up dust from the road as they turned off the highway and rattled across gravel toward them.

What's this, then?

Her heart fluttered hopefully. Maybe Mr. Friedmann had finally managed to talk the president into letting them out. Those trucks would take them into Havana; presumably, there would be some sort of accommodation waiting for them and hopefully something useful for them to do.

PLAGUE LAND: NO ESCAPE

The trucks came to a halt, then, one by one, turned and reversed toward the side of the court. She saw Tom Friedmann climb out of the Humvee and walk slowly to stand beside the three backed-up trucks.

Freya crossed the court, heading toward the vehicles. She waved. "Hey! Mr. Friedmann!"

He spotted her and offered her a muted nod. Freya reached the mesh, wound her fingers through and called out again. "Mr. Friedmann! Hey! Are we getting out today?" He looked distracted. An army officer was waiting for instructions from him. Heads nodded briskly, there was an exchange of words, then the officer strode away to pass on whatever orders had been given.

She tried to get his attention again. "Hey! It's Freya! Are we getting out of here today?"

He bowed his head and looked down at his feet.

Dammit. He heard me. He's ignoring me!

That didn't seem like him. She figured he was the kind who'd just come out with it if he had something awkward or difficult to say.

"What's happening?" she called out again, louder this time.

He remained as he was, still looking down at his own feet.

A voice barked out, and a moment later, the canvas drapes at the back of all three trucks were flung roughly aside. In their shadowed interiors, she could see movement going on—something shining as it was moved forward and into the sunlight.

She saw a bare, tanned forearm. A rolled-up sleeve. A gloved hand holding a fire hose. The gleam of a watch strap. The movement of arms and hands following orders.

175

ALEX SCARROW

"NOW!"

Jets of liquid emerged from all three trucks, arcing out across the court. For a fleeting second, she wondered if they were going to be treated to a cooling shower to wash away several weeks' worth of sweat and grime. Hardly the most dignified way of getting clean again, but—screw it—about time and more than welcome.

Then she caught the overpowering odor. Thick in the shimmering air and unmistakable.

Gasoline.

She screamed. "OH GOD, NO!"

The gas soaked her, stung her skin, her face. She backed away from the mesh fence as the arcs of liquid swept across the court, soaking everyone and drenching the asphalt. The air was suddenly filled with screaming, everyone realizing, like Freya, what was about to happen.

Freya, shaking, backed into a corner of the court, staring at her soaked hands and arms, feeling her clothes clinging to her skin, her long, dark hair matted, hanging and reeking of gas.

Oh God. No! Not like this. Not like this!

The hoses stopped. But the screaming didn't. Her voice and everyone else's pleading, crying, screaming, wailing as one of the marines stepped toward the mesh, produced a twist of paper and set it on fire.

Freya saw Mr. Friedmann turn away, head toward the Humvee, sobbing, not even man enough to witness what he was supervising.

The marine held the twist of paper in his hand until it had caught completely, then pushed it through the mesh and backed quickly away.

PLAGUE LAND: NO ESCAPE

Freya's scream became one long, ragged sound as, almost in slow motion, a wave of blue flame swept across the court like a vengeful ghost, engulfing her and everyone else.

"NO!"

She sat bolt upright in her cot, her scream strangled to a thick, throaty gurgle.

It was dark and very still. The stifling air in the warehouse was thick with the sounds of slumber, deep and even breathing, snores and rumbles. And there, perched on the end of her cot, like some fairytale troll, sat Grace.

"Freya," she said softly. "It's me."

Freya was still huffing air in and out of her lungs, like the bellows of blacksmith's furnace. She was still in shock, still half-immersed in the absolute certainty that she was on fire from head to toe, her skin blistering, bubbling, and sloughing from her bones.

"I saw your nightmare," said Grace. "It was horrible." She needed another few seconds to shake off the terror, to pull herself out of the confines of that dream and make sense of the context of this one. Was it another nightmare? Obviously, she was still sleeping.

"Grace?"

"Yes." Grace smiled. "It *is* me. I'm here. This is real."

"Grace," Freya said again. She looked around. She was still in the warehouse, the air still stank of tobacco, sweat, and feces. "How come you're here? How...? Where did—"

"I'm *inside* you, Freya."

"Inside me?"

"I infected you." Three words delivered as plainly and as simply as that. It *must* be a dream, then.

177

ALEX SCARROW

"I want to see Leon," Freya said. "Can I see Leon, please?"

"Freya, this isn't a dream. This is real."

"Uh-huh. Course it is."

"I infected you."

"No, you didn't."

Grace nodded. "I did."

"OK then. How? When?"

"On the way down to Southampton." She leaned forward, reached out for one Freya's hands. Freya instinctively recoiled and pulled her hand back. "Freya, this is not a dream. This is a construction. Like a mind trick. An illusion. It's an illusion I'm controlling."

"You're...controlling *this*?"

"Yes. Because I'm inside you. I'm with you."

"Well, that's just nuts. This isn't real!"

It certainly felt real though. Smelled real. Freya tried to remember if she'd ever had a dream where she could actually *smell* things.

"Freya, please...listen to me. I've got something very important to tell you."

"You...you're not here! You *can't* be here!"

"Not *all* of me is here, just a little. Enough to tell you what I have to tell you."

"This isn't making... I..."

"Freya, please!"

"Grace, I... Shit...this is—"

"You're *saved*. I saved you. You're one of *us* now."

"One of...?"

"And you have a job. A very important job to do."

"A job?"

"Let me explain it to you. Let me *show you.*"

CHAPTER
25

FLIGHT LIEUTENANT JAMIE CAMERON GLANCED AT THE FUEL display. "Ten more minutes of this, Steve, then we'll turn this old bird around."

"Good." His copilot nodded. "My eyes are starting to hurt."

Jamie tapped his throat mic. "Ten more minutes, guys." The rest of the crew acknowledged him.

Flying low at three thousand feet, beneath the top-heavy cumulus clouds, was tiring on the eyes, but the "floaters" had so far tended to hang at this altitude, pushed along more quickly by the lower and thicker air currents.

Ever since the outbreak, they'd been tasked with the same thankless job: flying endless, languid loops around New Zealand airspace looking for floaters.

The Surviving World had learned about the resistant effects of analgesics. The Surviving World had learned about salt—how to use it as a barrier, how to use it as a testing agent.

PLAGUE LAND: NO ESCAPE

The virus, however, was also learning to take better advantage of the world's high- and low-pressure fronts and prevailing winds. It had begun to produce more ambitious airborne structures: membranous sacks given lighter-than-air buoyancy by the methane and helium contained within. These sacks, some of them larger than weather balloons—swiftly becoming known as "poppers" or "floaters"—contained thousands of infectious spores. It wasn't enough to shoot these things down; they had to be shot down out at sea, so the fluffy, snowflake-like spores that erupted and descended from them hit seawater and died.

During the first year after the outbreak, there'd only been a couple dozen floater sightings, and those had been heading southwestward, having drifted a long way across the Pacific, presumably from the North and South American continents.

In the second year, the number increased radically, most of them drifting eastward from mainland Australia. There had been nearly two thousand logged sightings. Every single one of them easily popped with a burst of incendiary rounds, the flammable methane/hydrogen mix inside the sacks erupting with a satisfying bluish flash and the thousands of tiny spores sparkling like stars as they burned. In the last six months, the floaters had reduced to a steady flow averaging about a hundred per month. They were easy to see and quickly spotted on the radar. They drifted slowly enough to be less-than-challenging targets for the boys in the back of the plane.

"Sir, I'm picking up a signal, zero-four-seven."

That wasn't for Jamie; that was a message for the electronics officer, Lieutenant Talbot. The channels were all kept wide

ALEX SCARROW

open—unless Carling and Jessop way at the back of the plane started bitching about one thing or another.

"Got it on my screen now. Surface level signa— That's... *Whoa!* OK. That's big. Really big!"

Jamie tapped his mic on. "Talbot, what've you got back there?"

"We're picking up a signal on the radar. Something big on the surface."

Jamie hoped to God it wasn't another rogue oil tanker. There'd been one discovered over a year ago drifting listlessly on the ocean's meandering currents. A team in biohazard suits had gone aboard and found the ship's holds filled, not with oil but with tens of thousands of bodies, a last desperate bid to escape the outbreak. There'd been no sign of infection among them. But in a way that seemed worse. They'd died of thirst. They would have all been dead within a week of setting sail.

"Freighter?"

"Bigger."

"Tanker?"

"No, mate. This is way, *way* bigger."

"For Christ's sake, Talbot, stop pissing around and give me something more precise than 'bigger'!"

"What's on my screen is about three miles across, sir. How's that for *precise*?"

"Three *miles*?" He exchanged a glance with the copilot sitting beside him. "How far away is it?"

"Forty miles, at heading zero-four-seven."

About twenty minutes away from them, and judging by the heading, it was something that must have come in from the Pacific.

182

PLAGUE LAND: NO ESCAPE

"You sure it's not weather noise?"

"It's not *weather*." Talbot sounded irritated, like he'd been asked if he knew port from starboard. "It's solid and it's sea level."

For a cold-sweat second, Jamie wondered if he'd screwed up spectacularly on navigation. Satnav systems had ceased to function a long time ago. It was old-school navigation now, mark one, eyeballs, and time and speed calculations made on a paper chart.

His copilot anticipated his question. "Relax. We're right where we should be, sir, although...Talbot's picked up something that *shouldn't* be there."

"Right." Jamie checked the fuel display again. The detour was well within their range. "We'd better go and take a closer look at this damn thing."

A quarter of an hour later, his copilot made a sighting. "Jamie, you see it?"

He nodded. With a flat, uniform, deep blue sea, it was easy to spot—a block of faint gray on the horizon, "land" that shouldn't be there.

"Looks like a volcanic island."

Jamie adjusted the course slightly and reduced their altitude, so their first approach and flyby would be a relatively close one. The sea rushed beneath them, a glistening blur as they closed the last few miles.

After a couple of minutes, Jamie could pick out a lot more detail. The structure was shaped very much like a volcanic island—a central steep, column-like volcanic spout surrounded by an apron of ejected debris that would comprise the "lowlands."

Except...it wasn't colored the faint grays and greens he would have expected to see at this distance. Its overall hue seemed to be a deep red, the color of roasted beets.

"Could be it's a new volcanic island?" said one of the guys in the back.

"We'd have picked up the seismic activity," replied Talbot.

"Yeah right...like someone's still listening out for that kind of stuff."

"Pipe down," said Jamie. He checked their altitude and brought them a little lower, to a thousand yards. Low enough to get good detail as they made one large loop around the thing. "Cameras on. Let's get everything we can for the lab boys back home."

He studied the object as the plane dipped lower and their distance from the sea dwindled to less than two miles.

No way that's something geological.

And it didn't look man-made. Which left...

Viral.

He could see textures emerging from the side of the tall central cone: bumps and ridges that looked like thick tendons, circular ribs that ran around it like tide markers of growth. He could see motion on the far side of the cone, something large, flickering every now and then.

As the plane began to bank to starboard, beginning a large clockwise loop around the island, the flickering object gradually emerged from profile.

"Jesus Christ!"

He realized he was looking at a sheet of membrane, a *vast* triangular sheet of membrane, almost a mile on each side, fluttering like an impossibly large spinnaker sail. As the morning sun

PLAGUE LAND: NO ESCAPE

shone through it, it glowed a brilliant, bloody red, silhouettes of dark, branching veins spreading out across it, converging in a central knot of thicker, darker material. The gigantic "sail" was a crimson nightmare, and with the knot of flesh in the middle, it looked like an enormous bloodshot eye staring directly at the approaching plane.

"Looks like Sauron's Evil Eye," breathed Talbot.

Jamie nodded. Staring malevolently at their foolish approach.

Above the tall central cone, he could see hundreds of floaters all tethered to the structure, bumping and jostling together like the gathered party balloons of a carnival vendor.

The plane turned behind the island. Jamie could see a faint trail of white suds in its path, a line in the deep blue sea winding more or less in a straight line back toward the eastern horizon and the rest of the Pacific.

A wake—a telltale indication that this so-called "island" was actually *in motion*.

"It's not an island," he muttered. "It's a goddamn vessel!"

Freya,

The person who's in charge here is called Lawrence. He reminds me of the guy who was running the Oasis place. What was his name? Oh yeah, Carnegie. He seems like a pretty decent type. Not a total power addict like Everett. We have group chores just like at Everett's castle too—farming, fishing, cooking, foraging...repairing fishing nets (hate doing that).

According to Lawrence, right at the beginning, just after the outbreak, the virus grew feelers up to the gap in the bridge, hung around for a few days, then went away. He said the road on the other side has been pretty much clear of it ever since—as if the virus has decided there was nothing to see here.

But we think it knows there are people living here now. The old folks here are getting pretty anxious. They've had God knows how many town council meetings, each time it's the same thing: "We have to go!"

"Right, OK...but where?"

I get why they're so nervous. This is as close as the virus has ever gotten to them.

At the last meeting, I stood up and told them that the bridge and its six-yard gap is the best defense they're gonna find anywhere.

We've just got to stay calm and sit tight and stop the virus from growing across the gap!

That's me. How about you? Are you out there somewhere writing me letters I'm never going to read?

God, I miss you.

CHAPTER

26

"And...there's some of it sticking out over there," said Jake. Leon swung the hose to the left. He aimed the spray of seawater at a thick knuckle of viral growth that must have been missed by last night's shift or had a huge growth spurt as the shifts changed over. It had meandered nearly a quarter of the way across the gap and was now bending under its own extended weight. As the salt spray speckled the surface, its tough-looking, leathery skin began to crackle and break up like popping candy. The branch began to drool thick strands of gelatinous pink down into the lively waves and froth below. Every now and then, small and startled scuttling creatures tumbled out of the artery along with the slime and plummeted to their death in the sea.

Leon couldn't help a slight grin of satisfaction as his spray of seawater wore the thick root down and pushed it back to the far side of the bridge within a couple of minutes.

"Come on, it's my turn now," said Jake.

ALEX SCARROW

Last night's town hall gathering had ended with a resounding vote to stay put. If the one weapon they had against the virus was salt, then it made sense to stay right where they were, surrounded on all sides by an ocean full of the stuff.

It had been a tense meeting. Some of the residents had raised concerns about the "snow clouds" and "soap bubbles"—the airborne manifestations of the virus that had started appearing more regularly out at sea. But since everyone on the isle was still taking meds twice a week and they had a stockpile that was going to last years, stealthy infection seemed unlikely. A *swarming* was the main concern, and if they could keep the virus from establishing a bridge to the isle, they were going to be OK.

They had a four-person team working on it all the time now—two to take turns hand-pumping the water into a plastic tank, one to maintain the hand-pumped air pressure, and one to spray. The milder weather was cooling fast, and it looked like a long, hard third winter was on its way. If the virus followed the pattern of the last two, it would lie low and wait it out.

Leon passed the hose, rubbed his frozen pink hands together, then swapped places with Jake. He was now on the pump, pulling and pushing the handle to suck seawater up into the tank; it was backbreaking work.

Adewale was working the other handle, wheezing out a cloud of steamy breath into the cool air, exhausted from the exertion.

"It's enough now, I think," he gasped.

Leon looked up. Jake was spraying down the road on the far side to push the viral growths farther back.

Leon nodded and both of them stopped pumping. Finley

PLAGUE LAND: NO ESCAPE

followed suit and stopped working the foot pump that was maintaining the air pressure.

The hose died in Jake's hands, and he let out a groan of disappointment. "Crap, I was enjoying that."

"I didn't get a turn," complained Finley.

"You'll get a turn this afternoon," said Leon. "It'll only take a few hours for that stuff to start growing back across."

Adewale swiped the sheen of sweat from his forehead. "Is it growing across faster?"

"Faster and thicker," said Jake. "I wonder if it's trying harder to get across before winter kicks in."

Leon nodded. He hoped Jake was right about that. If it was trying harder, throwing its full weight into getting at them now, and this was its *very best* effort, then it looked like they were going to be safe while it "died back" during the winter, safe until at least next spring.

He wandered over to the edge and stared across the gap at the road to the town. Six weeks ago, it had been nothing but cracked asphalt and weeds. Now, it was almost completely covered with a lumpy and dark lattice of viral threads of varying thickness. Here and there were arteries that converged into a knot, from which small termite mounds had grown upward like thermal vents. The highest of them was about a yard tall and topped with puckering orifices that every now and then opened to release a small scuttling scout or to allow one in. The virus clearly knew there was something good to be hunted down nearby, but so far, it hadn't developed any sophisticated plans to get to them.

He wondered if it was testing them, perhaps even *toying* with them. Or maybe it had decided that the recent onset of colder weather was an indication that conquest of this small spit of an isle could wait until the next warm spell.

> Freya, even if you and Grace are alive, we're never going to see each other again, are we? Different islands in different parts of the world. I don't see airline flights being an option anytime soon. What do we do? We just go on existing on our islands forever? Is anyone anywhere fighting back, building up resources, reaching out to other groups? Are your rescuers coming back here anytime soon? Or was that it—one rescue attempt and now we've all on our own?
>
> Maybe I'll find my own way to reach you. Somehow.

"Ah now, Leon love, I'm getting to know that face."

Leon looked up from his bowl of fish chowder as Cora sat down at the table next to him.

"Huh…what face have I got on, then?"

"It's your *I miss her* face." She pulled a freshly baked brown roll into pieces and dropped them into her bowl.

Leon gazed out of the wide window, across the narrow cobblestone promenade at the wooden jetty beyond. The old seafront restaurant's "Ocean Spray Chippy" logo framed his view. Once, it had served cups of tea and the occasional bag of chips to senior citizens. Now it functioned as the community's cafeteria with two meals a day served to over a thousand hungry mouths. The kitchen beyond the swing doors was constantly alive with the sound of freshly caught fish being slapped down, gutted, and boiled or griddled.

"I looked for her as well," said Cora. "When we got down to the camp. I looked for that anorak too." She smiled. "I didn't see it either. I'm guessing she made it."

"I'll never get to see her again though."

Cora blew on her spoon. "No. I suppose you won't. But believing someone you care for is alive is something."

"True."

"I lost Iain, my husband of thirty years, in the outbreak. Then I met a lovely man called Dennis. And we survived the first winter, and then I lost him too." She sighed. "I suppose the lesson I should learn there is don't get too close to anyone or you'll break your heart again. When life becomes a matter of survival, best keep yourself to yourself. But…" She tested the broth with her lip and slurped some in. "But what's the point in going on if you can't allow yourself to love someone else again?"

"Time to move on from her?" He flung a hand loosely around. Apart from themselves, the isle was like one big nursing home.

"No. I'm just saying don't give up on the idea of there being someone else." She shrugged. "I was thinking about this last night."

"Thinking about what?"

"That nothing is *permanent*. We live for each day and can't plan for a future. Especially now."

Nothing was certain. Sure, it looked like they'd have the Isle

ALEX SCARROW

of Portland for the winter. But what developments would the next warm spell bring? Maybe next summer, the virus would've figured out a solution for its salt phobia. "You know," she continued, "I used to watch the news and see those stories of waves of migrants in their dinghies crossing the Mediterranean to get into Europe. I used to wonder why they'd put themselves through all of that. And now that I've been a refugee myself...I think I understand." She looked out of the window. "If there's a pretty good chance there won't be a tomorrow for you, or a next week, or a next year...if your life is a constant struggle for existence, you've got to grab any opportunity, haven't you? No matter how hard."

"I suppose so."

"And that tells me a lot about why they came. They were the ones who hadn't given up, the ones who'd figured out that the future *must* be made better, or why bother living in the first place."

She sank her spoon into the broth and stirred it. Steam wafted up between them. "When nothing is permanent or safe or guaranteed...you give up. Or you move on." She laughed. "Or you can just hope, I suppose."

"Hope?" Leon raised his brows. "For what? Another rescue fleet?"

"Who knows? The Americans and the Chinese managed to do it once. They might try again."

He shook his head. "They'll have enough of their own problems trying to survive to worry about rescuing pockets of people from around the world." He looked out of the window. "That rescue went badly. I don't see them trying it again."

PLAGUE LAND: NO ESCAPE

"Oh, buggeration." She let her spoon drop back into the chowder. "What?"

"I came over and sat down here to cheer you up. Now, all that's happened is you've got me feeling down!" She was joking, he suspected, but only half joking.

"I'm sorry. Before the world ended, I wasn't much better. My dad used to think I was a total emo."

"Emu?"

"Emo. It's what you call a self-indulgent, whiny-ass teenager who spends his life in his bedroom. Looking back, I think I probably was."

"Well, I certainly don't recognize *that* teenager. I *do* see a young man who stepped up when we needed someone to. I think your dad would be proud if he could see you now."

Outside, a fishing boat was slowly approaching the jetty. The boats went out half a dozen times every day, coming back laden with fish. The English Channel was brimming with cod, haddock, and mackerel now. Two years left alone, and fish stocks the world over were topped out. He watched as one of the fishermen hopped onto the jetty from the foredeck and began securing stern and aft lines.

They were never going to run out of food and drinking water here. If there was one outpost of humanity that stood a chance of outlasting all others, it was probably going to be this place.

Wait. That's all they were going to be able to do now: keep the virus from bridging the gap and wait for winter.

"It's good to plan, to always be thinking ahead," Cora added. "To be one of those ready to get on another boat if need be."

"I s'pose."

"Seriously, if you're not thinking like that, then what's the point?"

CHAPTER
27

GRACE WAS RIGHT; IT *WAS* UNPLEASANT. IT WAS A LOT LIKE climbing out of a soothing, warm bath back into a cold, drafty, and unwelcoming bathroom.

Jing felt his consciousness wading toward a distant surface of rippling shards of light. If he'd been the kind to believe in the idea of an afterlife, he might have interpreted those shafts of light as heavenly beacons. But he knew what they were—the reconnection of his supercluster cells with a tangle of optic nerves. He was in the process of disconnecting from the world within and reconnecting with the world outside. Grace had told him this process got easier to cope with and quicker with practice, but this being his first visit to what she'd referred to as her "bioverse"…it was hard.

He didn't want to return. She'd warned him about that too.

His foggy vision began to clear, giving him the blurred image of his own closed eyelids. He could now hear the soft fizz of the fluorescent lights and the hiss of the wall speaker. He could feel the cold, hard floor tiles beneath him and the shuddering cold blast of air on his skin from the air-filtration unit.

Jing opened his eyes and clenched them quickly shut again. The ceiling light was dazzling. It was overwhelming.

"Lieutenant Choi?" the wall speaker crackled deafeningly. Jing winced in response.

"Lieutenant Choi...can you hear me?" The speaker sounded painfully shrill.

Now his sense of smell was returning, his nose reporting in for duty. He could smell a festering, meaty, cheesy odor that was almost overpowering.

He fought an instinct to gag at the stench. *"Lieutenant Choi?"*

He nodded, if only to shut up the sharp crackle of the isolation room's speaker. "Yes," he replied hoarsely. "Yes...I hear you."

"How are you feeling?"

"Quiet, please," he rasped. "Give me...time."

The speaker remained mercifully quiet as the last vestiges of his *self* gradually re-inhabited the body lying on the floor. He turned his head to one side, away from the light above, and cracked his eyes open to see the bloody mess of his right shoulder and arm. In places, it had been dissolved right down to the bone, but it didn't shock him. Close up to it, he was witnessing repair work already going on: the rapid growth of fine strands of muscle tissue closing together to form thicker braids, the gradual creep of arterial tubes inching to join with each other. His cells all knew what to do, where to be, what to become.

I am becoming human again.

But calling this fragile, inefficient frame "human" felt as if he

PLAGUE LAND: NO ESCAPE

was cheapening the word. If it was possible, he'd felt even more human on the inside, more in touch with who he was, with those around him...with Grace. A sense of connection, communion— part of a whole that meant so much more than the mobile skin sack of liquid that was Lieutenant Choi in this outside world.

"Human" felt too generous a word for such an outmoded form of biological transport.

The speaker crackled again. "Lieutenant Choi? How are you feeling?"

He turned his head toward the observation window and saw their faces: Captain Xien, the prime minister, Dr. Calloway, and a dozen others, all staring at him as if he were some monster dredged up from a dark lagoon.

At this moment in time, he wanted nothing more than to go to back down into the rabbit hole, into the darkness, to the inner world, to Grace's bioverse. He wanted to climb back into that warm, welcoming bathwater and...connect with an endless community of minds. To talk, to listen, to learn. To understand more. To be more. To be part of more.

"How do I feel?" he rasped.

Their heads nodded, comically, in unison.

"Cold. Tired..." He wanted to add the word *lonely*, but his observers couldn't possibly understand what he'd mean by that.

He could choose to go back. And he definitely was going to go back there at the earliest opportunity, but first, far more importantly, there was work to do. A full debriefing. He needed to tell these men everything he'd experienced and what *They* had asked him to convey to these wide-eyed men waiting beyond the thick glass.

ALEX SCARROW

"Give me a little...more time." His throat and mouth felt bone dry. "May...I have some water?"

"Of course," a voice responded. A moment later, he heard the delivery hatch clunking. No one was going to fetch his drink for him, so he gathered his strength and sat up. His still-knitting arm peeled wetly from the floor, several small "feeding" tendrils snapping and falling away.

He clambered on all fours across the floor to the hatch and opened it, reached for the beaker inside and then poured some of the water down his throat, savoring the sensation of rehydration.

He felt a little more strength return to his cumbersome frame. He pulled himself up by grasping the edge of the table, and then he let himself down heavily onto the chair. In front of him, on the tabletop, he could see the spread-out construct of Grace's ocular organ. Before he'd gone under and joined her, he'd been repulsed by the sight of it: pink, purple, quivering, and glistening. It looked so fragile, exposed, and raw.

But now, he admired the economy of its structure: the simplest organic circuit to deliver Grace visual feedback of what was going on in this room, sending that data down to her consciousness.

Why make a whole eyeball, an ocular cavity, a skull, a brain, when just a small lens, a cluster of photo-sensitive cells, optic nerves, and a brainstem would do?

He smiled at the ingenuity of it.

"What's amusing, Choi?"

He shook his head. *They won't understand. Yet.*

"Nothing," he replied. He drained the glass of water. "Another water please...with sugar. Lots of it."

PLAGUE LAND: NO ESCAPE

He waited patiently for someone beyond the window to organize that. A few minutes later, the hatch clunked again. He reached inside, pulled out the cup, and, this time, drained the sweet sugar solution in one long chain of noisy gulps.

"That is better," he announced.

"Lieutenant Choi, are you ready to talk to us about this...uh, this *experiment*?" That was the prime minister's voice he heard.

Jing nodded. "Yes."

"Good. While you were...*gone*, we compiled a long list of questions that—"

"How long was I...*immersed*?"

"You were away for seven hours."

He arched his dark brows. "Seven hours?" It had felt like days.

"Yes. Now, Lieutenant Choi, as I was saying, a number of experts have assisted us in compiling a list of questions that—"

"I will answer your questions. But first...I must pass on a message."

———

Rex Williams regarded the men sitting around the long oak table—a mixture of the survivors of his cabinet from two years ago and an assortment of military uniforms. They were staring at him as if he had brought a sacrificial goat to the table, then slaughtered and gutted it right before their eyes.

He repeated what he'd just said. "I'll do it."

"That's absolutely senseless, Prime Minister!"

"Choi was returned unharmed, just as Grace promised he would be."

"We don't know for certain that he hasn't been changed in some way we won't be able to detect. He could now be weaponized—some sort of viral Trojan horse," said Dr. Calloway.

"I understand that. And we will continue to keep him in isolation for the foreseeable future."

"You understand, Prime Minister, that if you do this, you'll have to be quarantined too?" said Calloway.

"Of course."

"Possibly indefinitely." Calloway looked around the table for support. "You'll be rendered ineffective as leader of the committee?"

"I know. But we have to treat this as what it is. Unbelievable as this must sound—and God knows it sounds unbelievable to me—this is *an invitation from one civilization to another* to sit down and have a conversation. Now that we know the virus can cross the oceans at will, we *are* at its mercy."

"We have access to weapons, Prime Minister." Bullerton turned to look at Xien. "Subject to the Chinese agreeing."

"You're talking about using nukes?"

"Yes, sir."

"How many nuclear warheads in your arsenal, Captain Xien?"

The officer glared at Rex, poker-faced for a moment, then finally, he spoke. "Before the outbreak, I would have been court-martialed for telling you this. Most likely shot. But"—he offered a wan smile—"much has changed. We carry twenty-four warheads."

"Twenty-four?"

"Yes."

"Twenty-four warheads are not going to protect us for long."

Rex pointed at the fuzzy print of the long-range radar scan; they were looking at a tear-shaped blob off the northeast coastline

PLAGUE LAND: NO ESCAPE

of North Island. It was two hundred miles away and traveling their way very, very slowly—a little more than a mile an hour.

"In six more days, it'll land on North Island," said Rex. "It has *asked* to speak to us before it does so." He looked around. "It can wipe us out," he went on. "It doesn't *need* to talk to us...but it *wants* to." He spread his hands. "We're fools if we don't acknowledge that. It wiped out the rest of our world in just a few weeks. The only reason we're still alive here is that none of the first waves of infecting spores came to ground in New Zealand."

"We could evacuate."

"And go where?"

The room was silent. There was no answer. There was no place left to run. Rex would have been relieved if someone had raised a hand and suggested a viable alternative to submitting himself to the same process as Choi. Really. He would have been.

"It has invited me to go and talk with it. So that's what I'm going to have to do."

"What about the Americans?"

"What they decide to do is up to them." Rex shrugged. "If they're smart, they'll do the same thing."

Bullerton stood up. "Prime Minister, if you expose yourself to this virus, we will have to select a new acting leader. There's no way we can accept you back."

"I've already worked that part out," said Rex. "If I do this, maybe I can negotiate with the virus to leave New Zealand alone. Maybe I can assure it we're no threat. But if we respond to this request with a nuke, I suspect we won't last very long."

He laughed nervously. "Worst-case scenario, if it, you know..."

Kills me? Eats me? Turns me into slime? Jesus Christ. Am I really doing this?

"...just kills me, then you gentlemen will need to go and pick a new leader anyway."

CHAPTER
28

Clearance: 43kk Timestamp: 23.09.00.12
Source: radio, external. Encryption: Seleass34
Transcript for: President, Eyes Only

Message:

This is Rex Williams, spokesman and acting civilian head of the PNA speaking. And this is a message for acting President Douglas Trent. This communiqué is encrypted, Douglas. I know you're not anxious to talk with us, I'm guessing because we have the Chinese on board with the PNA. Fine. This isn't a conversation. It's a heads-up. One of our long-range recon planes has picked up a large viral structure that appears to have crossed most of the

Pacific just to get to us. We can now safely conclude the virus no longer seems to be held back by the sea. And that changes everything. I'm guessing another one may well be on a course toward you. If you have long-range planes and fuel for them, I'd get them up in the air to start looking for it.

There's something else you should be made aware of. One of the ships in the fleet that cooperated with yours, collecting survivors from Britain and Europe, picked up an infected virus carrier. A young girl. I'm sure by now you've been briefed on what happened over there? That this virus can make completely convincing facsimiles of people? The girl has presented herself to us as some sort of diplomatic ambassador with an invitation to myself to come and "negotiate a truce" with the virus in person.

What this means in practice is that I willingly submit myself to infection, to be partially broken down, "ingested" if you will, into its ecosystem.

I've been assured that I'll be returned to my former self once the talks are concluded, free of any harmful effects or any hidden infection. We have already had a volunteer undertake this process—ingested and

PLAGUE LAND: NO ESCAPE

returned—and while he is still in quarantine, it does appear that he's unharmed.

This is going to be a huge act of trust on my part.

Strange as all of this may sound to you, we're taking it seriously over here. If the viral structure approaching us reaches these shores, then it's going to be over for us. If we try to nuke the bloody thing, then we're presuming that it'll simply make another one. Plus, that may put an end to any further offers of negotiation.

If this plague can negotiate, if it wants to talk, I believe I owe it to the people here to go and listen to what it has to say.

If you've already been presented with a similar scenario, I strongly urge you to do the same and to think of it as a first meeting of civilizations. If you haven't yet been approached this way, then you may also have an "emissary" among your quota of rescued people, waiting to make contact with you.

Mr. President, I don't know whether this virus thinks the same way we do. It could be taking this meeting as an opportunity to determine whether we're a threat or an irrelevance.

That's [—unclear/indecipherable—] to begin with. Oh, there's one other thing. Our viral "ambassador" explained to us that she's some sort of hybrid of the virus itself and the person she was before she became infected. She's given us a name and claims that you actually know her? Whether confirming that fact gives you some comfort that the virus is leveling with us or not, I give you the name she gave us:

Grace Friedmann.

END OF MESSAGE.

Tom stared at the name printed at the bottom of the page, afraid to takes his eyes off it even for a second in case it became someone else's name when he looked at it again. He felt waves of heat and cold wafting over him, his skin and scalp prickling. He reached out for the back of the chair to steady himself, then finally he looked up at Trent.

"That's why I called you in here, Tom."

"My...my daughter?"

"Yes, your daughter. It seems she's very much alive."

"They're...saying she's *infected*?" That came out sounding more like a question. Like he needed Doug to clarify the point for him.

"Yup. Seems she is." Douglas Trent's hard, pinched face softened ever so slightly. "I'm sorry, buddy."

She's...infected? But alive. Alive!

"I've already given orders to lock things down, Tom. We've got spotter planes in the air. We need to know if one of these god-damned viral things is heading our way! I'm going to..."

Trent's voice was background noise right now as Tom looked down at the note again and reread the last paragraph. Single words stepped out of the blur of smeared print: *hybrid, viral.*

Hybrid. That one word gave him a shred of hope. Hybrid. Half of. Part of his daughter still existed, then a part of Grace was still alive. *Jesus.* He had no idea what that even meant.

He'd begun to think of himself as a grieving father, to concede the loss of both his children, accept that he was adrift, a loner for whatever time he had left to live.

Then *this.*

"...and if those sons of bitches can cross the sea, then that means those damned saline tests must be a load of bullshit," continued Trent. "We've gotta look at all those people you rescued again! We need to develop another kind of test. Shit! I need to get our people thinking about another kind of test we can use to..."

Grace.

Tom scanned the transcript again. The Prime Minister of New Zealand seemed to believe that there was an intelligence behind or within the plague, that his proposition wasn't as unbelievable as it sounded, that he was going to have a cozy chat with the common cold, smoke a peace pipe with a petri dish full of slime.

"...coastal defenses. Or maybe even set up an inner defensive area. Build walls, big ones, and then we just hold out and let this hellish thing hurl whatever it's got at us..."

"Mr. President?"

ALEX SCARROW

"...Jesus Christ. I need to know if we got one of these things coming our way and how long we've got to—"

"Doug!"

Trent stopped his rambling and looked up at him.

Tom waved the message in the air. "We might also have someone we can negotiate with, talk to? You know, someone right there in our holding pen?"

That part of the message seemed to have completely slipped Trent's mind. His eyes suddenly widened. "Christ! Shit! You're right!"

They stared at each other, Trent frozen to rigidity by the notion.

"I'll do it," said Tom finally.

The president didn't seem to hear that. His wide blue eyes were right through Tom and somewhere far beyond. "Shit," he whispered. "Shit. All those people!"

"There's about eight hundred of them, Doug."

"...all those people..." he muttered again, "crammed in that warehouse...*together!*"

"I know." For a moment, Tom wondered what the president was getting at. "I'll go in, Doug. I'll do it!"

Trent shook his head slowly.

"Look, I'm volunteering. I can find out who the infected messenger is and—"

"No." Trent waved his hand in a way that said the discussion was done. "No. No one's going in. No one's going anywhere near that... Dammit. We'll burn down the whole goddamn building and—"

Tom slammed his hand down on the desk. "Doug!" The sharp, aggressive tone silenced him. For the first time. Ever. "Rex Williams

208

PLAGUE LAND: NO ESCAPE

is right! If this thing is crossing over seawater, if it's coming for us, then we're totally screwed! It's over! It's all over!"

"I'll nuke the bastard."

"If it can cope with salt water, then maybe it's already colonizing everything under the surface right now! Which parts of the Caribbean Sea are you gonna bomb, with your remaining nukes, Doug? Huh? You got enough nukes to do the *whole* sea?"

"Or we abandon this island. We leave the goddamn Cubans and we get back on our ships and we—"

"Or we can negotiate!"

"*Negotiate!* Are you out of your mind, Friedmann?"

For the first time, Tom realized Trent had one of his hands spread across a firearm on the desk. Not holding it, but leaning on it, as if mere skin contact with the cold metal of its grip was what he needed to reassure himself, to validate his command, his authority. A comfort blanket.

He's losing it.

"Doug," Tom said quietly, "we've been invaded by something we never could have imagined existed. Something we could never have prepared for. This is the whole *War of the Worlds* thing, OK? It's just like that movie, and we got our butts kicked. All of us did."

Tom didn't want to look down at the gun.

"Just like a crappy movie. But…this time it's real, Doug. And you've got responsibilities. *We've* got responsibilities. To however many Cubans there are and to about thirty thousand Americans and eight hundred Brits."

Trent was listening. Nodding.

"If…we take what's in this communiqué at face value, and,

209

Doug, we *do* need to verify this, right? Get a reconnaissance plane and eyeballs up there in the sky?"

Trent's face remained impassive, still listening but not necessarily agreeing.

"Then, *if* it's true, Doug...it looks like it *wants to talk*. So let me handle that part, OK? Let me take that piece of it off your shoulders. Let me be the one to go into the containment building, find out if we have an 'ambassador' in there, and do whatever needs to be done to open up a line of communication."

"Yeah." Trent nodded again. "Yeah...maybe we need to get a line of communication or...something."

"And we should also be communicating with the guys in New Zealand. We've got to start talking to them."

The president's eyes seemed to be off somewhere, glazed over and a million miles away again.

"Doug!"

Trent's attention came back to him. He narrowed his eyes. "How? How're you going to do that, *amigo*? How're you going to open up a channel with this...*bug*?"

"Leave that to me."

Trent's face remained frozen and impassive, his state of mind impossible to judge. Then Tom saw the faintest hint of a smile widen his mouth.

"Do what you have to, Tom." He settled back into his chair, looking tired, his hands coming back off the desk, off the gun, and settling into his lap. He said again, "All right. You do what you have to. Meantime...I better go find out what sea monsters're coming our way."

CHAPTER
29

Freya,

I'm probably not going to do this anymore—
write these stupid damned letters. I'm not
sure it's doing me any good. Freya, just be
alive for me, OK? And if you're with Grace,
look after her.

Live long and prosper, as Spock says.

Love, Leon

IT WAS A COLD, FOGGY MORNING. THE WATER OF THE ENGLISH Channel lapped at the jetty, sulking like a scolded child. Leon and Jake were lining up outside the Ocean Spray Chippy for the second-sitting breakfast. The chalkboard set up ahead by the glass door showed they were getting something different this morning.

ALEX SCARROW

"Rhubarb and blackberry stew?" Jake made a face. "Is that even a thing?"

"At least it's not cod chowder."

Leon looked up the jetty and counted nine fishing boats tied up. Their fleet was back in from trawling last night, and their catch had already been taken into the restaurant to be gutted and filleted for dinner that evening.

"Something sweet instead of tasting of sea salt for a change," added Leon. "Count me in."

"Jesus, though. If they're gonna bother to grow stuff, why grow rhubarb?"

Through the window, Leon could see Adewale and Howard at one table. Finley and Kim, with half a dozen of the other kids on the island, were sitting together at their own table. Their little survival group had begun to fragment already, absorbed into the larger community. Which was fair enough. A good sign, really; they'd only been thrown together for a few days in that animal quarantine building—it's not like they were bonded together for eternity.

Leon imagined he and Jake would remain each other's wingmen; they seemed to have a lot in common and some indefinable camaraderie that worked. He also thought he would like to stay in Cora's orbit. He admired the older woman's can-do attitude. Cora reminded him a little bit of Mom—maybe that was it.

Through the glass, he could see Lawrence moving around from one table to the next with a clipboard tucked under one arm, smiling, laughing, stooping over, and cupping his ear every now and then. He used the breakfast sittings as an opportunity to pass

212

out the day's various job assignments, to catch up with everyone, to hear any grievances or settle them.

"Hey." Jake nudged his arm.

"What?"

"There! What's that?" Jake was pointing toward the end of the jetty. "Out there on the water." Leon turned from the bustling scene inside to look out to sea. The mist was shrouding the end of the jetty but wasn't thick enough to obscure it. He could see the faint outline of a mooring post at the end, the old flaking sign above it. He could just make out the lettering that announced: NON-PERMIT HOLDERS ARE REQUIRED TO REPORT TO THE HARBORMASTER UPON TYING UP!

Beyond the signpost and safety rail, across the flat, lifeless water, he could see something slowly approaching them. It looked like a low rowing boat. A dinghy. He could see the head and shoulders of a solitary figure bending slowly forward and pulling backward, the oars dipping and rising gently.

"Who is that?" said Jake. "The fishermen should be in for the day by now."

Leon shook his head. The seven boats were all tied up, their prows gently bobbing.

The row boat drew closer and clearer, and finally, as it reached the jetty, the figure stood up, wobbling uncertainly as it rocked, reaching out to grab the post as the dinghy *thunked* home under its own momentum.

"Someone go in and get Lawrence!" a voice called out from behind them in the line.

Leon rapped his knuckles hard on the window and the people

inside looked up. He pointed at Lawrence and crooked his finger to indicate he was needed outside. He saw a woman cup her mouth and call his name. Lawrence looked up from a conversation he was stuck in. Finally, he looked Leon's way, and Leon jabbed his finger toward the jetty.

The lone figure had slowly begun to advance down the wooden planking, passing the tied-up boats. There was something ominous about its ponderous steps. Leon instinctively felt trouble approaching. A dozen yards from where the jetty met the land, it stopped. The mist was still thick enough to shroud most of the details. From what Leon could figure out, the figure looked young.

The silence was broken as the door to the chippy was pushed open and Lawrence stepped out into the cool air. "What's the matter?"

"We have a visitor," said Jake, pointing at the figure.

"Hello?" called Lawrence. "Who's that out there?"

The figure remained perfectly still, perfectly silent.

"Who are you?" shouted Lawrence. His challenge came out amid a cloud of breath. He took several steps forward. "Can I help you?" The sound of his feet changed from the crunch and scrape of gravel to a dull creak as he stepped onto the first boards of the jetty.

He tensed up and turned. "Someone call the home guard," he barked. He turned to look back at the figure. "Are you alone? Is it just you? Or are there any others?"

The figure finally stirred and answered him. "I am...I am not one of your people. I am alone." Leon thought he could hear some kind of an accent in the words, the clipped ends to words that suggested a second language was being spoken. More than that—it was a girl's voice.

"Alone? Where have you come from?"

"I. Am. Not…a human." The words came out one at a time. Slow. Deliberate. It took another few seconds before anyone registered what she'd just said.

Leon heard gasps all around him. He heard the scrape of footsteps as someone hurriedly abandoned the line and ran away into the mist. "I am not human…but I *was*."

Lawrence was just a few yards away from the figure. "What do you mean by that? You're *infected*?"

The figure cocked her head slowly. "I am *remade*. I was once called Camille."

"For Christ's sake, get back, Lawrence!" someone shouted. Several others joined in. He waved his hand behind his back to shush everyone down. "Your name's Camille?"

The girl nodded. "I have a message for you." She looked at Lawrence, then over his shoulder at the others.

Leon's eyes met with hers momentarily as she scanned them.

"A message for all of you."

Lawrence backed up several steps and turned. "Someone get a bloody hose! Now!"

"WAIT!" Leon stepped forward. He joined Lawrence. "What's the message? Who's it from?"

"From all of us."

"Us? What do you mean by 'us'?"

"We." The girl looked to one side and tilted her head for a

moment, as if considering how to explain herself. Then she turned to Leon and continued. "You would call 'we'...the virus and all those who have been remade by it."

Leon heard more feet scraping on the gravel and receding into the distance as someone else decided they'd heard enough.

"So you're telling me...*you're* the virus?"

"Just a messenger."

"The virus...*sent a messenger*?"

"Yes," replied the girl.

Leon and Jake exchanged a glance.

Leon was well aware that those who were infected could talk, act like normal human beings, not even knowing they'd become *something else*. But he'd never considered the virus as something separate that could communicate on its own, have an opinion, have an agenda. Something you could communicate with.

"You're saying the virus can talk?" said Leon, doing his best to keep an even and calm voice. "Does this mean the virus is *talking* to you...right now?"

"I am disconnected right now. I am just a messenger."

Leon could hear footsteps approaching. Then, out of the mist, he saw two of the home guard dragging loops of a long hose between them.

Leon turned and held a hand up. "Just stay back for the moment. Stay where you are! We're talking here. That's all that's happening!" He turned back to face the young girl again. "Maybe you should tell us your message then?"

"The message comes from high-assembly-gathering cluster... with agreement from all advocates." The young girl's voice seemed

PLAGUE LAND: NO ESCAPE

to be modulating, fluttering uncertainly between feminine and masculine. "The message is..."

CHAPTER
30

"FREYA HARPER! PRESENT YOURSELF TO THE GUARDS AT THE front of the enclosure now!"

She jerked awake as someone grabbed her shoulder and shook her. "They're calling for you, Freya!"

She blinked sleep out of her eyes. Through the tall, barred window, she could see it was still dark outside. Every now and then, slashes of light swung across the high corrugated-iron ceiling of the old tobacco warehouse as a spotlight was swept along the outside of the building.

The announcement came across the PA speakers again, distorted, echoing, shrill, and now beginning to awake and annoy everyone inside. People were sitting up, groaning.

"You better go up front before you piss everyone off!" hissed Shay, the woman Freya was sharing a mat with.

Freya planted her hand against the flaking wall, hefted herself up off the thin mattress, and began to pick her way across the

PLAGUE LAND: NO ESCAPE

crowded floor lit only by the dancing light and shadows of the sweeping spotlights outside.

She made her way to the barred entrance at the front, miraculously managing not to step on anyone's outstretched hands or feet. There was a soldier in a biohazard suit waving around a small penlight to attract her attention. They'd all noticed over the last twenty-four hours that the marines had upped their biohazard precautions. Whether that meant good news or not was the subject of mutterings from one cot to another.

"You're Freya Harper?"

"Yes!" she hissed. "You can tell the idiot with the megaphone to stop barking out my name now!"

The soldier muttered something into a radio, and a moment later, the mix of a reverberating hiss and the hum of ever-threatening feedback snapped off.

"There's someone to see you."

"Who?" She guessed it was Leon's dad. She looked around. "Where is he?"

"Mr. Friedmann's out in the exercise area."

He produced some keys, unlocked the barred door, let her through. He nodded at the door that led out on to the basketball court. "He's out there."

She emerged into the cool glare of a floodlight standing outside the corner of the basketball court. She could see moths and flies caught in its beams and hear the *chhh-chhh-chhh* of the cicadas and the soft rumble and hiss of waves breaking nearby.

She wondered if this was another dream. She wondered if Grace was going to suddenly emerge out of nowhere again.

219

ALEX SCARROW

Savoring the coolness as the gentle breeze teased goose bumps onto her arms, she looked around for her visitor.

"Hey! Over here!"

It *was* Leon's dad. She walked quickly over toward him.

A soldier was standing guard nearby and gestured with a jerk of his gun that Freya needed to keep a few steps back from the mesh.

"Mr. Friedmann? Why're you here? What's going on?"

"Freya..." he began. He looked sideways at the soldier, then took a step forward until he was up against the wire. He lowered his voice. "We got a radio transmission from the other survivors in New Zealand. It's... I don't know how to say this..."

Her heart jumped as she realized it had to be something about either Grace or Leon. *Not Leon. Not Leon. Not Leon...not dead. Please...*

"Just say what it is...please."

"Grace."

"Grace? She's dead? She's alive?"

Mr. Friedmann said nothing for a moment as he stared at her. She sensed he was waiting for her to say something. But she didn't know what. "Tell me!"

He looked over his shoulder at the guard, then gestured for her to walk with him a few steps. "She's..." His voice faltered. He cleared his throat, lowered his voice to little more than a whisper. "She's one of *Them.*"

"Them?"

"The virus. She's infected. She's been turned into one of those copies. She's... Jesus Christ, she's been body-snatched or whatever the hell the term is!"

220

PLAGUE LAND: NO ESCAPE

Freya looked down at her feet. She realized she should have been rocked by that. Grace? But...she wasn't, and deep down, part of her had hung on to a suspicion that it was too good to be true— Grace, turning up like she had at Everett's castle.

Her mind was racing.

You knew, Freya. Come on, you already suspected this.

"How...how do you know Grace is infected?" she asked, stalling for more time to think.

"We got a message from New Zealand today. They say she stepped forward as some sort of ambassador on behalf of the virus. The virus wants to *negotiate* with them!"

Freya looked up at him. "Negotiate?"

He grabbed at the mesh, and it rattled in his grasp. "You came down to Southampton with her and Leon, didn't you?"

She'd told him that. "Yes." She'd told him they'd been holding out in a Norman castle. She hadn't told him about what had happened *before* that though.

"How long were you with them? When did you meet up?"

"We met sometime after the outbreak," she replied. An edited reply. A simple lie to avoid telling him about all the horrible things that had happened to his daughter.

"And you didn't know? Jesus! You were living with each other and you—"

"I don't know how or when... Are you even sure it's the same Grace?"

"It's my Grace," he croaked. "My little girl."

You suspected. Come on, Freya, you had your doubts. You just didn't voice them because Leon was so relieved to have her back. Right?

221

"Was she different, Freya? Was she"—he shook his head—"*wrong* somehow?"

Or maybe she'd never suspected back then...

But you suspect NOW, don't you?

There'd been a moment, back in Emerald Parks, a fleeting moment in that sauna when she'd thought she'd glimpsed something "wrong" dangling from Grace's face. And ever since then, Freya had written it off as something she'd imagined—that, or a lock of hair caught in the flashlight. Then everything had happened so quickly. They'd carried her away rolled up in a tarp, soaked her with diesel and set her on fire. And the screams, those human-child-burning-to-death screams had all but erased what she'd glimpsed.

When Grace had turned up at Everett's castle nearly two years later, the scars on her face and neck were all the proof she'd needed to confirm that here was Grace again. A miracle after that terrible fire, a shadow of her former self, but at least she was still alive.

"Freya?"

"It's true, then. She must have gotten infected at some point. I didn't know her well enough to be sure. But I guess it might—"

"When? At Southampton? Is that when it could have happened?"

"Maybe. Could have been, I dunno, earlier...maybe. I don't know!"

"Freya...*Freya!*"

She looked back at him. His fingers were gripping the mesh hard, his knuckles bulging and white.

"Listen to me! Is it possible she got infected and didn't even know it? Is that how this happens?"

PLAGUE LAND: NO ESCAPE

Corkie. Remember that grisly old bastard? That look of total astonishment on his face?

"Yeah...uh, yes. We had some people who had that. They didn't know they were infected. They just... It came out. They—"

"Were they acting differently? Oddly? What?"

She shook her head. "They...they just didn't know!"

"So any one of us could be infected. You? Me? This soldier behind me?" Mr. Friedmann lifted his chin at the tobacco warehouse. "What about in there? Is there anybody in there who could be infected?"

"Shit. I don't know! None. Maybe *everyone*. I really don't— They've been tested!"

He quickly put a finger to his lips. She closed her mouth. "The salt tests aren't reliable," he said quietly.

"What? How do you know?"

He leaned forward until his forehead gently bumped against the mesh. There was something in his gesture that worried her. Until now, he'd looked in charge, confident. The one person she'd encountered since the outbreak who looked like he'd survive it untouched. He looked defeated now.

"What is it?"

"The virus can cross the ocean."

"*What?*"

"New Zealand spotted some large viral island, or ship, on its way over."

"Ship? How?"

"I don't know any more than that. The point is the sea is not the barrier we thought it was. We're not safe here in Cuba."

"Oh God...we're not safe here!"

Come on, Freya...you already know this. That voice in her head was getting too loud to ignore.

"We're all in trouble, Freya. I know. But...listen, there's something else." He hesitated.

"What?"

"Trent thinks you're all *compromised.* That you're all infected. I think at least one person is, inside. One person who must be aware they're infected."

Freya? Come on...wake up.

"Shit."

"I don't know what Trent's going to do next. I need to get you out of there before he does something stupid to all of you."

"Like what?"

"He threatened to burn down the warehouse."

Her dream suddenly felt like a ghastly premonition. "Oh God. No. You need to get *everyone* out!"

"I..." He looked at the soldier standing nearby. There were others, a dozen of them, watching this conversation warily. "That's not possible. I've managed to stall him for now. But, listen, I'm going to get *you* out, Freya. Then I need your help. I need to find out if we do have someone in there who's here to talk on behalf of the virus! Before it's too late."

You know who that is.

"You've seen more of the virus up close than anyone. The copycat humans? Is there anything, *anything,* that gives them away? Marks them out?"

You know, Freya. Come on, wake up.

224

PLAGUE LAND: NO ESCAPE

That voice in her head. Grace's voice.

Yes. I'm not a dream. You are awake. This is real. I'm with you. I'm inside you.

"Oh shit, oh God," muttered Freya softly.

And we're not monsters, Freya. We can be negotiated with. We just want what's best. That's all. What's best for everyone.

"Freya?" Mr. Friedmann looked hard at her. "Are you OK?"

You're infected, Freya.

She slowly began to back away from him and the fence.

"Freya? Where are you going?"

"I'm..." She really didn't know. She was taking steps backward, recoiling at the realization. In shock. Confused. Frightened.

"Freya." He lowered his voice to a whisper. "Stay right there! Stay right where you are! I'm going to try and get you out." He turned to the soldier standing guard a few yards away. "Where's your CO?"

The soldier pointed across to the far side of the court. "Over there, sir."

"Go get him. We're getting this girl out of here. Right now."

"Sir? That's not—"

"This is on the president's personal authority, soldier! This girl has important strategic information. I need to get her in front of the president *right now*!"

The soldier looked from him to Freya, then back again.

"NOW!" barked Mr. Friedmann.

Freya wasn't entirely sure what had just happened. One moment she was in the basketball court, the next she was in a Cuban army

ALEX SCARROW

jeep with Mr. Friedmann frantically driving her along a dusty road.

The world outside her head suddenly felt distant, irrelevant even; she was inside her head looking out through eyes that no longer even felt like hers.

I'm infected?

Does this mean I'm still me?

Is this even me asking questions? Or am I something else now?

With each unanswered question, she felt as though she was sliding further down a slanting tiled roof, ever closer to the edge toward a drop into a terrifying abyss. If she stopped asking, maybe she'd stay right here, clinging to sanity by her fingernails.

She was dimly aware of Mr. Friedmann driving them through empty and dark streets, stopping several times at checkpoints manned by both U.S. and Cuban soldiers. She saw him pull out his ID on one occasion; at another, a soldier simply recognized Friedmann's face, wished him a good evening, and waved them through. The city, conserving energy and under martial law, was entirely dark. The vehicle's headlights picked out the signposts, the street names, and curious faces peering out from candle- and gas-lit homes.

Now that she'd acknowledged it, her mind felt violated, invaded, like seeing a burglar stalking silently through her home, touching things, examining things. Even though she "felt" it was not a stranger, but Grace, it was too much.

Your mind, Freya, just like everyone else's many voices.

Get out! Get out!

Freya! I want to help you. Listen to me...please!

226

PLAGUE LAND: NO ESCAPE

Finally, they were out of the dusty suburbs and driving on a potholed and empty road, flanked by chest-high ranks of swaying cassava plants on one side and grapefruit orchards on the other. Tom pulled over onto a dusty side track and brought the jeep to a halt. He switched the headlights off, and they sat in the moonlit darkness listening to the engine ticking as it cooled down and the persistent chirp of cicadas.

Freya dimly observed it all from afar and sitting right next to her, almost holding her hand, was Grace, explaining what was happening. Talking her through a transition that felt like descending into the deepest and darkest pits of Mordor.

And then, calmness.

After the calmness, the strangest sense of togetherness.

Finally, she accepted it. She had no choice. It was an inescapable truth.

"Mr. Friedmann...I think I'm the one you're after. The one with the virus inside."

She expected Mr. Friedmann to lurch back in his seat, away from her, to wrench the driver-side door open, and, almost comically, flee out into the night.

But he didn't.

"Did you hear me?"

"I heard you," he replied.

"Why...why aren't you...panicking...running, doing something?"

"Like what?" He glanced her way. "Do you want me to shoot you? Shoot myself?" He laughed bitterly. "What's the point, right?"

"You don't seem to care that much."

"There isn't much left to fight for, Freya. If Grace is infected...

227

ALEX SCARROW

Leon probably is too. *They* were my only reason to fight on, to stay alive."

She thought she heard his voice wavering with emotion.

They sat in silence for a while. She couldn't have guessed for how long—a few seconds, a few hours?

"You were in the pen at Southampton. You were on the ship. You passed all the tests. How certain are you that you're infected?"

"Certain. I can feel it...*hear* it...in my head." She turned to look at him. "The virus spoke to me."

He turned to look at her. "*It* spoke to you?"

She nodded. "I think it's been trying to talk to me during the last couple of weeks," she added. "In my sleep. Through my dreams."

"Are there any others who are infected in the warehouse?"

Freya shook her head. "I don't know."

"Have *you* infected anyone else?"

She shook her head. "No! Why did you get me out?"

He didn't answer immediately. He just stared out of the dusty windshield.

"Because...because you know about my kids, you've been with them. You're the only link I have to them." He turned to face her. "And I had a suspicion you might be the one."

"Since when?"

"Since we got the communiqué from New Zealand earlier. They mentioned Grace by name—she's with them down in New Zealand. She surrendered herself to them. Through her, they're going to try communicating with the virus."

And I'm here inside you too, Freya. I can be there and here at the same time. Tell Dad I'm here. With you.

PLAGUE LAND: NO ESCAPE

"Earlier, you said it spoke to you. The virus spoke to you?"

Tell him. Grace's voice. *Tell him I'm talking to you.*

"Yes."

"What did it say?"

"Mr. Friedmann, it's talking to me...*right now.*"

He nodded slowly. "OK, all right...then what's it saying?"

"It's in my head...the virus." She turned to look at him. "It's Grace."

Tell Dad...hi.

"A part of Grace is talking to me right now, Mr. Friedmann."

His brows knotted. She could see muscles in his jaw clenching, unclenching. "How? How's that possible?"

"It's hard to describe. It's...like, only a voice...like a memory of her, but a memory that can do its own thinking. She's telling me to say she's right here."

"How the hell is my girl inside of you?"

"She's...the virus...part of it..."

Freya, I'm going to come out and talk to Dad. He needs to see me.

She suddenly felt light-headed, like the time she'd accepted a playground dare and run in circles while staring straight up at the sky, only to collapse on the asphalt and scrape both her knees. It was like suddenly dropping, no ground beneath her.

Tell him not to be frightened at what's about to happen. Freya mumbled something. Hopefully Grace's message, but she wasn't sure what noises were coming out of her mouth now. The world was fading fast. Grace was taking over.

It was pleasantly dark.

Not a cold, intimidating darkness, but something comforting and warm, womb-like, welcoming.

So, this is it. This is how it feels?

The thought ran in lazy circles around her, the most cogent thought her foggy mind could manage. *Not so bad after all, Freya.* She settled back in the darkness to rest and to consider her circumstances. Infection...the world was full of far worse things than that.

Infection felt just like a lovely, warm bath.

CHAPTER
31

GRACE OBSERVED THE MEN SITTING IN THE HELICOPTER WITH her. There were seven of them, all wearing biohazard suits and masks.

On one side of her sat Jing. She'd insisted he come along. He had entered her world and returned to this one to reassure everyone, particularly the prime minister, that it was OK. He was unharmed and unchanged. Since his short exploratory trip, he'd been kept in isolation and prodded and poked, giving daily blood and DNA samples. The emergency research facility was reluctant to let him out, but they had their samples to continue inspecting under a microscope. Prime Minister Williams had overruled their objections but allowed one of their team, Dr. Kevin Calloway, to come along as a scientific observer.

All it had taken was a glimpse of Life 2.0—the possibilities, the endless bioverse...*infinity* defined within a droplet of water— for Jing to comprehend how limited his life had been. He spoke now like an evangelist touched by something indescribably wonderful and yearning to return to it. Even with Jing's glassy-eyed assurances that something wonderful awaited him, the prime minister was terrified of the process he'd agreed to undertake. In the dimly illuminated cabin of the helicopter, through the slightly tinted glass of his mask, Grace could see his eyes were wide, his skin waxy with sweat. She'd tried to reassure him, Jing had too, but...Williams had already seen the whole process in great detail through a thick glass window, seen Jing reduced to the product of an acid bath...

The other four men in the helicopter's crimson-lit cabin were Williams's security unit. They were here to escort the PM to the safe care of the hostile force's representatives, then wait for his return. They looked as though they'd rather be anywhere else.

They were also here to record everything. Absolutely everything. Cameras and lights had been attached to their masks and everything they filmed would be beamed up to the P-3K2 Orion circling above.

Grace had her concerns about this being filmed.

Most of the people living in New Zealand had only heard secondhand accounts from survivors of the outbreak or seen grainy, shaky smartphone footage. The virus was a frightening, apocalyptic, yet distant presence to them. The purpose of this meeting was to educate, not to terrify.

The red light in the cabin blinked off and on, and the four military men stirred in their seats and began to check their cameras and equipment.

"Grace?"

PLAGUE LAND: NO ESCAPE

She looked up at the prime minister perched across from her. "Are you OK, Mr. Williams?"

"I...uh...I'm actually quite terrified."

"You have no reason to be. I promise. It's going to be OK."

"So you say."

"It is very brave of you," Grace added. "To agree to do this."

"It's..." She heard his breath catch. "It's not like we have a lot of choice, is it?"

"We all need to talk. Together. It's really important you see for yourself."

"You understand, Grace...that even if I come back singing your praises like Jing, the people I've been leading will regard me with suspicion, see me as a Trojan horse." He pressed his lips together. "I can see for myself and report back, but one thing I can't promise you is that anyone will trust, or even listen to, what I have to say. And anyway..." He looked at Jing. "How do I know I'll come back as me and not some copy of me?"

"You have to trust us," replied Grace.

Rex shrugged. "Right. Trust. Again. How about answering me this." Rex grinned anxiously. "Is this going to, you know, *hurt*?"

"Prime Minister?" Jing's voice. Rex Williams turned his way. "I assure you, there is no discomfort. It is a completely painless process."

"Right."

She could see his gloved hands balling into fists and relaxing. "But will I feel *anything*?" he asked. "Will I sense anything?"

"It is like a grand descent," Jing replied. "Like Alice going down into the rabbit hole."

233

The helicopter began to bank as it made its final approach. Jing was sitting beside the cabin's small round window and twisted in his seat to get a better look.

Over the comms system, she heard the soldiers and the helicopter's pilot.

"Jesus Christ!"

"What the f—"

"It looks like Tracy frickin Island!"

The "island" had something that looked like the stack of an active volcano in its middle: a tall and tapered stovepipe that appeared to have a stationary cloud tethered above it, dark and turbulent, rolling in and around itself. As they drew closer and began to descend, the cloud revealed itself as a swarm of dark-colored spheres.

"What are those?" asked one of the soldiers.

"Those are free-floating membrane sacs that contain infection spores," explained Dr. Calloway. "What we call 'floaters.'" He turned to Grace. "Are they produced within the chimney-like structure?"

Grace shook her head. "I don't know."

"You're a viral. How can you not know?"

"You're human, Calloway," said the prime minister. "Do you know how to build a suspension bridge?"

"What? No. Of course I—"

"Right, so this girl doesn't know everything."

"It's not a girl, sir. It's a viral construct. We have to treat it with extreme caution."

A couple of the soldiers in the cabin nodded at that.

PLAGUE LAND: NO ESCAPE

"Or treat her with courtesy," added Williams. "Keep in mind this is a *diplomatic* mission. We're here to say hello. And so are They."

Grace was impressed with the prime minister's manner. She wanted to reassure them all that, despite the hellish appearance of the approaching island, it was a benign structure. It was here to listen, not to conquer.

The water around the leading edge of the island was beginning to spray as the long reach of the helicopter's downdraft hit. They were descending very slowly now, the pilot doing his best to make the helicopter, with its deafening noise and disruptive blasting air, appear unthreatening.

Grace looked down. She saw the surface of the viral island twitch like an elephant's leathery skin in response to the tickling claws of a settling bird. The helicopter continued slowly forward, settling down gently with barely a bump.

"We're down," reported the pilot.

"All right. Mr. Williams, your attention please, sir?"

The prime minister turned to the officer leading his security team. He was holding the handle of the cabin door's lift bar.

"Me and my lads will exit first, sir. We'll scan the perimeter around the helicopter. When I'm happy we have no hostiles about to jump us...then I'll give the word for you to come out. Is that clear?"

"Yes. Yes. Of course."

"Pilot?"

"Yes?"

"Keep her take-off ready until I say."

"Roger that."

235

The officer looked directly at Jing. "Lieutenant Choi, you're coming out alongside us. You're infected already. I'm guessing you can tell the crawlers to back off."

Grace answered before he could. "No. He's not one of us. He's been infected and then returned uninfected. Just like I said."

"But the virus will treat him as a friendly? One of them, right?"

"No," she replied. "The scouts are not intelligent. They'll see Jing as just the same as you. Let me come out with you. I *am*... infected. They'll know that as soon as I take my mask off. Jing and I will come out with your soldiers. Then I need to remove my mask and my gloves. I need to *touch* tissue, to let it know who I am."

"No way," said the officer. "She's our leverage. If she escapes, we're left totally vulnerable." He looked at Grace. "We're hanging on to you." He nodded at one of his men, who was holding a flamethrower. The gesture was pretty clear: *Try and make a run for it, and we light you up.*

"I'm not here to *escape*. I'm here to help Mr. Williams meet my...*friends*."

"Captain," cut in Jing. "You should trust Grace. She has no agenda. She just wants us to meet them and—"

"The safety of the prime minister is my only concern. So this is *my* call." The officer nodded at his men. "Steve, Chris, your boots down first. Then the girl and Choi go out, then it's me and Ross. Clear?"

His men *yes sir*ed.

"Then, when I'm completely happy, and *only* then...it's your turn, Prime Minister."

"What about me?" asked Dr. Calloway.

"You're an observer. I don't give a shit what you do."

"All right, that seems sensible," said the prime minister. He turned to Grace for assurance. "Grace...you do what you need to do."

CHAPTER
32

REX WILLIAMS WATCHED AS THE OFFICER OF HIS SECURITY unit lifted the bar lever and the cabin's door slid open on its rails. The confined space was suddenly filled with the roar of the helicopter's engine, the *thwup-thwup-thwup* of the spinning rotors, and the rush of air blasted inside by them.

"GO! GO! GO!"

The first two men jumped out swiftly, scooted across the uneven surface, and dropped to their knees. He pointed to the girl and the Chinese officer. "Your turn!"

Rex watched Choi and Grace step out, followed by the other two soldiers. He could hear short orders being barked over the communications system.

"Steve, go left. Chris, right!"

"Yes, sir!"

He could hear their labored breathing, all four men encumbered

PLAGUE LAND: NO ESCAPE

by their biohazard suits as they got into position, dropped to one knee into ready-to-fire postures.

Rex leaned forward, poked his head out of the door, and looked around. They were parked about fifteen yards from the front of the "island." He could see waves splashing over the top, and where the spray landed, the rich, chocolate-colored ground looked like the raw and frayed texture of whiplashed skin. He watched as another lively wave broke over the messy fringe, and immediately, the dying skin closest to the edge started bubbling and blistering.

This thing isn't *immune to salt. It was* scarring *itself in order to cross the sea, tolerating biomass loss.* He wondered if it was feeling pain as it did so.

"Anybody eyeballing movement yet?"

A chorus of negatives crackled back in response.

"I'm going to remove my mask and say hello," said Grace. "Is that OK?"

"Sir, are we really letting her do this?" That was Calloway. The question was directed at Rex.

"Yes, we are. Grace...go ahead. Let them know we're here."

He stepped out through the cabin's door and put a foot down on the ground. It gave subtly beneath his boots, like walking on freshly spread tar.

"Prime Minister! Please stay inside until—"

"For God's sake, I'm fine!" snapped Rex. He ducked low as he stepped away from the helicopter's downdraft and walked over to stand by Choi. He could see their surroundings more completely now. The ground was uneven, with gentle bumps and dips that made it look as though a thick, wet blanket had been draped over a hidden landscape of giant sinews and bones. He noticed the ground began to slope upward gently toward the giant "volcano" in the island's middle. It was impossible to judge the height of it since there was little recognizable or familiar to use for scale. As high as a ten-story block? As high as a water tower?

Grace was down on her knees, unclipping, then lifting the mask's plate away from her face. She leaned forward until one side of her face was pressed against the ground.

"Jesus...like the Pope kissing the—"

"Shut up!" barked the officer. The communications channel went quiet again.

As Grace knelt with her cheek against the ground, her eyes settled on Rex. She smiled at him "You look totally terrified!"

"I'm...uh, I'm doing fine, Grace. Can you tell me what you're doing right now? Is this about making contact?"

She closed her eyes. "I'm knocking on the front door."

They waited in silence for a minute, then finally she stirred. She slowly lifted her head from the ground, leaving a sticky, jelly-like strand dangling for a moment before it snapped back down.

"They know we're here. And They know why." She turned to look at him, revealing the side of her face that she'd held down. The flesh of her cheek was gone, exposing tendons and bone, gums and teeth. Her smile was a zombielike sneer, a cheap movie-world prosthetic.

"What will They do?" asked Rex. "What's going to happen?"

"They're coming," she replied. "Relax. All They want to do is show you."

"Show me? Show me *what*?"

"What They have to offer."

"What does that mean, Grace? What can They 'offer' us?"

"Movement!" one of the soldiers barked suddenly. "Three o'clock."

Rex turned to his right and scanned the marbled, brown terrain. He could see a portion of the ground puffing up like a blister. Its color lightened as it ballooned, stretched, and thinned. The membrane popped softly, the skin rupturing and falling to the ground to reveal a ribbed orifice that descended into darkness.

"Shit!" gasped one of the soldiers.

They waited and watched for another few seconds before spotting movement within the cavernous interior.

"Grace? Talk to us. What's happening?"

"Shhh," she replied, smiling again. "It's OK, Mr. Williams... Just wait and see, OK?"

Rex squinted to try and make sense of what was emerging out of the gloom. He could see the top of something pale, tall, slim.

"What the hell is that?" said Calloway.

There were five of them, growing taller, like calcium stalagmites in fast-forward. Rex realized they weren't growing; they were advancing up an ascending ramp into the open. He understood with that, that this structure was more iceberg than ship, with an unknowable mass hidden below the water's surface.

How big is this thing?

The pale objects emerged from the orifice into the sunlight and began to cautiously advance across the undulating ground toward them.

"Steady, lads," said the officer. "Fingers *off* triggers."

ALEX SCARROW

Rex could hear a faint hissing, skittering sound above the gentle splash of the bow waves nearby. The tall objects, a little closer now, appeared to be pale columns, like tree trunks freshly stripped of bark, at their bases, a froth of pale movement that he began to recognize as a swarm of the small scuttling creatures.

"Grace?"

"Yes?"

He pointed. "Those crab things, they know who we are as well, right?"

"Everyone knows who we are by now," she replied. "You're among friends."

The five trunks and the surging carpet of pale creatures drifted closer, riding over the humps and dipping into the troughs.

"You should lift your mask or remove a glove," said Grace, "so they can taste you."

Taste? This was starting to feel like a bad idea.

Their welcoming party was now just five yards from them and had come to a halt. The carpet of scuttling creatures settled down, retracting their tiny legs and claws into their pale, pearl-like shells until they looked like thousands of glistening pebbles. The tree trunks, he could see now, were not solid but a woven rope of slender, glistening, eel-like creatures, writhing and twisting around each other as they appeared to struggle upward to the very top.

"What now?" Rex asked.

"Grace? May I go now?" said Choi.

She nodded. "Go on, Jing."

The Chinese officer removed his mask, his gloves, then

PLAGUE LAND: NO ESCAPE

unzipped his biohazard suit, shrugging it off his body and stepping out of it. He turned to look at everyone.

"I am not afraid," he said. "This is what I am choosing—to pass into this other world."

"You're not coming back, Lieutenant Choi?"

He shook his head. "This is our future. Embrace it, Prime Minister."

"Christ. What's it going to feel like?"

"There is no pain. No discomfort. Only a sense of unity." Jing smiled. "You will see."

God help me.

Choi turned to Grace. "I thank you for your friendship and your invitation."

"I'll see you inside, Jing."

He stepped forward, crossing the small distance between them and the writhing trunks, removing his shirt, then his undershirt, and discarding them in his wake. He stepped onto the carpet of glistening, pale pebbles and stopped before the nearest of the trunks, looking up at it like a pilgrim at the end of a long journey. He carefully removed his trousers and underwear and stood naked before them, his arms spread wide.

The trunk advanced until it was pressed firmly against him, then the eel-like shapes suddenly ceased their endless, squirming race to the top, changed direction, and swarmed over his body. Within seconds, he was engulfed.

Rex could hear one of the men cursing quietly, someone else's breath hitching nervously.

"Steady, men," said Rex. "Those things..." He could hear his

ALEX SCARROW

voice shaking. He was sure he sounded like a ten-year-old school-boy, a figure of authority no more. "Those things didn't *attack* him. We're still good. We're still good." He turned to Grace. "What happens now?"

"Do you trust me, Mr. Williams?"

I don't have much choice, do I? He was here now. If he turned and ran for the helicopter, he wasn't sure what would happen. Would the crabs chase him down? Would running now undermine his role as the ambassador for what was left of humanity? Trigger an aggressive stance from the virus?

He cracked an uncertain smile. "Yes."

She held out her hand to him. "Take my hand, and we'll step in together."

"I'm not going to lie... I'm really very, very bloody scared."

She smiled, a scary Janus-like expression—on one side warmth, compassion, on the other, a wraithlike sneer.

CHAPTER
33

"The truth is…we can cross the water to get to you. We have been able to do this for some time. You are not safe here anymore," said Camille.

Leon watched the young girl as her gaze swept across the people crammed into the fish-and-chip restaurant. She looked every bit as human as anyone else. Only, *unlike* everyone else, there was an odd serenity about her.

"So, if I spray you"—Leon was holding the hose in both hands—"you're saying it won't do you *any* damage?"

"It *will* hurt me," she replied. "Please do not. You will kill many in my community. And I am only here to help you."

"Help us?" Leon started forward.

"Take it easy, Leon," said Lawrence. He took a step closer. Most of those in the small restaurant had stood up from their chairs and backed well away. Lawrence, however, had come forward. He looked at Leon, then at Jake, standing on the other side of the small narrow-framed girl, with a salt-water-filled fire extinguisher ready to use.

"My name's Lawrence. I suppose you could say I'm in charge here on the isle."

The girl studied him for a moment before answering. "I am Camille."

"So"—the old man narrowed his eyes—"starting from the basics...you're saying you're one of Them."

"Do you need proof of that? I can disassemble if you want?"

There were gasps at that. Leon turned to see heads shaking, eyes wide—Cora's, Finley's, and Kim's the widest; they knew how that looked when it happened.

"You really don't want that happening in here, Lawrence!" called out Jake.

"That's what happened at Southampton?"

He nodded. "They break down into crabs, hundreds of them. There's no way to fight them."

"In that case, we'll take it for now, Camille, that you're infected then. Please...don't *disassemble!*"

"Don't even move a muscle!" added Leon.

Camille shook her head sadly. "You are all so frightened. You do not have to be. They came to help us move on to the next stage of life, to absorb us. They are like librarians. Gatekeepers of information."

"You say your name is...was *Camille*?" said Leon.

"I *am* Camille. And I am human," she replied with a hint of indignation.

"You're *not* human," snapped Lawrence. "You're a copy. A rec-reation, a—"

246

PLAGUE LAND: NO ESCAPE

"I am Camille Ramiu. I am a proud Hausa. I lived in Niger. I lost one parent to disease and one to militiamen. I always dreamed of going to school, but I had to care for my brother and sister, or they would starve." She inspected her hands. "These are my hands, my fingers, and they are as much mine now as they once were before." She turned to look at Leon. "*Leon...*you said that is your name?"

He nodded.

"Leon, yes, you *can* hurt me with the salt water. But it will not kill me. It will kill the flesh it touches. If enough of my colony structure is damaged, I would have no choice but to disassemble into smaller constructions. And these smaller creatures are not able to communicate with you in the same way I can. They are simple. They work on instinct."

"We don't want that," said Leon. "We really don't want that happening!"

"Why did you come here?" asked Lawrence.

"I have a message, but it is very complicated, Lawrence."

"What's the message?"

"It is better, perhaps, if I can *show* you?"

"NO!" He shook his head quickly. "Don't do anything! No one's doing anything! Just tell us the message!"

"As you wish." She locked her fingers together and raised both hands to beneath her chin, looking like a little shaman in prayer. "They are ninety-nine percent of life on Earth. They are made up of all the humans, all the animals that existed here on this world. There are now only a few small groups like yours around the world."

"Where are they?" asked Leon.

"The ones who came to rescue you, they came from places

247

called Cuba and New Zealand. There are a few others, but they are struggling, dying."

"How many of us left?" asked Leon. "Do you know?"

She shrugged. "I have no number, but most of them will not survive for much longer. Their food is dwindling. This world will continue to grow colder as the climate has been changed by our *reach*. They, and *you*, will die out in the next few winters."

"We're doing just fine as we are!" cut in Lawrence.

She shook her head sadly. "It will get much harder for you to survive. Your food will run out..."

"No, it won't. We have an endless supply of fish, for God's sake!"

"Not for very much longer."

"Hang on! What do you mean by that?" asked Leon.

"The sea creatures will also be absorbed soon. We are learning ways to filter the salt from their chemistry. There is so much life in the sea for us to bring into our world."

"We can go on foraging for supplies," said Lawrence. "Indefinitely."

"This is true. But those supplies will also run out one day." Camille looked over to the restaurant, then at the window, at more faces peering through the scuffed glass. "Your population will die out." She turned back to him. "Death is your enemy. Not me. Not us."

"Not our enemy?" said Lawrence. "Your flippin' virus wiped us out."

"No. We have not 'wiped out' anything. We have *preserved* it."

Lawrence shook his head, exasperated and out of his depth.

"Yes. Every form of life has been broken down, read, and

PLAGUE LAND: NO ESCAPE

stored. Kept safe. If you want to know who has done more wiping out of life on Earth, it is humans."

Leon had heard enough of "They." He wanted to know more about them than just that one mysterious word.

"Camille? Who are *They*?"

She turned to look at him. "Yes, that is a much more useful question to ask." She paused for a moment. It looked like she was listening to an unheard voice, seeking advice. "They...like to be seen as *facilitators*, that is all. Helpers."

"Yeah, but *what* are They?" pressed Leon. "What? Not why are They here. *What are They?*"

Camille shrugged. "Helpers. They have instructions that are stages that take Them to a final goal."

"So, what's that?" asked Leon. "What's this 'final goal'?"

"To achieve on a different scale what cannot be achieved now."

"What the hell's that supposed to mean?"

"It is easier for me to show you than it is to explain it to you."

Lawrence raised his hands. "Don't do anything! Just stay right there!"

"I came here to invite one of your group to come with me."

"Now listen here! No one's going to go anywhere!"

Camille shook her head. "I will not *force* anyone. I am here only *to ask* for one of you to volunteer."

"When you say 'come with' you," said Jake, "what does that mean exactly? What's going to happen to them?"

"They will be absorbed. They will have a chance to witness *my* world." Camille smiled. "Then they will be allowed to return and explain what they've seen."

ALEX SCARROW

"Great," said Leon. "You're going to infect them, let us take them back in, and then we're all going to be sneakily infected!" He turned to Lawrence. "This is bullshit!"

"No. No infection. We do not wish to 'sneak' in." She nodded at the window. "We do not need to *trick you*—we could sail across and land on this place quite easily. We could force you, overrun you, but we do not want to. We choose to ask you instead."

CHAPTER
34

TOM FRIEDMANN STARED OUT THROUGH THE DUSTY WIND-shield. A pallid gray light was threatening to steal back into the night sky. He had no idea what time it was now. His watch was back on the bedside table in the small room he'd been assigned in the diplomatic apartment block.

He looked down at Freya, curled into a fetal position on the seat beside him. Her dark hair was splayed across her face. She appeared to be utterly exhausted and fast asleep.

He had been talking to this girl for several hours. But it hadn't been Freya.

He'd been talking to *Grace*.

She'd been sitting right there, on that seat. His daughter. Not the Grace he last saw over three years ago, but a girl who was now a teenager. Her face had gradually grown out of Freya's. Maybe in full daylight, the transition from one face to another might have been horrifically disturbing, but by the wan light of the moon, it had seemed like a magical transformation. The bridge of Freya's nose had thickened slightly, her jaw had become more oval and pointed. The skin around her eyes had shifted almost imperceptibly, one moment Freya's, the next, unmistakably, he was staring into Grace's eyes. Freya's hair, however, remained unchanged, as did her body. It had been an odd and unsettling experience for him to see his daughter's face transplanted onto another person's frame.

As she spoke to him, he *knew* it was Grace; her voice had the slightest trace of her New York accent, the hard corners of it knocked away by the short time she'd been living in London.

He sensed it could only be her—not a copy or an impersonation.

Dammit. It was her.

You look like crap, Dad.

That was the first thing she'd said.

She told him about how the outbreak had happened in the UK, in London. That after their last phone call got disconnected, things went south on their train up to Norwich. How Mom did her best to keep them both alive, finally having a breakdown and Leon stepping up to look after them both.

She told him about their months hiding out in a mothballed nuclear bunker from the Cold War, eating tin cans of food. Then eventually emerging into daylight, into a world transformed by the virus, stripped bare of everything that had once walked, flown, crawled, slithered.

She shared with him how Mom had died in the service station, ambushed by spiderlike creatures—Grace referred to them as "scouts." How Jennifer had fought to ensure both her children escaped through a smashed window before being overrun by the creatures. Jennifer fought to save her kids. She didn't get "preserved." She was torn to pieces.

Tom listened to his daughter try to persuade him that she was one of the *lucky ones*, not like her mother. That infection was the way "They" *preferred* to invite their victims.

...They've learned the best way to preserve humans. The pathways that need to be taken, the particular order in which a body is disassembled and broken down to ensure the valuable parts of the mind—what makes us us—remain unharmed and perfectly encoded...

She explained that the scouts—the crablike creatures—were like dumb robots, simple, disconnected automatons. Constructed for scouting, foraging, and, if necessary, killing. Running, resisting, fighting the virus was going to draw them like tiny, voraciously hungry assassins.

Dad, you have to understand, the virus isn't the enemy.

Death *is our enemy.*

She gave him a phrase that seemed to work well in summing it all up for him. *There* is *an "afterlife," you know? A heaven. But it's not up in the sky—it's deep down. It's within us.*

A biochemical afterlife.

The real tragedy, she said, was all of those who lived *before* the virus came to our planet. All the generations of people before them, come, gone, and then lost forever—their memories just fading photographs and footnotes. The people still alive now, right here on this island and far away in New Zealand...they faced the same fate—the terminal end of the natural life cycle. From the moment you're born, you're on a clock ticking down to death and decay, then gone…lost forever.

He'd asked her about Leon. She told him he'd been there at Southampton.

Dad, if Leon is still uninfected, and he dies…he'll be gone. Gone forever. Like Mom.

Her eyes focused, her face set with a determination. *Dad, now listen closely. This is really important…* And then she told him why she was here, why she'd surrendered herself to the Chinese aircraft carrier.

That had all happened an hour ago. Then, Grace's face had faded away and Freya had returned, slumped down in the passenger seat, exhausted by the process.

She stirred now, swiped her hair back, and blinked sleepily.

"You OK?"

She nodded. "Feel sort of hungover."

"I…I spoke with my daughter. I actually spoke with *Grace*."

Freya smiled. "I know."

"She said the virus is coming this way. It's coming to us. It wants to *meet* with us."

Freya didn't seem to hear that. She certainly didn't respond to it.

"Freya? Did you hear? It *is* coming this way!"

"I know. I know." She flapped a hand to hush him. "Grace is telling me that right now." She tilted her head like a cat listening for mouse squeaks beneath an old grandfather clock. She nodded to herself, then finally seemed to realize Tom was waiting.

"They're afraid of the survivors here on this island," she said. "Very afraid of them."

PLAGUE LAND: NO ESCAPE

"Afraid? Why?"

"Weapons. Bombs."

"You're talking about the nuclear warheads?"

She nodded. "They're well aware of the technology humans still have at their disposal. That they can still use on them." She paused again. She pulled herself up in the passenger seat and tilted her head once more. Listening. "Grace is telling me They're undecided about how to deal with you. Some want to reason with you, to get you all to submit and join. Others don't want to risk a mass death from the bombs—They want to strike hard and fast and wipe you out."

"If the virus is coming our way," cut in Tom, "what'll it do when it gets here?"

Freya shook her head and looked at him. "That's what she's saying. They don't know yet. They're still trying to decide."

He rubbed a hand along his jaw. *Jesus Christ. Maybe I'm hallucinating all of this?*

"You know, Leon and I made a pact back in England. A deal."

He turned to look at her. "What deal?"

"We wouldn't let ourselves die this way...you know? Become infected." She closed her mouth, shook her head. "I'm beginning to understand how stupid that was. How wrong we were." She turned to look at him, frowning at something, maybe at herself. "I've seen what it's like. While you were talking to Grace...I saw...it."

"Saw what?"

"The *inside*...I suppose." She looked around at the worn and scuffed metal dashboard of the ex-Soviet military vehicle. Then held her hands up, staring at them as if they belonged to someone else. "Did you ever play computer games, Mr. Friedmann?"

"What? No. Maybe a little bit of Pac-Man as a kid."

"You ever try one of those virtual reality helmet things?"

He shook his head absently.

"It's weird, so weird," she said, staring at her hands, flexing them. "Coming back *out*...that's kind of what it feels like. Like I'm wearing stupid virtual reality goggles. The outside world"—she patted her hand along the dusty dashboard—"that's the part that feels...*fake*. But inside? That's what feels *real*."

She shook her head. "Back in England, Leon and I both agreed we'd rather shoot ourselves than end up like everyone else. The thing is"—she looked at him—"they are guessing that's how everyone on this island feels. And They know the survivors here have bombs...*nuclear* bombs. They're scared for themselves, for us. They're scared the survivors will do something stupid."

"Which means we have some leverage. Something to negotiate with. Maybe if we let off another warning shot—"

She twisted in her seat, reached out, and grabbed his wrist firmly. "No! *No!* You mustn't!"

"What?"

"You drop a bomb on them and They won't have a choice! They'll swarm you. Wipe you all out!"

"Freya, we're not just going to simply lie down and let them crawl all over—"

Her grip tightened. He could feel her nails digging into his skin. "You *have* to convince Trent. You *have* to convince him to meet with them!"

PLAGUE LAND: NO ESCAPE

"There's no way! Even if I agreed with you." He tried peeling her fingers off his wrist. "There's no way I'd be able to convince him. Freya, let go of my arm!"

"You have to see."

"What?"

"You *have* to! You've got to see what I've seen!"

By the pallid gray light of approaching dawn, he could see a glistening fervor in her eyes.

"Freya! You need to calm the hell down! I'm not going to..." He tried to jerk his arm back.

She shook her head. "Not until you understand. Not until you've seen what I've seen!"

He tried to shake her off. But her grasp was surprisingly strong.

Then he felt a sharp stab into the underside of his wrist. "What the—"

"Don't struggle!" she hissed. "It's OK...It's OK!"

"—*hell* are you doing?" He managed to wrench his wrist free of her hand, and as he did, he saw something thin and glistening, like the needle of a syringe, pull out of his skin. The "needle" dangled from her palm, still pumping drops of a milky liquid onto the car seat.

"Shit! What...*what have you done to me?*"

"I'm sorry." She held her hands up before her. "I'm sorry. But... They're right. We *need* you. We need you to reason with Trent."

He looked down at the pale underside of his wrist. The small puncture in his skin was already puckering and reddening.

"What the...! You...you just *infected me*?"

He could feel warmth traveling up his arm, and it reminded

him of a childhood sensation: helping his mom with the dishes. A cold kitchen but hot, soapy water, his arms and hands blissfully warm while the rest of his scrawny body was enviously goose-bumping.

She's killed you. The bitch just injected you. Shit. Shit.

A part of him that sounded like his younger self, like Technical Sergeant Friedmann, was screaming at him to get off his ass and do something quick. His eyes settled on the glimmering metal of the handgun sitting on the dash. He reached out for it quickly. The crosshatch of the grip felt reassuringly rough against his palm, the cold trigger even better against his index finger.

"*No!*" screamed Freya, reaching out to snatch it from him.

He placed the barrel against his temple. Hard. It hurt. It would leave a bruise there, if he was still alive tomorrow.

"DON'T DO IT!" she was screaming.

DO IT, asshole! screamed Sergeant Friedmann in his face. *You wanna be slime? You wanna be a shitty crab? DO IT. DO IT!*

That cozy warmth was spreading across his shoulder now, across his chest. He could feel his body losing a war. He had one good arm left and, at the end of it, a good, solid, reliable gun.

DO IT! NOW!

His finger tightened around the cold trigger. He could feel the hard edges of the grip pressing against his soft palm—the last sensations his functioning mind would register as he squeezed.

The trigger wasn't moving. It was locked. His mind dimly recalled the safety was still on.

Shit. It wasn't a Beretta. His fingers knew every contour of the standard-issue M9. It was Russian. Not a gun he could

PLAGUE LAND: NO ESCAPE

unlock by touch. He needed to look at the damned thing to find the safety.

Shit.

And that's when he felt his resolve beginning to ebb, a marine's honorable way out fast receding as an option, becoming a hazy notion, as the warmth of invasion spread down his arm.

"Don't fight it," whispered Freya.

He slumped back in his seat. He could feel that warmth descending down his chest into his upper torso. Whatever was inside him was making use of his vascular system to get where it wanted to go. Traveling quickly and intelligently. He could feel the heat inside traveling upward now, propelled by his pounding heart.

His face suddenly felt hot, then numb.

"It's OK," he heard Freya whisper. "It just wants to get to your brain as fast as it can."

No shit.

He could feel his surroundings—the dusty dashboard, the smeared windshield, the threadbare driver's seat, the dark silhouettes of trees outside, and the lightening predawn sky—all pulling away from him. Receding. Strangely, it felt like he was shrinking. In a few seconds' time, he'd be the size of an action figure with a funny, squeaky voice to go with it.

His vision was clouding, dimming. Fading.

Freya was still talking to him, but he could only hear the muffled tones of her voice, just like ducking your head underwater in a bath. He could hear the thumping of his own heart, the roaring of his own veins like the hiss of distant traffic on a free-flowing highway.

ALEX SCARROW

It felt like a descent. Like a deep-water submarine sinking away from the shimmering light of the surface into the dark abyss below.

CHAPTER
35

LEON LOOKED AROUND AT THE OTHERS. THEN AT LAWRENCE and Jake. "This is nuts. No one's going. No one's actually giving this a thought, right?"

Camille shook her head. "We are not monsters. We are you. We *were* you. All we want is what is best. We just want someone to come and see."

"No one's doing it!" said Leon. "No one!"

"We want someone to come to us willingly. No one will be taken by force."

"Lawrence! For Christ's sake...*tell* her! No one is going! No one is—"

"I'll do it," said Jake. "I'll go..."

Leon looked at him. "*What?*"

"I'll go."

"Don't be a frickin idiot!" He turned to Lawrence. "Tell him! We're not doing this. We're not looking for volunteers!"

ALEX SCARROW

"What if she's right?" said Jake. "What if everyone I knew…" His voice faltered. "What if *Connor's* in there somewhere?"

"Not *everyone*," said Camille. "There were *some*…far too many…who got lost in the process. But They did the best They could. They tried to save as many as possible."

"This is complete bullshit," said Leon. "They just want us to lower our guard."

Jake placed the extinguisher down on the ground beside him. "You're saying I get to return back here? And I'll be uninfected?"

"Yes. I promise," replied Camille.

"I won't be, you know, *changed in any way* or anything?"

"Any scout cells left in your bloodstream will switch off their self-defense mechanism. Your immune system will destroy them quickly and easily. They will die to ensure you return as you were. Unchanged. Uninfected."

It's a lie. It's a trap! Leon wanted Lawrence to step in. Bring this farce of an exchange to a close. And if he wasn't going to…

"Jake! We've both fought to stay alive this far! And you're just going to lie down and let her infect you?"

Jake shrugged. "What if she's right? We're hanging on, that's all we're doing…hanging on. If the food runs out, if we can't catch fish, if this winter is going to be worse than the last two… Shit, Leo, if They can just wander up to us like this girl has, we're already screwed!"

"For Chrissakes, we'll relocate! That's what we'll do!"

"What if she's right though? What if being infected is like being uploaded to the internet or something? What if it *is life* but different? Something better than this? *Life 2.0?* I volunteer."

PLAGUE LAND: NO ESCAPE

"Hold on!" cut in Lawrence. "Look, how will—"

"My choice," said Jake firmly, turning to Leon. "My choice, mate. Don't worry. I'm good with this."

"Jake. Don't!" It was Cora, standing with Howard, Adewale, Finley, and Kim. They had instinctively grouped together, an old allegiance resurfacing. "We escaped the warehouse together, love. We got so far. Don't give in now!"

Jake shook his head. "I'm not giving in. I'm just... I need to know." He glanced back at Camille. "She's made it sound OK. What if it isn't that bad?"

"Shit, Jake!" said Leon. "You've seen it with your own eyes! We all did! Those things were monsters! Those things were screwed up!"

"I'm just going to see, mate. Then I'll come back and tell you what's going on."

Leon shook his head slowly and took a few steps toward his friend. "You won't be able to come back to us, Jake. You go, then you're gone for good."

"I think this girl's right. We're on borrowed time. It's just going to get worse and worse until we die out."

"Jake is correct," said Camille. "In my world, there is no death. Not anymore."

"Immortality," added Jake. "Come on, that sounds better than this."

Not as a bug. Or some twisted mutant.

"I'm staying human, Jake. Right to the bitter end, if it comes to that." Leon wanted to grab him and shake him. Scream at him that they could just burn this creature and run. Get their stuff, get off the isle, and go find somewhere else.

"Leon?"

"This..." Leon felt his throat tighten, his eyes brim, threatening to spill a tear. "You know, this is just...*giving up.*"

"You know what she's just described?"

Leon shook his head, not sure where his friend was going.

"*Heaven*, mate. That's what it could be."

"Or hell," Leon whispered.

"Or...the other alternative, a bullet in the brain, and then it's just nothing forevermore." Jake held out his hand. "*Nothing* just sounds like shit."

"If you return...you know we won't be able to trust you. You'll be a viral. That's it."

"And you'll burn me?"

Leon didn't know what he'd do if Jake came back among them and started evangelizing like Camille. Looking like Jake, sounding like Jake, but talking about the virus like it was some hippy-dippy chill-out zone.

"Yes. If we have to...whatever the hell you come back saying, you're gonna be one of Them." He bit his lip. "I'm staying human, Jake. Right to the end."

Jake reached for Leon's hand and grasped it. "Look, if I come back, at least gimme a chance to try and say something. OK?"

"Don't do this."

Leon turned to the faces lining the back walls of the restaurant. "This is complete crap. *Isn't anyone else going to goddamn well say anything?*"

He got nothing back. Cora had tried, and the others gathered around her said nothing. The rest of this morning's diners shook their heads.

PLAGUE LAND: NO ESCAPE

He suspected they all wanted Jake to go. To be the sacrifice... until next time. Until Jake came out of the goo and asked for another volunteer to come and join him. And one by one, they were all going to be led like pigs to the slaughterhouse.

Jake turned to Camille. "So what happens now?"

"We will both leave on my boat." She turned to Lawrence. "I can see you have men outside and they have gasoline. Please, will you ask them to back away? To let us go?"

Lawrence nodded. "Uh...all right." He cleared his throat and raised his voice. "All right, everyone, listen to me. The girl and Jake are leaving us. Everyone just stay where you are. Stay calm while I go inside and explain what's happening."

Leon watched him as he went over to the door, pulled it open, then stepped inside to address the crowd with the same message. Through the foggy window, he saw their response. Their eyes suddenly widening, peering through the window at their visitor, then starting to back away.

"Hey, Leon?"

He turned to his friend.

"Just don't burn me, Leon. OK?"

They flamed Grace, remember? They didn't stop to ask her a damned thing, did they? They just burned her because they were frightened. Is that what you are now, Leon? Frightened? Ignorant?

"I think you're an idiot agreeing to this."

"I'm taking one for the team, mate. If it's a crap deal...I'll let you all know."

Leon huffed out a dry laugh and offered his hand. "You do that."

Jake grasped it. "And if I don't come back, for whatever reason, you stay safe, bro."

"I'll do whatever it takes."

"You're a real fighter, mate."

Not always. Leon let him go. "Good luck."

The crowd had cleared back far enough, and Lawrence stood before them, arms spread wide.

Camille turned to Jake. "We will go now."

Leon heard Lawrence telling someone to calm down and stay well back.

He watched his friend and the viral creature walk down the long jetty, slowly becoming indistinct silhouettes amid the fog, and then, finally, they were gone from sight.

Leon heard them stepping into the dinghy, oars being dropped into their holes, and the gentle *dip* and *splash*, *dip* and *splash*, as the small boat pulled away.

CHAPTER
36

FOR A WHILE REX WILLIAMS FELT WEIGHTLESS. THAT WAS THE only word he could use.

Weightless. Disembodied.

It was a pleasant state. However, if the virus had tricked him into allowing himself to be infected and this state of being was to last forever, how long would it be before he began to feel this nothingness close in on him, suffocate him?

He became aware of sensations beginning to stir. First taste and smell together. He suddenly had the distinct impression that he could smell or had just eaten something flavored with vanilla. One of his favorite flavors.

Then he thought he could hear waves breaking softly on a beach: a gentle thump of water and a long hiss as it withdrew. Other sounds faded in: the occasional call of a seagull, the soft *clink-clink-clink* of halyards against a mast.

The sounds informed him that he was on a beach; then finally,

ALEX SCARROW

the darkness lifted, and he *was*: a beach that looked familiar from his youth—the Turnball Sailing Club. He could see the dinghies drawn up farther down the golden sands, deck chairs and beach umbrellas and the clubhouse farther along. The Pacific Ocean was warm, turquoise, and in a placid mood today.

"Hello."

He turned to see Grace sitting on a bright-red beach chair beside him.

"This is really nice," she added.

"How...? This...this..." Rex shook his head. The Turnball Sailing Club didn't exist anymore. When he was in his teens, it had gone bust, the clubhouse was demolished, and the beach was built up with apartments.

"I read your memories," she replied. "I liked this one. And it seems you like it too."

Rex nodded. He'd been ten when his parents first joined. Those were maybe the happiest few years of his life, coming here virtually every day.

"Why...why are we sitting here?"

"We could be anywhere, any-when. But I thought you'd like to see this again."

Rex nodded slowly. "I spent so much time down here." He looked at her. "But this isn't here. This is a...some sort of halluci-nation, isn't it?"

"Not really. It's real in every sense that matters."

"But it *isn't* real. It can't be. The sailing club doesn't exist anymore."

"What we see, hear, taste, touch, smell, feel, Mr. Williams, all ends up as electrical signals converted to chemical messages

268

PLAGUE LAND: NO ESCAPE

before we're even aware of them. Our minds interpret the chemistry and decide what that means, where we are, and how we feel." She leaned over and ran her fingers through the coarse sand. "To be honest, the only things that are real—that you can rely on being *true*—are those you experience *inside* your head. Everything outside is just…information."

"But"—he gestured at the sea—"this is either here, or it's not. It's not a matter of *opinion*."

"You know, the real sky outside could be green, the sea could really be bright orange. But we've all decided to interpret the information our eyes gather in a certain way. We are told the sky is blue, so we all see the sky as blue. All that matters on the inside is what you decide is true."

"So this is…inside? We're inside…*what* exactly?"

"We call it the *bioverse*. It's a good name. I don't know who first came up with it."

"Is everyone who got infected…in this *bioverse*?"

Grace nodded. "Most of them."

"Where are they?"

She shrugged. "Nearby."

He looked around. "On this beach? In the clubhouse? Beyond these trees?"

"No. This is a private space. Just you and me. I made it from your memory, so you didn't panic when you reassembled."

"Reassembled?"

"Your mind. Your consciousness."

Rex had an unsettling image of his brain floating like a cauliflower in a jar of jam.

ALEX SCARROW

"You're talking about my...*brain*?"

"No, your *awareness*. That's such a tiny part of you. I think only fifty or sixty million cells of the brain. It's so small. The rest of that organ, the billions of cells, they're just storage, they're housekeeping, they control body processes."

"I don't understand."

"Someone explained it to me this way: awareness is like your CPU. The rest of the brain is the hard drive, the cooling fan, circuit board, power unit...all that stuff. It follows you around, and sometimes it all assembles together—one complete mind. Sometimes it's just your awareness you have with you." She smiled. "That's a lot to take in, I guess."

"So...how much of you is here with me?" he asked.

"Not all of me," she replied.

"Just your *awareness*?"

"Not even all of that." She smiled. "You can share yourself out, be in two places at once, duplicate, then recombine. It's—"

"My God...*duplicate*?"

"Uh-huh."

"So then...if you can do that, which one is the real you?"

She laughed at that. "I am not the cells themselves, Mr. Williams. I'm how they talk to each other. I know that must sound weird."

"You're not kidding."

"Are you religious?"

He shook his head. "My father was Catholic. I never believed in any of that."

"Well, I was going to say it's easier to understand this if you think of yourself as a spirit."

He spread his hands. "And what? That makes all of this...
heaven?"

"Yup." She shrugged. "Kinda. Or nirvana, whatever you want
to call it."

He was about to laugh at her reply, but then he realized she
was serious, and she was right. Looking at this strangeness *that*
way, yes, it made sense.

"This is a...microbiological afterlife?"

"That or you can call it inner space or the bioverse." She
shrugged. "Everyone seems to have a different name for it."

"If I accept your religious metaphor, and you and I are *spir-
its...*and this is heaven? Then, does it follow that there's a *God*?
Someone or something in charge?"

"Not in charge." She smiled. "Not really. But They're certainly
here to help."

"Who?"

"Them."

"*Them?*"

"It's really hard to describe who They are." She pressed her lips
together as she thought about it. "They found their way here sort
of randomly, I guess, but They came with a mission." She turned
to him. "Would you like to meet one of Them?"

He wondered if he was going to regret it. "That's why I'm here,
isn't it? So we can meet? Negotiate?"

Grace shook her head. "They don't *have* to negotiate with
you. We could wipe out the last survivors easily. We could swarm
ashore and get this over with very quickly. But then many would
die in the process and their minds lost forever. No one wants that."

"So what do They want from me?"

"Just for you to see for yourself. Decide what's best. Then go back home and tell everyone. That's why you're so important, Mr. Williams. People trust their leaders. You know, the same thing is happening with other groups around the world. We're getting other leaders to see for themselves."

He understood. He was pretty sure she was telling the truth about swarming them too; if They could make that vast floating structure and tolerate the salty Pacific, They could probably find a way onto the two islands of New Zealand without any trouble.

"So?" She looked at him. "What do you think? How about it?"

"Meet...one of *Them*? One of your facilitators?"

"Yes. Just one."

What the hell am I agreeing to do here? Meet God?

"Anything I need to know first? Dos and don'ts...that kind of thing? Wear a tie or something?"

"No." She laughed softly. "They're not judging you."

"Right."

He looked around once more at the bay, at the clubhouse, at the inviting turquoise waves. "I suppose we'd better get on with it and have this meeting."

He was standing in a dark void. Floating, in fact.

It took him a while to realize that it wasn't just more blackness—it appeared to be a projection of space. He began to pick out the faint, steady light of distant stars, the subtle brushstrokes of the Magellanic Clouds.

"Grace. What's going on?"

PLAGUE LAND: NO ESCAPE

He heard Grace's voice even though he couldn't see her anywhere. "Just a moment." Her voice filled the universe around him.

The luminosity of the stars and gas clouds increased until what was once the blackness of a dead universe was awash with color, like a watercolor painting left out in the rain. At college, he'd studied a module of cosmology. From the little he remembered of it, he realized what he was looking at was a universe much, much younger than the present one.

"Why am I seeing this?" She didn't reply. "Grace?"

No response. He looked down at himself and saw nothing. He was simply present in this place, in what he presumed was another bioverse simulation. He was a wandering spirit, witnessing the incredible adolescent years of the cosmos.

Presently, the gas clouds began to move, to swirl and spin into what looked like weather systems, and Rex understood he was watching millions of years accelerated into seconds. The clouds swirled and compacted, glowing brighter with energy. The scene suddenly zoomed in on a random tendril of gas, and Rex felt panic for a moment as he found everything rushing past him. He was pulled toward a small segment of the universe, to inspect it more closely.

He saw clouds of gas and dust that had fallen in on themselves and formed into a cluster of baby stars. Rushing forward again, descending into even greater granular detail, he found himself hurtling toward one particular star as the rest receded into the background.

The color washes of distant gas clouds drained away, and once again, space was a black void peppered with faint pinpricks of stars. His view zoomed in, and now he was hovering above a world.

My God.

Another world. He could see beige oceans and dark land masses that began to distort and change shape. He realized, once again, time was being accelerated and he was seeing this planet's geology finding its form, tectonic plates sailing like ships across the incomplete crust. The land masses settled, or maybe time was being slowed down. He saw the planet's hue change, become cooler. He saw the beige oceans change to more of an olive color; he saw the envelope of an atmosphere thicken and green-tinted clouds begin to form like milk curling in a stirred coffee cup.

"Is this...*Their* world?" he asked, hoping Grace, or someone, would answer him. "Is that what I'm being shown?"

But still nothing. Silence. He remained on his own.

He watched the world below him settle now that it had an atmosphere; time was being slowed down yet again. He saw the marbling of colors changing across the land masses, ecosystems rising and falling to be replaced with new ones as global temperatures changed.

He watched a smear of white spreading down from the top and up from the bottom of the world, almost meeting at the equator and then drawing back like theater curtains, and realized he'd just witnessed a complete ice age. It might have lasted tens or hundreds of thousands of years, but for him, it had been mere seconds.

Time slowed down still further. And that's when he saw it.

One flash of light on the world as day and night looped the

PLAGUE LAND: NO ESCAPE

planet. One flash, followed by another and another. Artificial light, surely.

Life? Is that Them?

The pinpricks of light increased across the surface, at first random, isolated dots, but as the number grew, they began to link up into weblike patterns that could only suggest an intelligent structure.

They're showing me their history.

The webs of light within the night side became hair-thin gray lines on the day side of the planet. Roads? He saw the lines converge and thicken and the blotches of grayness expand like bruising on an apple. The oceans began to show their own stains of color. The whiteness at both ends of the planet began to recede farther, until they eventually vanished. The discolored oceans began to rise, encroaching on the land masses, the gray cities quickly vanishing beneath the advancing olive seas.

Rex noticed the atmospheric envelope thickening to become foggy, and he realized he was seeing this world rise in temperature, starting to cook itself within a hot and humid blanket.

Global warming. *Not just us, then.*

For a moment, he wondered if he was being shown a history of Their world or given a cautionary lesson with some hypothetical planet. The fog now thickened and became a featureless, solid, opaque envelope.

The world began to recede beneath him and he sensed its story was over. Suddenly, he was whisked with a disconcerting blur to somewhere else. The sun here was warmer.

Is this a different system?

Another world was rushed toward him. The palette of planetary colors was more earthlike. The seas were turquoise, the land bluey green. Hair-thin lines raced toward weblike networks that converged on discolored stains of construction, and Rex watched as they began to break up and disappear, the dark stains of what had to have been vast cities fading to nothing. It didn't disappear beneath a superheated blanket, which seemed a more positive thing, but its intelligent life vanished. This world's story ended with a lush and verdant planet-scape, but no sign of civilization.

Someone was here once. They tried to reach out beyond their world, but only got as far as orbit before...?

Before what? They wiped themselves out? They ran out of resources? They were erased by a virus?

Rex was jerked away again and found himself floating above a third world. Like the first two, the telltale signs of intelligent life were there: the crisscrossing trellis of lines, the golden glowing of artificial constructs on the night side. He wondered what fate was awaiting these poor souls.

He wasn't kept waiting long.

His eyes picked out movement, something tumbling, approaching fast.

An asteroid. It looked the size of a grain of rice to him, but if this planet was Earth's size, then it could easily have been the size of Manhattan. It smacked into the middle of an ocean with a blinding flash of light.

As the glare faded back down, he could see the atmosphere recoiling as a shockwave pushed it back, revealing a growing ring of planet surface exposed directly to the vacuum of space. He saw concentric rings of ocean racing out from ground zero; tsunamis that had to be hundreds if not thousands of yards high.

A mushroom cloud rose from the point of impact, an enormous spout of ejecta that spread out and began to create a shroud that would, he suspected, end up coating the entire planet soon enough. He saw the delicate concentric rings of seawater meet the land and turn into pale white brushstrokes that kept on going. He saw lights on the dark side blink out. And the shroud quickly spread like spilled ink across tissue paper.

Rex Williams had just been shown a sequence of worlds, dying in different ways.

Intelligent worlds.

CHAPTER
37

IN ANOTHER DARK VOID, IN ANOTHER PLACE FAR AWAY, A young man named Jake Sutherland understood what he'd just witnessed too. Unlike Rex Williams, he was much less self-conscious about voicing his thoughts out loud.

"So. You've showed me lots of civilizations dying. Is that a warning or something?"

His words hung in the darkness unanswered.

"I was told to come and see. Is this what I was meant to see? Is there more?"

The darkness remained unresponsive.

"Hey, Camille? You there?"

There was no reply from the girl who'd brought him here. He was alone. The sun, the dying world below him, were gone now. Even the faint stars...all gone. A plain, black canvas once more. He was beginning to wonder if that was the show. All done, and *please pick up your trash as you exit this auditorium.*

That's it? He hovered, bodiless, and waited, wondering how long he could exist in this nothingness before his mind caved in on itself, leaving him utterly lost. A day? A year? A decade? A century?

I.

A whispered voice. Jake's attention jerked away from his growing panic. He waited for the voice to say something more.

I...am...They.

He looked around but saw only black. It was impossible to tell where the soft, sibilant voice had come from.

"You...are you one of Them?"

Them. Yes.

"Where's Camille? Where's the person who brought me here?"

Not here. Just you. And Us/I.

He realized he was asking pointless, panicked questions. He'd been shown things, *important* things, and the next few words needed to *not* sound stupid, needed to be about what he'd been shown.

"You showed me some alien civilizations? Real ones?"

What is "alien"?

"Alien? It means not from my world," replied Jake.

Then yes.

"Why? Is it a warning? Is it—"

It is history-truth. What has been.

He was vaguely aware the voice had spoken a word he'd never heard before, but somehow his mind had automatically done it's best to translate into a hybrid English: *history-truth.*

Many. Civilizations. They come, they go. They never last.

"We...up until you came, we thought we were *alone* in space."

ALEX SCARROW

Jake had the feeling somebody more qualified in astronomy or physics might have been a better volunteer. "We've been listening and looking for aliens for decades."

Very much time, very much space. Very little life like us. Like you.

He played that reply through his head a couple of times before he got the sense of what He-She-They-It was saying.

"You're saying there's so much time and distance between us all?"

Yes. Never a chance to discover-share.

Another one of Their hybrid words. The second half of the definition moved subtly like a digital circuit in his mind between the words *share* and *bond*.

We/I, one of these. Once. We/I would last only a short while. Like you.

"Why? Why only a short while?"

The nature of complexity. Short-lived. It is fragile.

Destroys itself. Or is destroyed.

"But...you've just destroyed us!"

Saved you. You are preserved-stored-alive.

"You've 'stored' us? What do you *mean* by that?"

Encoded. Reduced. Compressed. Now we can discover-share. Together.

Camille had talked for a while with him before this dark void. Preparing him. They'd been sitting in a bizarre but pleasant setting of *her* choosing—a playground. She'd talked about what she called a "bioverse." A shrinking down of all that mattered on this world into a much smaller space. But then, she'd added, *small* was really just a redundant word now. Like *large, here, there, up,*

280

down—language that was inevitably going to fall out of use among the billions that now lived here.

"You're saying…this place, this bioverse thing is…?"

Bioverse is…universe abstraction, minus distance, minus time.

"It's the universe?"

All civilizations, encoded and saved. Ours also.

Jake let that sit in his head for a moment. "Are you saying what's happened to us…the infection, the deaths, everything? That also happened to you?"

Yes. And all others. Transformation-gift to us is now our transformation-gift to you.

CHAPTER

38

"High Tower, this is Eagle One. I've got eyes on it!"

Aviation Pilot Warren "Hooch" Moffat tapped his F-15's joystick lightly. The horizon swung, his left wing dipped obediently, and through the Plexiglas canopy, he was now looking down at the flat table of the deep blue Atlantic Ocean. The only feature on its surface defied Moffat's ability to describe it.

"That's, uh...that's a big-ass mother!" He was a pilot, not a poet.

His wingman, Juice, kept formation beside him, rising up on his right as they both banked left together, describing a wide counterclockwise loop around the distant object far below.

"Jesus Christ, Hooch...that thing's made by the virus?"

Moffat shrugged and shook his head. Their briefing had been hurried and, he felt, not entirely complete. "Maybe."

It looked like a floating theme park. That was the phrase that jumped into his head. The pinks, reds, purples, the swirls. The tall

PLAGUE LAND: NO ESCAPE

central structure looked like some cartoon island volcano ready to spray a geyser of M&M's up into the sky.

Holy crap. It even had big bunches of what looked like pink and red party balloons floating above it.

"Goddamn freak show," said Juice.

"Eagle One, Eagle Two, this is High Tower. Just tell us precisely what you two are seeing!"

"Copy that." Moffat puffed his cheeks out before replying. "OK, well it looks like a...like some kind of island. It's shaped sort of like a kidney bean. Mostly flat, but then there's a...what looks like...a central funnel shape. Similar configuration to a volcanic island."

"Eagle One, is the object in motion or stationary?"

Moffat and Juice were coming around toward the back of the island. He could see the white of breaking water at the front and a long, fading trail at the rear.

"High Tower, affirmative. This thing's definitely moving. It's doing it slowly, but it's moving."

"Eagle One, can you give us an estimated speed?"

He shook his head. At this altitude, it was virtually impossible to gauge. "Hard to say—less than ten knots certainly."

"Less than ten knots, copy that."

He looked again at the wake it was leaving behind. The fading trail of foam seemed to be doing a good job of sticking around in a receding straight line, which meant a calm sea. But there was something else he could see there. Something beneath.

"Juice?"

"Yeah."

"Check out the wake. What do you see?"

They were now passing directly over it, and Moffat could see his wingman straining forward in his seat and looking almost vertically down.

"I see..." Moffat heard the soft clunk of his friend's helmet against the canopy over the radio channel. "There's something else down there...beneath the wake."

They were over it now. The wake was rushing away behind them. They were going to have to do another lap around the island before they got a second look at it.

"I saw something trailing below the surface. That what you meant, Hooch?" added Juice.

"Yeah."

"Eagle One, this is High Tower. Repeat your last."

"Juice and me were just saying it looks like this thing's dragging something behind it. We're going around to take another look. Lower this time."

"Copy that."

Moffat kept his joystick tilted left as they made an even arc around the structure, several miles long, slowly descending three hundred yards in altitude as they did so. Finally, they were coming back around again to approach the viral island. As the front of the island slipped past his left side, Moffat could see much more detail on the surface.

The flat "ground" at the front looked like several dozen acres of an open slaughterhouse.

"Looks pretty damn gross down there," said Juice.

"Uh-huh, you can say that again." He could see blisters and

boils, ropes of what looked like intestines, ribs and folds of dry flesh, all of it sunbaked and leathery.

The cone shape in the middle of the island loomed toward them. Hundreds of thread-fine tethers emerged from the volcano's crater, holding the party balloons in their big, jostling clusters.

As they zoomed past, several dozen of the tethered clusters were released, a cloud of red and pink orbs detaching from their threads, rising quickly and spreading into the sky like a flock of startled birds.

"Jesus!" He instinctively twitched his joystick to the left to give it a wider berth.

"Jesus!" echoed Juice in his earpiece.

"This is High Tower. What just happened, Eagle One?"

"Floating objects, like balloons...a whole bunch just detached and scattered."

They were past the cone-shaped central structure and now fast approaching the rear of the island. He craned his neck to look down again at the leathery, organic landscape. This time, though, it seemed to be alive with movement.

"Shitty shit!" gasped Juice. "You see that?"

He could. A number of dark orifices in the ground had puckered open like whale blowholes and squeezed out what looked like soap foam. As the foam spread out and diffused, he could see that he was actually looking at a swarm of creatures of varying sizes.

"Eagle One, what are you seeing?"

"Creatures. Everywhere. Thousands. *Millions* of them!" replied Juice.

ALEX SCARROW

"High Tower, this is Eagle One. The structure must have a substantial portion below the waterline. That's where they're all coming from."

The two F-15s roared over the rear of the island, and Moffat craned his neck to look down to his left at the island's long wake.

He could definitely see something down there under the water—something thick and pale, the faint ghost of an object that seemed to extend back, beneath the bubbles of the wake, as far as he could see, becoming lost in the flash of the sun on the ocean's rippling surface.

"Looks like it's dragging a thick line or something," said Juice.

"Repeat your last."

Moffat replied, "The island seems to be dragging some sort of thick cable behind it."

"Cable?"

No, that wasn't the right word. "More like an umbilical cord."

CHAPTER
39

"WILL THE PRESIDENT EVEN BOTHER LISTENING TO YOU?" asked Freya.

Tom hunched his shoulders as he steered the jeep slowly along the Via Monumental. The road was busy, not with cars, but with ox- and horse-drawn carts and rickshaws stacked high with goods for trade. He honked the jeep's horn to clear a space through the logjam and began to weave his way forward.

"He may do. We go back a long way. We used to be army buddies."

"But if there's a viral formation approaching Cuba, this island thing, he's going to be really twitchy? Nuke twitchy?"

"Uh-huh. If I can't reason with him, I might be able to take him down."

"You'll get shot, won't you? He's got guards, right?"

"Well, let's hope plan A works. If the virus is on its way, Trent needs to be convinced to talk with it...or..."

ALEX SCARROW

Be taken out.

Ahead of them was the Castillo de los Tres Reyes del Morro, a stone castle that dated back to Spain's colonial times. Before the outbreak, it had been a well-visited tourist spot just outside the city with a large manicured lawn out front. Now the area was being used daily as a contraband marketplace where supplies of homegrown and undeclared food supplies were being brought in to trade.

"Dammit!" he cursed.

They should have headed back into the city sooner. It was eight o'clock already, and the roads going into and coming out of Havana were clogged. Less than an hour ago, Tom had woken up, emerged from the "bioverse," to find himself in this jeep, parked at a rest stop beside a field of cassava plants. He realized he understood *everything*—why the virus was here, why it had done what it had done. It was wary of the human survivors and the damage they could inflict with the weapons they had left.

He had to get to Trent before Trent made a terrible mistake. But if the president knew he'd been touched by the virus, he was likely to order Tom shot and burned without a second's hesitation.

Seeing was the only way to comprehend it all.

He now understood what had happened to Earth. And why. His journey into that bizarre inner universe had been like a visit to a planetarium or a wild virtual-reality ride in a theme park. But it had made *perfect sense*. If isolated pockets of life existed across the impossible-to-travel expanse of the universe, then the only chance they'd ever have to meet would be in a much smaller one. A microscopic cosmos.

"You OK?" said Freya.

He nodded. "My mind's still reeling from all this."

"It's a total head trip all right."

He nodded. "Our language just can't explain it. We don't have the words." He honked the horn again and cleared a space down the side of a short line of tethered sheep. "I don't know how the hell I'm going to convince Doug to allow himself to experience what I have." The jeep rode up on the curb, then bounced down to the road beyond. "Freya, when did you first suspect that…that the virus had gotten inside you?"

"Before we got to Southampton, I was using a cane. I was getting almost to the point where I needed a wheelchair."

"What was wrong with you?"

"I had MS."

"Multiple sclerosis?"

"Yeah. The symptoms were getting worse quickly. Then, on the ship, I noticed I was feeling better." She turned to look at him. "I don't know when the symptoms started turning around. Could be months back. Maybe Grace infected me back at the castle!"

"What about Leon? Do you think she infected him too?"

He realized how bizarre his question sounded. He was actually hoping Freya would say yes.

Unbelievable.

Since the outbreak, he'd been praying that his children had somehow escaped the plague, that they'd dosed themselves up on enough medications to survive the clouds of spores and been smart enough to make it through the intervening years.

Now he was praying that Leon had succumbed to it.

ALEX SCARROW

"I don't know. I suppose if I could be and not know about it, so could he. I just can't think *when* it could have happened. We were together pretty much all of the time."

Tom steered the jeep onto the rough shoulder to bypass several rickshaw drivers and the line of traders now peeling off into the grounds of the marketplace. Tom picked up some speed as they headed into the large entrance to the Túnel de La Habana.

"Trent might not even agree to see me," said Tom. "I think I used up most of whatever we have between us on getting him to send ships to Britain. He thought the whole effort was a waste of time and resources."

"That was all *your* doing?"

"My nagging. I convinced him we could cherry-pick from the British survivors—engineers, doctors, medics—and boost the numbers of the non-Cuban population. We're unwelcome guests here, as I'm sure you're well aware. Especially since Doug seized control."

At the far end of the tunnel, where the road ramped upward to rejoin the street level of Havana, he could see a military checkpoint.

Tom slowed, lowered the window, and produced his ID card. The U.S. marine glanced at it quickly, recognizing his face and name.

"Mr. Friedmann, sir. What are you doing *outside* the city perimeter?"

"I needed to get some headspace."

"You should've taken a marine escort out with you."

Tom shrugged. "I know. I just needed to get some air."

"Sir, you know the president announced a lockdown on security this morning?"

PLAGUE LAND: NO ESCAPE

"No...no, I missed that."

"The British evacuees are going to be moved off island. The president wants to get all U.S. personnel—"

Just then, Tom heard a voice raised in alarm. He looked over the marine's shoulder and saw one of his comrades looking up into the sky. He heard another voice and another, more heads turning up, fingers pointing.

"Oh, Jesus Christ, no..."

Three vapor trails were arcing up into the sky from the bay. He realized what they were. Nukes.

God no. One of the spotter planes must have located the viral island coming their way. *And Trent's reacted the only way he knows how...*

He turned to Freya. She was looking up at the arcing vapor trails, her mouth hanging open at the sight of them.

"We're too late, Freya."

"Are those nuclear bombs?"

"Tactical nukes, yes."

"Oh..."

"What's going to happen?" he asked. "What's that mean? How's the virus going to respond to them?"

She shook her head at all his questions. "I think this is going to end badly."

CHAPTER

40

REX WILLIAMS RETURNED.

It felt like a birth of sorts, emerging fully formed, into daylight from the womb-like smothering of soft tissue, as he stepped from the interior world of the artificial island.

Fifty yards ahead, he could see the four men from his security team, their faces hidden behind the reflections of their faceplates. Dr. Calloway was farther back, the helicopter sitting still and quiet behind him. He blinked at the harsh light of day, shivered with the cool air blowing across the viral structure's vast "foredeck."

"Prime Minister?" called out a muffled voice. "Are you OK, sir?"

Rex nodded. "I'm OK," he replied. "I'm fine."

The figure gestured. "You have to put the suit back on, sir!"

He could see his biohazard suit had been laid out on the ground nearby, ready for him to step into. He realized he had

PLAGUE LAND: NO ESCAPE

to accept now that he was no longer going to be thought of as Prime Minister Williams, instead as a potential impostor, a viral agent.

He nodded. "Of course."

"The girl and the Chinese guy—are they coming out too, sir?"

"No. They're staying here."

They're home.

"It's just me."

He put the suit on, pulled the hood over his head, sealed the faceplate, and connected the air supply, then the soldiers led him back to the waiting helicopter, its engine beginning to whine in pitch as the rotors turned and began to pick up speed. He clambered back inside the cabin and sat down across from a wary-looking Dr. Calloway.

The speaker inside his hood crackled. "So, Prime Minister?"

Rex looked up at him.

"What happened in there? What did you see?"

And that's when he realized why the girl, Grace, had insisted he *come and see.* Words of explanation just weren't going to be enough. He looked around at the cramped and clumsy confines of the helicopter's cabin—its hard, primitive edges, the grime and small blisters in the gray paint, the faint blooms of rust—and realized right then that he was seeing the crude mechanics of a redundant form of humankind.

The men in the cabin with him were just lumbering water-sack giants held in an approximate shape by clunky, brittle, calcium frames and protected—barely—by a pink membrane sheath that creased and sagged and mottled and aged all too quickly. He was looking around at the crumbling remnants of the past.

Mankind 2.0 is waiting patiently for us down there to wake up and join them.

"What did I see?" replied Rex.

Calloway nodded eagerly.

"I don't even think I can begin to describe what I saw. But I know what I'm going to say when we get back."

"What?"

Rex was aware the soldiers were listening in on this conversation too. They were on an open channel inside the helicopter. "We shouldn't be afraid of the virus."

The tips of all three nuclear missiles dipped further, and their altitude began to rapidly decrease in twenty-yard increments. Their paths, parallel for the majority of their journey, began to diverge slightly, one heading to the rear end of the viral island, one to the front, one to the very middle.

Two seconds before impact with the leathery, lumpy ground, they detonated.

For a few moments, three miniature suns blinked into existence above the empty ocean, dazzling in their intensity. They rose up, lifted carefully by columns of superheated steam and framed by concentric garlands of shockwaves that stirred and combed out the few natural clouds in the vicinity.

The entire mass of the viral island above water was incinerated in a nanosecond, tens of thousands of tons of nearby water instantly converted to steam. In the superheated area of ground zero, a void was left behind by the rapidly rising balls of flame and columns of steam.

The nanosecond passed. The sea crashed in on itself, covering over the gory, excavated gouges of the island.

The enormous underbelly of the viral structure, having survived the initial heat and shockwave of the blasts, now had salt water cascading down through its delicately built insides. Raw organic fluid, un-leathered, unprotected, began to bubble, boil, and disintegrate. Flow tubes a yard in diameter that were this living structure's arterial system ruptured and spilled their super-highways of liquid traffic into internal spaces. Scout, maintenance, storage, research, and message virals in their trillions were inundated by a descending tidal wave of salty ocean water as it roared downward from cavity to cavity, internal walls of flesh and fiber corroding and tearing along the way.

The island might have been over three miles from tip to stern, but beneath the water, it had hung down like a large, fleshy polyp five miles deep. Within ten minutes, this subsurface leviathan was catastrophically dissolving on the inside, a bloody carnage of viral creatures screaming as they frothed and corroded. Outside, the dark calloused envelope of dead tissue began to twitch and convulse like a heart shredding, the surface tearing and spilling a cloudy pink broth into the ocean.

From the rear of this dying mass there was another thick flow tube: the three-thousand-mile-long "umbilical" that had been trailing behind it. It began to detach itself from the dying organ. As water began to flood into its open end, it contracted on itself, sphincter-like, muscle tissue instinctively understanding there was an opening to close. Several dozen tons of seawater got in and wrought havoc, killing trillions of cells floating in its highway carrier fluid and burning huge stretches of the tunnel wall. But with the breach now quickly and effectively sealed, the damage was contained.

The seal was reinforced with raw scar tissue and finally tore itself away, jettisoning this section to face its own doom as it dissolved from the inside out, ruptured, and spilled its guts into the sea, joining the remaining large fragments of the island's underbelly in their doomed descent to the bottom of the Atlantic.

Within the now-sealed flow tube, billions of cells coalesced together, forming a temporary supercell cluster, a large jellyfish-like coalescing of soft tissue floating in carrier fluid and gathering information and awareness.

After a few minutes of internal discussion, a chemical message was settled upon. Agreement reached.

The Outsiders are a threat.

CHAPTER
41

WAITING IS WHAT IDIOTS WITHOUT A VALID PLAN DO. WAITING is for dumb cattle lining up to be slaughtered.

Dad used to have a saying for everything. That was one of his. However, he was equally likely to say *better to do nothing than to do stupid.* So no help, really.

Leon decided to opt for Dad's first piece of wisdom. If the virus could now just walk up and announce it was meeting to think about what to do with them, then...it seemed pretty damned stupid for them all to be sitting around waiting to find out.

Jake Sutherland had wandered off down the jetty and into the mist with that girl twenty-four hours ago. And they'd heard nothing since.

Doing nothing felt like stupidity; it felt like he was laying his head on the block and urging the executioner to get on with it.

"You guys ready?"

He'd only spoken to those he'd arrived with: Cora, Adewale,

ALEX SCARROW

Howard, Finley, and Kim. All five of them felt exactly the same. They'd escaped together once before, and they could do it again. Sitting around and just waiting for their fate to be decided for them was not an option. The truck was still parked up at the far end of the broken bridge, still had supplies, guns, and half a tank of fuel.

Cora nodded. "We're ready, love."

Everyone had a backpack stuffed with water bottles and dried noodles plundered from the community's waterfront supply house. That was all they were stealing. Once they were in the truck and on their way, they would figure out what they should do next.

Leon checked his watch. It was eight in the evening and dark enough to get going.

The plan—for what it was worth—was simply that they were going to make their way down to the bridge. If some of Lawrence's unsteady home guard were on duty, they'd deal with them first, then slide the plank across the gap and make a run for the truck. Each of them had a one-liter sports bottle loaded with kerosene and a lighter. If any snarks started to emerge from the roots zigzagging along the bridge, then squirting burning kerosene might be enough to allow them to reach the truck.

Leon nodded. "OK. Let's go."

They crept out of the terraced council house Leon and Jake had been living in, into the drizzling rain, and walked in silence down the narrow lane toward the seafront road. Normally there was no one out and about at night in this little community. They'd grown so used to taking the sea on all sides as an impenetrable

PLAGUE LAND: NO ESCAPE

defense that Lawrence had long ago abandoned the idea of a night security team. But tonight, it seemed, at least half the island's population was outside, some with flashlights, some with lanterns, some wandering up and down the coastal road, some down on the beach and staring out at the calm, rain-speckled sea and the drifting fog.

No one was sleeping.

They trooped past a cluster of old boys gathered around a wood burner, holding their hands toward the flames and rubbing them every now and then.

"You all right there?" one called out to Cora.

"Aye," she replied casually. "Can't sleep."

"Don't blame you, love. Everyone's out and watching for spooks in that mist."

"We're going to keep watch farther down the beach," said Leon, his breath puffing out into a cloud.

"Well, lad, just make sure you stay in sight of someone else, in case you spot something. All right?"

"Right. OK."

They walked up past the chip shop; the lights inside were still on as tonight's cooking team cleared up. Leon could see several lamps on at the end of the wooden jetty and people standing guard there.

Adewale drew up beside him. "Leon?"

"What?"

"We're leaving Jake behind. It feels wrong."

"He's dead."

"He might return."

ALEX SCARROW

Leon looked up at him. By the moonlight, he could see the gleam in Adewale's eyes. "But it wouldn't be Jake anymore. It'd be a copy."

Ahead of them, looming out of the night, was the barricade wall that ran right across this spit of land. They approached, and no one challenged them, so they pulled the gate open and stepped through.

Beyond the barricade, Portland Road veered to the right, while the long beach continued on. They followed the road as it curved, and then ahead of them, Leon could see the old abandoned boatyard, the portable toilet, and the bridge.

There was a light on in the cabin. As they drew up outside, Leon poked his head inside to see who was on duty.

Peter and Dereck. They had halfway finished a bottle of rum on the table, and a cloud of cigarette smoke was hanging above them.

"Hey, young man," said Peter, spotting him. "You coming to join us?"

Leon shook his head. "We're leaving."

He wasn't sure how the old man would react, and maybe it was stupid just coming flat-out with it, but he couldn't imagine either of them pulling a shotgun on him.

Peter sighed. "Leaving the sinking ship, eh?"

They're drunk.

"The virus doesn't need to try growing across this bridge anymore. It can reach us from any side now. It's not safe here, Peter."

"Aye. True."

"So...yeah, I'm leaving."

"And yer friends too?"

"Yup."

Peter reached for the bottle of rum and took a slug, swished it around his mouth before gulping it down noisily. "In that case, take good care of yerself, lad."

"You're not going to stop us?"

He shook his head. "Why would I? If they're coming for us all soon, it'd be daft to force you lot to stay, wouldn't it?"

Leon was about to duck back out but hesitated. "What are you going to do?" He stopped short of offering both old men an invitation to join them.

"Well now, we got another one of these," he said, tapping the neck of the bottle, "and we got our shotgun. We'll be fine, lad, if it comes to it."

Leon nodded. "Don't let it take you alive, Peter."

"No plans to, boy." He looked at Dereck, and the other man nodded. "We'll be fine. You better get off before the party starts."

Leon lingered in the doorway.

"Go on, lad," said Peter, "before I change my mind."

Leon nodded and ducked back outside. "Let's get this gang-plank across."

Adewale, Finley, and Howard maneuvered the plank across the gap. In the still of night, silent except for the pattering of light drizzle and the lazy sloshing sound of the sea below, the rasping of the wood against the asphalt sounded worryingly loud.

In the background, Leon could hear both old men murmuring quietly inside the portable toilet, chuckling at something.

"What's waiting for us out there?" whispered Cora.

He looked where she was staring. The mist was lingering

beyond the ragged gap, thick and ominous, the army truck barely a dim outline in the distance.

"Just our truck," he replied quickly. "That's all."

"Do you have any idea where we're going once we get in it?"

He looked at Cora. "No. But at least while we're driving, while we're moving, we're safe."

"We can't just drive forever, Leon."

"Why not?"

The plank was now across, and Adewale, the heaviest, tested it to make sure it was stable. "It is safe."

All eyes settled on Leon. He gazed out at the mist on the far side, his breath curling in the cold night air. "Right..."

Come on, MonkeyNuts...the truck's just there. You can see it.

It's what he couldn't see that worried him.

You run, Son. And you keep running. OK?

"Let's go."

CHAPTER
42

CAYO CRUZ DEL PADRE IS THE NORTHERNMOST PLACE YOU CAN go in Cuba. Beyond the tip of this marshy island, it's Caribbean blue water all the way until you hit the bottom of Florida.

Private First Class Germaine Lewis, for his sins, was standing on a coarse block of whitewashed concrete that had been dumped here three years ago as a secure base for construction cranes that had never had a chance to arrive. According to Jorge, one of the Cuban soldiers posted to stand in this humid swamp-like hellhole along with him, this place was once upon a time going to be built up into a luxury vacation resort.

Lewis really couldn't see it. Looking around, this island off the north coast of mainland Cuba was several hundred square miles of stinking marsh that would be better served as a landfill or a cesspit. But clearly, more imaginative people than him had seen the potential in this place. They'd put money into it and appeared to have gotten things started.

ALEX SCARROW

"Nuked them?" said Jorge. "You shit me!"

Lewis nodded. "That's what the boys are saying back in the barracks. Something like a dozen warheads were launched this morning, taking out viral concentrations in the Bahamas, Dominican Republic, Haiti. It's part of the president's *fightback*."

Jorge made a face. "Your president thinks he can do this?"

Lewis shrugged. "Why not? If we've got the weapons, why not use the damn things? These virals can burn just as easily as firewood. So, if we have to, we'll take this world back scorched mile by scorched mile."

"Kings of a scorched kingdom?"

Lewis could see Jorge was needling him. "Well, buddy, you gotta start somewhere. Baby steps, man."

He turned to look back at the other three. They were sitting beneath a green tarp erected as a sun shelter and throwing dice onto a garbage can lid. The clattering sound was irritating as hell, and he wondered what they were using for betting chips, since neither Cuban nor American dollars had any value or purpose now. Cigarettes, probably.

Jorge nudged his arm. "Lewis?"

He turned back around to see him pointing out toward the sea. "You see that?"

His finger was pointing toward an ochre bloom of shallow water and coral reefs.

"What is it?"

Jorge leaned closer, so Lewis could sight down the length of his outstretched arm. "There! Right there!"

Lewis narrowed his eyes as he tried to make sense of what

PLAGUE LAND: NO ESCAPE

Jorge was pointing at. He could see the crests of waves breaking over a coral head. That was all.

"What? I see waves, dude."

"It is moving!"

Lewis studied the oddly colored patch of sea again. The gentle southerly waves were breaking over a hump of coral that he guessed was only half a yard or so below the water. So far, so normal. Pretty, actually. But...

Shit.

It *was* moving.

The faint beige discoloration in the water was growing more distinct, and it was definitely slowly advancing toward them. No doubt about it, that "coral head" was on the move.

For a moment, he imagined it might be some gnarly old parasite-covered whale that had decided to find a way through the corals and beach itself on the shingle right in front of them. It continued its gradual advance toward them and finally broke the surface.

"Shit! What the hell is that!"

Instinctively, he reached for his assault rifle. Jorge called out to his compatriots.

It surged forward. Lewis could see it was the front end of something long—*very* long.

"*¡Dios mio!*" cried Jorge.

The other Cuban soldiers were on their feet now, scrambling for their guns.

"Crap!" shouted Lewis.

It was surging up onto the beach before them; its front seemed to be bulging out, expanding, the encrusted old surface crackling and flaking as it did so.

"¡Válgame Dios!"

It finally slowed down and then stopped halfway up the beach, twenty feet from them, like some creature too exhausted to pull itself any farther out of the sea. Its front continued to contort and expand, flakes of darkened scab-like material dropping away and revealing a lighter, pink, and raw-looking substance beneath it.

The other three soldiers joined them. All five of them pointed their guns at this squirming kraken, none of them knowing whether it made sense to open fire on it or not.

"The virus," hissed Jorge. "It is here!"

Without warning, the front of the beast suddenly tore open: three pink flaps of skin folded back on themselves to reveal the dark, ribbed, glistening walls of some giant throat. From way back down inside, he caught the gleam of something—some *things*—scrambling toward the light.

"Oh crap."

The glimmers of reflection became a clearer impression of form as the things inside surged forward and finally emerged from the ragged mouth into the evening sunlight: pale crustaceans, like spider crabs, long-limbed, small-bodied, pale shellac shells like mother-of-pearl and—*good God!*—they were huge.

All five men started firing a volley at the exact same moment. The first few creatures exploded, ejecting shards of shell and strings of mucus. But behind them were dozens more.

No, hundreds more.

Lewis's finger was locked down on the trigger until his M16

PLAGUE LAND: NO ESCAPE

clattered uselessly, the clip empty. He fumbled in his webbing for more ammo, muscle memory guiding him as he ejected the exhausted clip, flipped around the new one, and slapped it into the base of his gun.

Just as he started firing, the Cuban soldiers' steady fire began to falter as they ran out of bullets. Lewis turned his fire from a constant panicked spray into short, targeted bursts at the nearest creatures. Their bodies erupted in a satisfying way; if this had been a computer game, he'd have been raving about it.

The first to finish reloading was Jorge. Like Lewis, he was firing short and aimed disciplined bursts now, conserving what ammo he had.

The creatures' bodies were beginning to stack up on the sand just beyond the mouth, becoming an obstacle that was tangling with them and slowing them down. But then the creatures began to wise up and fan out, spreading around the tangle of weeping limbs and broken shells left and right.

Ah, shit. We're getting flanked.

"BACK UP!" he shouted. "BACK UP! BACKUP! BACKUPBACKUP!"

His order came too late to make much of a difference. One of the creatures leaped forward from the side, landing on the leftmost Cuban. Lewis was vaguely aware of the man going down, the sounds of his screaming, the sound of ripping material, then flesh, then bones cracking.

Screw tactics now. He realized they were beyond army training and down to simple survival: run or die.

One more clip. Again, by finger touch and muscle memory, he found it in his webbing and slapped it firmly into his gun. "Jorge! I'm running!" he shouted.

"I'm out of ammo!"

"Then for God's sake, go. Go. Go. Go!"

Jorge backed up, out of his view. Just then, another of the Cubans to his right went down, the man and the creature rolling across the sand in a wrestler's embrace, his two arms outnumbered by far too many appendages to keep him from being gutted from the groin upward.

Lewis fired four and five round bursts to his left, then to his right, until finally the gun rattled uselessly in his hands.

He hurled it at the nearest of them, then turned and ran across the concrete parking lot toward the M3 half-track parked by the canvas awning. He allowed himself a glimmer of hope that he would be faster across firm ground than these spindly nightmare things behind him and that, once he got to the vehicle, Jorge would already have the half-track fired up and belching clouds of diesel exhaust.

Lewis's hopes were short-lived.

He felt his feet whipped out from beneath him as something long swiped the ground behind him. He tumbled forward, landing face-first. A moment later, something dropped heavily onto his back, knocking the wind out of him. He could hear skittering, clicking sounds right next to his ear.

"Screw you!" he snarled between gritted teeth as he gathered himself and pushed up to try to get his legs under his body again.

He managed only one more step forward before feeling something close quickly and firmly around his neck. Rough against his

PLAGUE LAND: NO ESCAPE

skin. It felt sharp, like the blades of a large pair of scissors. It hesitated a moment...

And then...

Snip.

CHAPTER
43

OUTSIDERS ARE A THREAT.

The message propagated quickly, spreading from one artery to another, the synaptic links of a brain lighting up like a Christmas tree. Its journey began at the cauterized end of the giant umbilical that snaked its way across miles of ocean to northwest Africa. It traveled at the speed of chemistry, which is to say faster than the speed of cellular migration. Within eight hours, it had reached the shores of a place that had been called Algeria *before*. There, the message followed numerous paths: northward, across the Strait of Gibraltar into Europe; eastward along the Mediterranean coast of Africa; south, into the beating heart of the continent.

The counterreaction by Them was simply to protect the billions of innocent human lives shrunk down to fit into Their almost-infinite biological universe. There was no knowing yet how many complete conscious entities had been incinerated in the three nuclear blasts, not to mention how many Earth species might just have been lost from Their consolidated memory, the residual trace memories of species from ancient worlds.

They had followed mission instructions and permitted the native intelligent species to come together and decide the fate of those stubborn few of them left behind. That decision had been difficult and contentious—not to absorb them by force, but to *convince them to join.*

The detonation of three nuclear warheads had changed things. *They* were taking matters into their own hands. *They* now had no choice but to follow their encoded mission orders. Safety first.

Preservation was essential.

The reaction was immediate in the wake of the mass incineration of life. The other umbilical cords that had grown ahead of the island, running along the seafloor and sloping upward as the waters warmed, surged forward toward the source of the threat.

Within a few hours of the apocalyptic blasts, those cords farthest forward had extended their reach and broken the surface. Inside, within their brittle, salt-resistant walls, unthinking automatons in their tens of thousands were hurriedly being fabricated from biomass. In many cases, their shells would still be as soft as shoe leather as they emerged into the outside world, hordes of glistening newborns programmed with very simple instructions now—not to scout for resources, not to map the lay of the land, not to detect further sources of carbohydrate fuel.

They were simply instructed to *kill.*

That same reactive instruction spread throughout the global network. They could only do what was best for the mission now; the majority-data was important, the minority-data represented a threat; a binary switch was unequivocally flipped and would remain so until this job was done.

Then—and only then—would They return to their role as knowing and benign chaperones.

CHAPTER
44

LEON HURRIED DOWN THE ROAD TOWARD THEIR PARKED truck, his flashlight picking out the way ahead through the mist. He carefully stepped over the shriveled veins of several abandoned viral threads, an all-too-serious game of Don't Step on the Cracks. To his eyes, they looked like the roots and limbs of plants left to die and fossilize in a dusty old greenhouse. However, they might still contain enough of a thread of life within to alert the virus to their presence if he clumsily stepped on one.

The truck was right there, where they'd left it weeks ago: two wheels up on the curb, two on the road. He paused, waiting for the others to catch up as they cautiously picked their way forward in his wake. Before he got too close, he ducked down and shone his flashlight at the dark space beneath the vehicle.

That's where they'd be hiding.

If they were lying in wait, that is.

ALEX SCARROW

Adewale came to a halt beside him. "Can you see any of them under there?"

There'd be glimmers of reflection of their shells if they were, like fragments of broken glass. "No. I think we're good."

He made his way forward again, flashlight aimed down at the road, picking out the thin, black, snaking lines, looking very much like random saving stones. A few more yards of careful steps and he finally reached the truck. He walked around to the back of it, steadied himself with a *one, two, three*, then quickly lifted aside the green canvas awning.

His flashlight picked out nothing but the supplies they'd left in the back.

He let out a puff of air, and Adewale, beside him, hissed an edgy breath out of his nose. "It is like a game of dice."

The others were now joining them around the truck. "Does it still work?" asked Kim.

"Don't know," said Leon. "I hope so."

"Let's just get in and get going!" hissed Cora.

Leon nodded. He was surprised at how easy it had been to get to the vehicle, but the virals had to be out there in the swirling, gray mist, somewhere nearby, waiting for the right moment to catch them off guard and swarm them.

"Come on, everyone," urged Cora. "Get in! Get in!"

He watched Finley, Kim, and Howard climb up, Adewale holding out one of his big hands to help them. Cora clambered up into the cabin on the driver's side and Leon was just about to pull himself up when he saw the silhouette of a lone figure picking its way down the bridge road toward them.

PLAGUE LAND: NO ESCAPE

"Hold on a sec!" he called to Cora before she could turn the engine on.

Leon wondered if it might be Peter or Dereck. One of the old men might have had a change of heart.

He hurried forward, holding a hand back at Cora to indicate he wanted her to wait.

"Hello? That you, Peter?"

The figure stepped nimbly over a thick root. Clearly not an old man, by the way he moved. Leon snapped on his flashlight and shone it at the figure.

"Hey, Leon."

Jake.

Jake stopped dead in his tracks.

Leon ran his flashlight beam up and down him. "Jake...is that you? I mean, really *you*?"

"Yeah, Leon, it's me." He stopped where he was, just ten feet away. Close enough to talk without shouting but still a wary distance between them. "But I'm not going to try and tell you I'm virus free, because I'm not. Yeah, I'm infected."

"OK." They stared in silence at each other for a moment. "You know we can't take you with us?"

"Duh." Jake smiled. "I'm not here trying to catch a lift."

"You're a fool," said Leon. "You didn't *have* to do it."

"You sound really pissed off with me."

"I am. I...we *needed* you."

"I'm so glad I did it. I see what Camille means now."

Glad? The word made hairs on Leon's neck stir.

"Leon, there really is nowhere to go, mate. Nowhere."

"That's up to us to find out."

"Something happened. I'm not sure what, but now They feel threatened by you. Time's up. Time to join us or..."

"Or what?"

Jake shrugged. "What do you think?" He turned to look back over his shoulder at the bridge and the community beyond. "It's all going down over there. You obviously guessed we were coming tonight. The virus will try its best to preserve as many of you as it can. If you don't fight, if you don't run..."

"Is that what you're asking us to do? Lie down and let ourselves get infected?"

"*Infected*. It's a shit word for how this feels. And I know it looks horrific. I know! It's not an easy thing to ask. But...can you trust me, Leon? Can you just hear me out?"

"No way." Leon backed up a step. "There's no way I'm dying *that* way."

"It's not death, Leon. It's *life*."

Leon pointed at the dried-out network of lines crisscrossing the road. "That's not life. The creatures, those roots...that's not any kind of goddamn *life*!"

"Those things are, like...they're just the infrastructure. But what's inside is *life*. Life 2.0. It's the *future of life*." Jake closed the distance by several steps.

"Jake..." Leon backed up. "I *told* you...if you came back, there's no way we could trust you."

"Leon, please! Just listen to me for a second. This is a new beginning!"

"You sound like that girl Camille. Except she wasn't a girl, was she? She was a viral impostor."

"She was—*is* a 'girl.' So am I. I'm human *still*. I'm Jacob Sutherland. But I'm a lot more than that now."

"Leon!" Cora called out across the dark. "Get back here! WE GOTTA GO!"

"Time's up, mate. This really is the last chance." Jake took another step forward. "After this, if you run, They're going to hunt you down."

"That's what the virus has been doing since the beginning. Hunting us."

"No, Leon. There's a difference. Getting *infected* is getting invited, absorbed. That's the important part. But getting *hunted down* by these stupid-ass crabs means you're gonna end up as meat chunks. Dead. That's it, mate. Biomass material, bits and pieces to be used to make more of them."

"We're running, and we'll fight for as long as we can."

Jake nodded his head slowly. "I was really hoping I could convince you...but I'm wasting my time, aren't I?"

"Yeah."

"Then I'm just going to *do it*." Jake turned to his side as if he were whistling for a dog. Immediately they appeared, clambering over the sides of the bridge. Through the handrails. Crabs, big ones—monsters designed to move quickly and kill efficiently.

Shit. They must have been hiding right underneath the bridge.

Jake stepped forward and held his hand out. "Take my hand!"

"Screw you!" Leon backed up.

"Take my hand, mate! Please!" He glanced at the creatures

pulling themselves over the railing onto the road. "Those crabs don't do invites. They just kill!"

Leon stared at Jake's hand, just a yard or so away from him, fingers outstretched, desperately beckoning him.

He shook his head. "I'd rather die."

Jake grimaced. His arm straightened out, and his hand seemed to explode. The skin of his palm burst open, and out of the jagged wound uncurled a loop of tendon. It happened so fast. It uncoiled like a cracked whip, lashing out and curling around Leon's right wrist.

Leon tried tugging his hand back, but the hold was too firm.

"Don't fight me, mate!"

Leon jerked his hand again but realized another tendon was beginning to protrude from the opening in Jake's hand and uncurling, ready to wrap around his forearm and consolidate his grasp.

"Just say yes, Leon. Please! Say yes first...*then* I'll do it!"

Leon dropped his flashlight and reached deep into the pocket of his anorak. He felt the plastic sports bottle, liquid sloshing around inside. He whipped it out, thrust the neck of the bottle into his mouth, and wrenched the cap off. He filled his mouth with kerosene until his cheeks ballooned.

Jake's eyes widened as Leon threw the bottle at his face, reached into his anorak, and pulled out the lighter.

"Leon! Shit! No..."

Leon spurted the kerosene out across the short space between them in a messy cloud of droplets over his left hand which was held up, thumb poised on the lighter.

PLAGUE LAND: NO ESCAPE

He flicked.

The aerosol cloud of liquid erupted into a plume of flame that singed Leon's hair, his eyebrows, burned the tip of his nose.

"NO!" Jake screamed as the flame reached him and ignited the kerosene spattered over his face. His head was instantly engulfed with flames and his last human word morphed into an inhuman, multivoiced scream.

The tentacle loosened its grip, and Leon jerked his hand free and turned...

To see the few yards he'd put between himself and the truck were now filled with a wall of large crabs.

They closed together, squeezing out the gaps between them. No longer acting like mindless arachnids scrabbling to be first to a prize, they acted as one, like trained footmen. The screaming behind him intensified as the flames began to dwindle, and Leon realized Jake was shouting an order.

The creatures began to advance on him.

He opened his mouth to yell for help, but nothing but a throttled gurgle came out.

Crap. This really is it. Game over.

In just a few seconds, he would feel the sharp teeth of one of those claws biting into his scalp, cracking into his skull, then compressing until his head burst like a watermelon.

There were too many to fight. He closed his eyes and began to crouch down to a kneel.

I'm ready. Let's do this.

Light blazed through his closed eyelids. He opened them to see the dazzling glare of twin headlights hurtling toward him like a high-speed train, throwing the creatures' advancing battle line into a momentarily frozen silhouetted image.

The truck crashed into them, rolling them over and squashing their bulbous bodies so that they erupted like ripe and swollen boils probed by a needle, spraying gobbets of liquid into the glare of the headlights.

The truck screeched to a halt directly in front of him. Close enough that the growling engine and the radiator grille were just an arm's reach away.

"GRAB HOLD!" screamed Cora.

Without thinking, Leon reached out, wrapped his fingers through the vibrating grille, and stepped up onto the front bumper.

Then with the sound of gears grinding painfully and a lion's roar of complaint coming from the engine just beyond the rattling, shaking metal grille, he felt the blasting hot air of the engine on his face as the truck lurched into reverse, bouncing back over squirming bodies.

CHAPTER

45

THERE WAS AN OLD SUN-BLEACHED WOODEN BENCH THAT HAD once been painted a cheery yellow but now only showed flakes tucked into the grain and the knots of the wood. Freya was sitting on it and watching the end of the world—or what was left of it—unfold before her eyes. The jeep was parked a dozen yards away on a patch of gravel beside the winding road. Mr. Friedmann had driven them up here, into the hills overlooking Havana.

It was so pretty up here. So peaceful.

"And so it begins," she said as Tom Friedmann sat down beside her.

There were several thin plumes of smoke rising from the buildings, and now that the last of the day's light was draining from the sky, they were beginning to see the flicker of flames here and there, the sporadic, faint blink of muzzle flash. It was quiet enough to hear the distant rattle of gunfire above the soft hissing of the trees around them.

ALEX SCARROW

"You think this is it? All over?" he asked.

"I would say so. If those were nukes we saw going up...I'm guessing the virus is pretty pissed off with whoever's left. No more Mr. Nice Guy."

He laughed humorlessly.

She looked at him. "It all makes sense." She nodded at the distant city. "We're like the dinosaurs—too big, too inefficient, too clumsy, too wasteful, and now it's our time to go."

They watched as a dozen or more U.S. Navy ships began to maneuver themselves away from the waterfront and out into the middle of the bay. "They were never out to destroy us. They were trying to *archive* us."

"Just like copying all those old tapes and vinyl records to digital, eh?"

"Yes." She nodded. "Exactly like that. So they can exist forever online and not fade away."

"Making us museum exhibits."

"No." She looked at him. "Come on, you glimpsed it. You spoke to Grace. She's alive. She's never going to die. You'll be with her... and everyone else. Maybe even Leon too."

"That's what we're doing, then? Giving up?"

"Even if we had a chance of escaping..." She nodded at the distant gray ships getting in each other's way, churning up boiling wakes of white foam behind them. "Even if we had a choice to be aboard one of those, I think I'm ready to choose this."

"*Choose* this?" He looked at her. "Is this *really* a choice? What if I want to fight back or run? What happens then?"

"They'll catch you eventually."

PLAGUE LAND: NO ESCAPE

They sat in silence for a while, watching the winking lights of flames sprouting up here and there, the staccato flicker of gunshots.

"We saw this back in England," said Tom. "I was much closer. It was horrific."

Freya nodded. *It was.* She'd never been so terrified as she had been that night.

"How do things go for us?" he said. "I'm presuming They'll get up to these hills soon enough?"

"We're infected. We have a little bit of their chemistry in us already. I think They'll figure that out as soon as They make direct contact with us." She looked at him. "Hopefully."

"And what? They'll just leave us alone?"

She didn't know. A part of her was listening to Grace's voice assuring her everything was going to be OK. Everything was going to be just fine.

"Grace is saying, if you run or try fighting back, the creatures will *instinctively* react, they'll be thinking about killing you rather than preserving you."

"*Grace* is saying that?"

"Uh-huh." She cocked her head and listened for a moment. "She says when the snarks come, we should stay put, stay calm. We just let them reach out to us and do what they need to do."

"What? Swarm over us?"

"I guess."

He was silent for a moment, then she heard him whisper, "Screw that."

"Remember how it felt in the car? A sting, one little sting…that's all. Then they do all the hard work. You just sit back and rela—"

323

"You're not doing a great job at selling this to me, Freya."

Freya laughed.

"What?"

"Grace just told me to tell you you're being a total wimp. She said going to the dentist is ten times worse."

"She never much liked the dentist." Tom smiled. "If it's a choice between having a tooth taken out or being turned to human mush? I'll take the first one."

Freya could see where Leon had gotten his dry humor from. "Come on, you've been inside once before. It's not as bad as that."

"It feels like a *surrender.*" He turned to her. "It pulls against every instinct I have inside me. Like giving up. Like suicide."

"Trying to run...fight, that really *will* be suicide though."

You entirely sure?

She only had Grace's word for that. Freya's infection had been slow and stealthy—more to the point, in complete isolation. She wondered if the virus inside her was making assurances it couldn't guarantee. What if the rest of the virus had a very different opinion about her? What if the scuttlers decided they were just meat to be chopped up and digested?

She tossed that thought to one side. Grace had been so clear; preservation where possible was a core instinct, a cornerstone of the virus's behavior, its purpose.

Freya? Grace's voice. *Don't be a threat to Them. Trust Them. Trust me.*

"I'm not sure I can do this," said Tom. "You know, I've got a pretty well-developed fight-or-get-the-hell-away reflex."

"All the old army training?"

"Maybe."

"Do you want to see Grace again?"

"Yes."

"Do you want to see Leon again?"

Now here she was, making a promise she couldn't guarantee—Leon. By now, the virus must have found him. But had he surrendered? Or had he run? Or worse, taken his own life before it had reached him?

"God yes. Leon? More than anything."

"Then give me your gun."

Tom looked down at the sidearm tucked into his belt. "What are you going to do?"

"Throw it away."

"*What?*"

"No gun, no threat. When They come, we lie down and let them know we're OK with Them."

The last stain of daylight was fading fast, and she saw floodlights from the various logjammed ships in the bay switching on, their sharp beams crossing each other, the water churning and boiling around them. She sensed all was not going well for their escape attempt, that the virus had figured out a way to scale their sheer metal hulls.

"Shit," muttered Tom.

CHAPTER
46

THE MARINE SERGEANT POKED HIS HEAD THROUGH THE DOOR-way and glanced in both directions down the passageway. "The way ahead's clear, sir."

Trent had insisted on hearing the helicopter's engines starting up and the blades turning before he committed to making a run for the roof. He wasn't going up there to wait in the open for some dull-witted pilot to go through a pre-takeoff checklist.

The two marines beckoned to him that it was time to go, and as Trent left his luxurious presidential office, he glanced quickly back at its grandeur with a hint of regret. If there'd been more navy, army, air force—more nukes—at his disposal, he was sure he could have commanded the great "take back" of planet Earth from there.

They hurried down the passage. Red lights were flashing on the walls and warning fire bells blasted his eardrums as he ran past them. He could hear the rattle of gunfire echoing from the

PLAGUE LAND: NO ESCAPE

other buildings around the courtyard, voices raised in alarm and panic. Less than an hour after the nuclear detonations had been confirmed, the virus had arrived on the island, emerging from beaches and coves all the way along the northern coast.

He was certain that had been the virus's intention all along. In which case, he was glad he'd fired those three nukes.

"Which way now, Sergeant?"

"We're turning left up ahead, and then we'll see the emergency exit that leads out onto the roof, sir."

"Good. Lead on."

The passage had doors open wide on both sides that led onto the public radio broadcasting suite and telephone system monitoring stations.

Of course this morning's preemptive strike had been the right move. The pilots had reported a huge structure coming their way. What the hell was he supposed to do? Give up? Broadcast to everyone to make their peace with God?

He'd made the call—a very calm and logical one; they had a clear and vulnerable target sitting out there and the means of taking it out.

This isn't my fault. I did the smart thing!

The marine sergeant in front of him held out his hand to bring them both to a halt. He peeked around the corner, then looked back at them. "Gonna go check ahead. Stay here!" he bellowed above the shrill blast of the fire bells.

I did what I thought was for the best, for Chrissakes!

The sergeant disappeared around the corner, leaving Trent and the marine private with the deafening ringing coming from a speaker on the wall above and the flashing red lights along the low ceiling.

The marine looked quickly back at him. "Stay down."

Trent nodded, holding back an urge to reproach him for forgetting to add the "sir."

You gonna let that go, amigo? *Let a lowly pissant grunt disrespect you like that?*

Trent's wandering mind was jerked back by the loud, echoing rattle of gunfire. The dimly lit walls flickered back staccato images of the sergeant's silhouetted figure from around the corner. A moment later, he heard the man scream, another couple of shots, both projecting a haunting shadow image on the corner walls: a man down on his back, a hand held up defensively, something spindly, tall, with many legs and appendages rearing up to deliver a fatal blow.

"Back! Back! Back!" yelled the private. He swung around and shoved Trent hard with a clenched fist to his chest to get him reversing the way they'd come. He staggered backward, nearly falling over.

"What the fu—!"

The way they'd come only moments ago was blocked. The private let rip with half a dozen rounds right over Trent's shoulder. The nearest creature exploded, showering them both with shards of skeleton armor and dabs of sticky gunk. Trent fell backward onto his ass; his peripheral vision registered another half a dozen flickers of gunfire just above his head.

Another creature, its body the size of a basketball, with spider-thin legs that lifted it up to the height of a man's head, lurched

PLAGUE LAND: NO ESCAPE

backward from the impact of the rounds, spattering the floor, the walls, and Trent's crisp, expensive white shirt with more strings of gore.

Behind the creature, filling the passage as they spilled out of an open doorway like toothpaste out of a tube, came more and more of them. The marine stepped over Trent and continued to fire shorter bursts as he advanced several steps toward them.

Finally, he was out of ammo. The gun was tossed aside as he reached with the other hand for his sidearm. He wrenched it out of its holster, and just as Trent thought he was going to fight on until the last round, he turned it on himself.

One flicker of muzzle flash and he dropped heavily, boots sliding in the gore on the worn carpeted floor.

Trent was *alone...*

And the creatures advanced slowly toward him. He felt himself let go, the warmth running down his leg, and he was vaguely aware that the shrill sound filling the corridor was his own screaming voice.

His eyes widened as he caught the gleam of the flashing red light on the serrated blades, the barbed spines, the lobster-like claws.

"NO!" His shoes scuffed and skidded in the blood as he tried to shuffle backward. The nearest creature began to raise its body high on its thin legs as it drew closer.

The creature had a pair of pincers—a powerful-looking cutting implement, industrial shears that jarred open like a spring-powered trap, ready to close again.

On him.

CHAPTER
47

FREYA GAZED UP AT THE NIGHT SKY.

It was completely dark. The sparsely placed, old, fizzing streetlamps had winked out an hour ago as the power failed, leaving Havana illuminated only by fires dotted across the city, taking a steady hold in the absence of any firefighters.

Above, she could see stars. It was a clear sky, a perfect tropical night, if a little chillier than one would expect from a country like Cuba. But then, of course, *everywhere* was colder these days. She'd overheard someone in the warehouse theorizing that the complete absence of human activity and *all* of the world's animal life would explain the radical drop in global temperature. She vaguely recalled from her school days that 1.5 billion farting cows added up to a third of the world's methane emissions, so that kind of made sense.

The distant sounds of gunshots had died away. There were no more signs of life in the city. Every now and then, she heard a

PLAGUE LAND: NO ESCAPE

scream come from the stepped hillside of fancy houses and private gardens, the virus working its way systematically out into the suburbs.

Toward them.

She panned her flashlight out through the windshield at the gravel of the rest stop. No sign of them here just yet. She snapped it off and settled back in her seat. Mr. Friedmann was beside her, silent. He'd withdrawn into himself. She wondered if he was the praying type.

Will I be safe, Grace?

You will, Freya. I promise.

But you said the snarks are just dumb-ass "machines."

They are, but they know blood chemistry. They know "friend-lies" when they taste them.

I don't want to end up as crab food!

You won't.

She gazed at the logjam of ships in the distant harbor. One of them seemed to be burning. Shafts of light from another's flood-lights swept the water around it.

This is happening everywhere, isn't it, Grace?

I think so. Everywhere.

They're finishing us off?

Finishing what They came to do, Freya.

"Saving" us all, right?

Grace didn't reply immediately. *Saving those They can.*

And Leon?

The pause was even longer. *We will soon pass inside. Then we can try and find out if Leon's with us.*

331

"Freya!" Mr. Friedmann jerked forward in his seat, snatched the flashlight from her hand, and panned the beam out through the windshield. "Shit! *Look!*"

She sat forward in her seat and stared at the ground where the beam of light rested. A carpet of tiny, pale crabs was emerging from the undergrowth on to the gravel of the rest stop.

"They're here!" he whispered.

"OK," she whispered back, aware that her heart was suddenly pounding in her chest. "We need to stay calm."

The carpet of creatures slowly inched toward them, a shimmering, gleaming tide of scouting virals, like army ants on the march across a jungle floor.

"Grace says we should step outside and—"

"No way. No goddamn way!"

"And lie down."

"No. No. Shit!" He glanced quickly at her. "I can't. I can't just..."

Just then, something drifted into the beam of the flashlight. A solitary, fluffy snowflake seesawing lazily down until it settled lightly on the hood of the jeep. Then there was another. And another.

"It's snowing," he whispered. "Virus flakes."

The gentle flakes reminded her of that night so long ago. She'd been in her bedroom looking out of the window at the flakes descending on her cul-de-sac in King's Lynn, knowing that however much it looked like a white Christmas come early, it was death descending.

"Grace says that's a good sign."

"Why?"

PLAGUE LAND: NO ESCAPE

"These flakes are made for infecting." She reached for the door handle.

"Freya!" Tom grabbed her arm. "What the hell are you doing?"

"It's time." She tried to pry his fingers off her. "Look...Grace is right. The snowflakes are a *safer* option. Safer than the *snarks*."

He gazed wide eyed at the slowly advancing blanket of shining shellac. "I can't."

"Come on. We have to!"

He shook his head. "It's suicide."

"No. It's not." She twisted the handle, and the door unlocked with a dull clunk. "If we stay inside this jeep—if the snarks have to *smash* their way in—they'll do it."

She saw him glance at the gun sitting on the dash. "Really? You're thinking of doing *that*?"

He breathed deeply in and out, through his nose. His eyes remaining on the gun.

"I want to go look for Leon. How about you, Mr. Friedmann?"

He didn't answer, but he let go of her wrist.

"Are you coming?"

He shook his head. "This is...completely absurd!"

"I'll go first," she replied. She offered him a reassuring smile. "Show you it's gonna be OK." She opened the door, stepped out onto the gravel, and held out her hands.

"It *is* gonna be OK, right, Grace?" she whispered.

Yes. Once it enters your main arterial system, it will "know" you.

A single flake settled onto her palm and began to "melt," breaking down into a small droplet of thick syrup. She gazed down at it.

"What's happening? Freya? Talk to me!"

333

"It's just saying hello," she replied.

The droplet began to grow fine, pale threads across her palm, exploring its new terrain, millimeter by millimeter. She could feel her skin tickling where the droplet sat and knew another thread was growing downwards *into* her, overpowering skin cells and rendering them a compliant, malleable material.

Meanwhile, the crabs had come to a halt just short of the vehicle, fanning out, spreading around it as their hair-thin antennae twitched like cat's whiskers.

"Freya?"

"It's OK," she answered him. "It's gonna be OK."

"I...I'm not ready to do this!" he barked.

She turned to look at him through the open passenger-side door. "You *have* to."

"Dammit! *I can't!*"

She could see his chest heaving. He was hyperventilating in there. Terrified.

"It's OK. I'm scared too."

It'll be fine. Tell Dad...it'll be just fine. I'm waiting right here for him.

Freya stared at the reddening skin of her palm, already beginning to soften into a gel-like substance. "Grace is waiting for you, Mr. Friedmann."

"Really?"

Freya nodded. "I promise."

Just then, she heard a skittering sound from across the road. She turned to see larger creatures emerging from the gloom, similar to the ones she and Leon had encountered in the Oxford

PLAGUE LAND: NO ESCAPE

overpass, the size of small dogs. She wondered if there were even larger ones out there beyond the reach of their flashlight, waiting patiently to determine how this encounter with survivors was going to go.

Tom turned the jeep's headlights on and her suspicion was confirmed. Farther down the road, they stood there on spindly legs, bobbing and swaying gently, ready to charge forward and tear to pieces anything that presented a threat.

"Shit! Shit!" hissed Mr. Friedmann. He snatched the gun off the dash.

"No!" she whispered. "Don't fire it! Please! *Don't!*"

He had it gripped tightly in both hands, the aim wavering, undecided between the gathered creatures outside and himself.

"You pull the trigger," she hissed, "and it's over for you either way. Maybe me too!"

A trickle of dark-brown liquid rolled out from her clenched fist and down onto the pale skin of her wrist and forearm. "This isn't the end, Mr. Friedmann. It's a *change*! That's all!"

She watched him agonizing over his decision, his lips drawn back, teeth clenched, the barrel of the gun arcing between himself and the open window like the pendulum of a clock.

A small string of liquidized skin began to sag from the heel of her thumb.

"Grace is begging!" she whispered. "She's begging you. *I'm* begging you...please, don't!"

Freya *sensed* the invasion of the virus in her bloodstream.

She could feel a reassuring warmth spreading throughout her body. Grace was no longer whispering. She imagined Grace had other things to do... Maybe somewhere deep inside her body, a simple negotiation was taking place—Grace explaining to the invaders that this body was already taken.

"Freya! I've got to go now. I'm gonna get out of here!"

"Don't..." She felt light-headed now. Freya could feel herself beginning to slide into that warm bath, felt the world drawing back from her. She tried to plead with him again, vaguely aware that her words were slurring like they used to, that the strength was ebbing out of her legs. That she really needed to sit down.

She slumped to her knees. "Please don't..." she pleaded again. "Please, put the gun down, come out here...join me..."

The world around her felt like a movie screen shrinking in size, receding, leaving her with the sensation of floating in a dark and empty auditorium. She settled back until she could feel the coarse bite of the stones against her shoulders.

Now she was seeing stars and tumbling snowflakes glowing brilliantly as they descended through the headlight beams toward her. There was something so beautiful about how elegantly they danced.

She heard something moving, the whine of unoiled hinges, the rasp of footsteps on gravel. She was dimly aware of something flickering across the headlight beams, then of his face appearing, looking down at her.

So far away, as if he were looking over the lip of a well and she was at the bottom staring up.

"Please...don't..." she whispered, aware that her voice was changing somehow, weakening, becoming softer, becoming someone else's.

"Please...don't...*die...Dad...*"

The world was a dwindling round window, shrinking, shrinking, the soft hiss of the trees, the skitter of spindle-thin legs shifting impatiently, her own labored breathing—the world slipping away and becoming increasingly irrelevant.

Fading fast. Fading. Fading.

Then her window on this world was finally gone. Darkness. She knew They had control of her eyes and her optic nerves now. But not her ears. Not yet.

She could still hear Mr. Friedmann's panting breath.

"Please..." she slurred. Her lips felt numb, ungainly, cumbersome, making her sound stupid.

"Please..."

Her ears began to fill with the dull roar of internal traffic, the superhighway of cells racing through an arterial motorway system. A city alive in rush hour.

The last of the old world was leaving her. Or she was leaving it.

She thought she could feel some movement beside her.

Then a male voice. Mr. Friedmann's voice. His words were indistinct. Muffled. He no longer sounded frantic or frightened.

Just resigned. And—as the last portions of her mind fought to hold on and understand what was happening *out there*—she thought she could just about figure out what he'd said.

"This. Is. Completely. Nuts."

CHAPTER
48

Three Days Later

REX WILLIAMS WOKE UP FOR THE SECOND MORNING IN A row with no one there beyond the thick glass to observe him. The light still fizzed softly from the ceiling of his room, the monitor still flickered in the observation room beyond. There was no one on duty.

Again.

The last piece of information he'd received had come from the pleasant young navy ensign just before she'd handed over her watch duty to someone else. There'd been reports of floaters over North Island. Not revelatory news—the spotter planes had been shooting those damn things down for the last two years. But coupled with two days of no-shows through the observation window and, more importantly, no meals slid through the hatch, Rex felt it was fair to say he might end up dying in here.

PLAGUE LAND: NO ESCAPE

There was water still available from the tap. The toilet still flushed. And, of course, the power was still on. But for how much longer? And when it *did* stop, the flow of filtered air would cease. He'd die of suffocation within a few hours. He was getting a little concerned.

If only he could see what was on the monitor. The internet still worked in a limited way for those on North Island; there was still enough of a digital infrastructure for the news station to post sketchy bulletins.

Rex had been thoroughly debriefed on his return. Treated with a wary skepticism as he laid out everything he'd seen, felt, and heard. He'd known going in that this would happen. That on returning, they would have to consider the prospect that he might be some form of manifestation of the virus, not to be trusted. During his short absence the shape of the crisis committee had changed. Now it was being jointly led by the deputy PM and Captain Xien.

They'd allowed him to record the announcement he wanted broadcast publicly. Filmed him through the thick glass as he explained to the camera that the virus was intelligent. That it was not a malignant force, and that it was interested in discussing terms by which both "civilizations" could live alongside each other.

Whether they'd actually broadcast it, he had no idea, but he doubted it.

Maybe Grace had fooled him, then. Convinced him to allow her to be freed and taken to the approaching island so she could rejoin Them. And now here he was, locked in a clinically clean "dungeon," waiting for the power to fail, the lights to go out, and to die alone in the dark.

So...it's come, then. The virus must be here.

He could only imagine the horror of what was going on in the world outside. That enormous floating scab picking its way down Cook Strait, drifting into Wellington Harbor, and unleashing on the inhabitants whatever hordes of nightmare creatures it had stored in its bulk below water.

Rex closed his eyes against the glare of the ceiling fluorescent light. If his luck was in, the power would trip out and he'd suffocate in his sleep.

Something woke him.

He wasn't sure what exactly. The light was still on. There was still power. He turned his head on the pillow to look left at the window, hoping to see someone in the observation room. But there was no one.

He heard a crackle of something over the intercom. The speaker was still on, of course, quietly filling the silence of his room with the soft hiss of nothing happening.

Then again. *Something clacking.*

"Hello?" called out Rex hopefully. He stared at the small wall-mounted speaker as if looking at its grille would tell him more. "Hello? Anyone out there?"

Another clacking sound. Then something that sounded moist, like a wet towel slapping and dragging gently against a wall.

He sat up on his cot, half-terrified and half-relieved. "I'm in here!" he shouted.

He thought he saw a shadow in the observation room,

something tall lurching just beneath the ceiling light, casting a momentarily splayed outline down across the wall and onto the desk. Something big, misshapen, inhuman.

The noise ceased. The double-door entry was a pressurized airlock that needed someone able to read the instructions to turn the…

Clack.

He could see the blurry shadow again. Tall. Limbs flexing and curling from a mound near the top, a Medusa-like crown of writhing snakes mounted on top of a twisted totem.

Clunk. Hissss.

Rex's heart jumped. He pulled his bare legs up to his chest and wrapped his arms around his knees. That was the outer door. That was air pressure equalizing.

Clack.

Much clearer now. Not just coming out from the speaker—he could hear it transmitted through the inner hatch too. Something fumbling just behind the door. Right outside.

"Oh God, help me," he whispered. He knew this was the virus coming for him. As such, he should have been thinking of it as a rescue, but his heart was pounding in his chest as he listened to the form shuffling around outside.

Click. Clunk.

The heavy door swung slowly inward, revealing something that filled the doorway.

Amid the contortions of bloody skin, purple muscle, and pale shellac, amid the confusion of human and animal and crustacean, he saw something emerging from soft tissue. It formed like sculptor's putty manipulated by an invisible artisan's hand.

341

ALEX SCARROW

A face he recognized. The face managed a wet, rigid smile of barely firmed-up flesh and unready sinew and spoke with a voice that sounded like a witches' quartet. "There you are."

"Grace? Is...is that y-you?"

"Yes. Come on...join us."

PART

III

CHAPTER
49

Three Months Later

9/29

Freya,

Even though winter's pretty much starting to kick in again, the virus seems to have stepped things up, instead of going dormant. We've been constantly fighting bugs all the way down the coast.

Big bastard ones.

It's like the virus has decided we're a nuisance that needs to be cleared out of town once and for all!

ALEX SCARROW

We've been upping our meds, twice what we were normally taking. We've all been scratched, cut, spiked, God knows how many times now. So far, thank God, I think we're keeping the infection out. I wonder whether the virus actually wants to infect us anyway.

Maybe we're just food now. Or sport.

10/7

Freya,

It's getting freezing cold again. October and it's started snowing heavily already. We're staying warm though. We've got a space heater—one of those big cylinders on wheels that looks like a jet engine. A couple of minutes of that every hour and we're good for a while.

Oh, and we found a lighthouse!

It's perched on a large cement "plug," on top of a rocky outcropping in the middle of the English Channel. We found a battered, old tugboat and a couple of motorboats pulled up and stored in the lighthouse's basement floor. Cora's worried that in a storm the tugboat might get smashed to

PLAGUE LAND: NO ESCAPE

pieces, which is a good point. But we haven't had any stormy weather in years, have we? Not since before the outbreak. Which makes me wonder if Finley's right that the world's climate has been "equalized" by the virus somehow.

If so, then I guess you're not tanning yourself on a beach right now.

It's not bad here really. We live mostly on a floor about two-thirds of the way up in the lighthouse. For some reason, it feels warmer than the other floors, but also, the higher up you go, the less damp it is.

10/15

The virus can get across the sea. We know that. I guess you must know about that too by now. I often wonder whether it's continuing to develop, getting smarter all the time while we sit here and shiver in our ivory tower.

Don't laugh, but I wonder if one day a helicopter will come over and land on the roof and virals will emerge with guns and stuff. Why not? The virus seems to have access to the minds and memories of everyone it's turned to mulch. I'm guessing that more than a few helicopter pilots got turned into slime.

Seriously.

Crabs, growth roots, spore clouds—none of them seem to have anything like human intelligence. What does that mean? Are they all linked? Or is it like a whole new ecosystem or something? How do you reason with an ecosystem? Who's in charge?

It's questions like that that we discuss each night over the cooking stove.

November

Cora died today. You met Cora, by the way. She was that nice lady who brought over something for us to eat in the compound at Southampton. Remember her? She slipped on an icy rock outside the lighthouse. She just slipped and fell into the sea. Kim saw her go in from a window halfway up. By the time we all made it down to the bottom, she was gone.

No sign of her. She was gone beneath the slush and ice.

The sea is freezing cold here now. I mean, completely freezing. She would have lasted a minute or two at best, gone into hypothermic shock and drowned. The sea just took her away quickly and quietly. No fuss, no muss.

Sounds really wrong to say this but—I think Cora was the worst person for us to lose. I mean, it wouldn't be good if it happened to any of us, but it's particularly bad it was her. She was the heart of our little group I think, the Survival Mom.

December

We're going through our diesel supplies faster than we thought we would. The space heater does a great job, but, Christ, it's a thirsty bastard. We're about a third of the way through our stock! We've switched to keeping it on most of the time but turned down to its lowest setting, so at least there's a constant trickle of heat on our floor. We plugged up the ladder entrances top and bottom to kill the draft and conserve our heat. But then nearly killed ourselves because of the buildup of carbon monoxide fumes! So, there's a life lesson learned! We unblocked the entrance to the floor above, so there's somewhere for the toxic fumes to go and some way in for fresh air.

Duh.

OK. So we're playing Risk way-y-y-y too much. You know, the board game? The one where you've got the map of the world, and you have to conquer it? Finley made a copy by drawing the world map on the floor with a piece of chalk and we're using screws and bolts we found in the lighthouse's workshop for the pieces. I carved several wooden dice, which work pretty well, although some have a habit of rolling higher than others.

Which of course causes total meltdowns as I'm sure you can imagine.

December/January (not sure)

Howard cut his hand on one of the iron railings last week. It's been getting steadily worse ever since—all pink and puffed up. He's been on antibiotics, but I don't think they're working. I don't know whether it's the wrong kind of antibiotic, or whether they've just out-of-date. No one knows what to do to help him fight the infection.

Kim's really upset and worried. She's grown

really close to him. She sees him as like a father figure or something.

Freya, I don't know if we can survive losing someone else. Cora hit us hard. And it's so hard being the leader, constantly having to try and boost morale. Constantly assuring the others it's going to be Ok, that we're going to be fine.

Only I'm beginning to wonder if we are. The arithmetic of our situation is only going to go one way, right?

I'm exhausted trying to be positive in front of the others all the time.

Feburary-ish

Howard passed away last night. Finley said it must have been sepsis. We wrapped him up in a tarp. Adewale carried him down to the concrete foundation and said a prayer. Then we tipped him over the handrail and gave him a burial at sea.

For a moment, I thought his body was just going to stay there, resting on the icy slush, but eventually it slipped through and disappeared.

So we're down to four now. Not so good. But, I

suppose, trying to look on the positive side, that's still enough people for a decent game of Risk.

March

We've got enough food and drinking water for a few more months, when it should, in theory, warm up again, hopefully for the ice/slush to break up enough so we can do another run ashore for supplies. But—and this is a huge goddamn "but"—we're getting low on diesel for the heater. At the rate we're burning through it, we'll run out in a couple of months.

So, pretty soon, we're going to HAVE to try another supply run, whether the sea's cleared or not.

It's something we keep discussing that we need to do, but we keep putting it off. I'm thinking we can wait until we're down to two months' supply, then we should really go and get some more.

April

We need better balanced dice. It led to a fistfight. I actually hit Adewale. I punched him in the face. I can't actually believe I did that. I feel so bad about it. We were fighting over Europe. I was invading it, he was defending it, and there's this one particular dice that delivers sixes pretty much every time.

Jesus.

May

Just want to wish you a happy birthday. (I think it would be about now, right?) I miss you so much, Freya. I think if it was just you and me here, I'd be fine with that. I'd be happy here until we died of old age, to be honest. (That or froze into an ice sculpture.) Our little safety bubble. I could go with that.

In other news, I have a fractured ankle. I missed a step coming back down from a piss trip. Typical. I've spent, what? Over four years surviving the apocalypse and the end of the world without a single broken bone, then I go bust my ankle going for a leak!

I can't even blame ice and say I slipped on an icy step. I simply _missed_ a step and...crack! We have plenty of painkillers of course, which I am merrily munching my way through (well, maybe not so merrily), but it's keeping the pain down to a dull throb that I can cope with. I'll be honest though, I'm petrified I'll end up like Howard and die of sepsis and an overenthusiastic immune system!

For the moment, I've got my leg up in the air and Kim insisted I move my sleeping bag right next to the heater, since I can't move around to keep myself warm.

Which is kind of her.

May

They're going for a foraging trip ashore without me. I feel, like, useless sitting here with my dumb-ass broken ankle.

May

Shit. Where the hell are they?

May

It's been three days now. It's not a weather thing. There's no such thing as "weather"

PLAGUE LAND: NO ESCAPE

these days. No storms. No blizzards. One day's the same as the next—gray sky and a flat, white sea.

Something must have happened to them. The virus.

Probably.

Summer

I'm alone. I was hanging on to hope for a few weeks that maybe the boat had gotten damaged and they needed to go find another one. But I guess the truth is they're gone. The virus got them or the boat sank or something.

"Alone" is going to be hard. I have food and heating and water, and, really, I can last a long time here. But I wonder if there'll come a time when I choose—you know—NOT to hang on.

Shit.

Winter

I think I've been here a year now. Winter's come again, Big Time. It's much harder than the last three. Really, really cold now. The snow on the helipad is at least a three feet deep! I'm worrying about how much weight the helipad and this old tower can take. I wonder if I should be shoveling it off.

Winter

I'm really going to have to start rethinking my heating plans. There's fuel for just a few months if I keep burning through it like I am. I'm going to have to ration it. Maybe there's some stuff I can find that I can burn. There are old stores.

There must be something down there I can use. I'm going to freeze to death otherwise.

Winter

I just managed to hobble downstairs and came across a stash of coal bags. I'm not sure how long it will last or if I'm going to end up choking myself on fumes in here, but I'm gonna use it anyway. I might even heat up some of my meals on it. In other news, I found a bunch of old books on the floor downstairs.

PLAGUE LAND: NO ESCAPE

I'm guessing that's from when this place wasn't automated and had a crew. The choices are interesting. There's a bunch of books by someone called Jilly Cooper and a guy called Archer. But there's also a whole load by Stephen King. A writer I've actually heard of!

I think I'm going to start with him.

Spring

OK. Listing in descending order of favorite Stephen King books: The Dead Zone, Firestarter, The Stand, It, The Shining, The Tommyknockers, Cujo, Needful Things, Christine. Speaking of The Dead Zone, I can't believe Stephen King predicted a total ass hat like Trent!

Sheesh. Now for the Archer guy.

Spring

Seriously? OK I'm gonna do it. I'm going to have a go at those Cooper books.

Winter

Winter's here again. Does that make it two years now? Or three? I'm losing track.

Winter

So, Freya, I think today is the day. I've been listening to Dad's advice. And he's right—at some point, you've just got to admit when the game's over. So...this is me signing off. Which is nice timing really, since there's only a few more pages left in the notebook.

I love you, Freya. Always have.

CHAPTER
50

LEON SET DOWN THE PEN AND CLOSED THE COVER. WRITING down a long, protracted goodbye felt stupid. It would've felt like he was stalling, delaying the inevitable.

"Today *is* the day." His words spilled out amid a cloud of evaporation and echoed off the hard, concrete walls. Pale daylight leaked from the ladder well of the floor above. Leon had no idea what the time was, other than it was *day*.

It was day and night, that was all. The days were best used for sleeping, the nights were for keeping moving and eating and using a few minutes' worth of fuel to boost his small, dark world above freezing for a few hours.

But the last liter and a quarter of red-tinted diesel fuel was sitting in a milk carton. There was enough there for two or three more blasts of the heater. Then, that was it.

Really it.

ALEX SCARROW

He could hear Dad's voice. *Your core body temperature's not going to last very long once that heater goes out for the last time.*

"I know, I know."

Leon looked up at the ladder. He and Dad had discussed the options last night. The drop from the helipad would be certain. No mistaking that. But Leon wasn't sure he could do it, to *will* his body to take that last step and lean forward.

There was the gun, lying on the ground; all that was required was the twitch of one finger.

Dad shook his head. *I heard stories of idiots who screwed that up. Took an ear off, lost an eye...ended up paralyzed or in a coma. You make sure you aim straight, Son.*

Leon nodded. "I will, Dad."

He pulled himself slowly to his feet and let the mound of sleeping bags and blankets fall away from him onto the floor.

Today's the day, Leo. Don't leave it too late. Don't leave it until dark. Don't leave it until you're too cold to hold the gun straight.

"I won't," he croaked.

He picked the gun up and tucked it into the inside pocket of his anorak, safety on. The last thing he needed to do was shoot himself in the gut or the groin and bleed out painfully.

He cleared the debris away from the well leading down. He didn't want to do the deed in the space he'd been living in these last two years. It had served him well. It felt vaguely disrespectful doing it here, leaving a mess that wasn't ever going to get cleaned up.

He wanted to go down to the bottom. Open the door of the storage room and step out on to the concrete base, lean against

PLAGUE LAND: NO ESCAPE

the handrail and do the thing there. He hoped he'd go over and leave no mess behind. No fuss, no muss.

Like Dad said, if somehow he flinched at the last moment and ended up unconscious, at least the freezing-cold sea would finish the job quickly.

"Anyway, it's not like I'm giving up," he mumbled as he took hold of the ladder and began to climb down.

No way, Son. I'm so frickin proud of you. You held out, Leo. You're the very definition of a born survivor. Marine material for sure.

"Thanks, Dad," Leon replied. "You remember that time you told me I was a waste-of-space loser?"

I do. I was so, so wrong, Son.

"Yes, you were."

He began to make his way down the creaking, old spiral stairway. He realized he hadn't actually descended this far since last summer. It had been six months since he'd last tried limping down these creaking, old, rusty steps.

"Echo!" His voice echoed around the cavernous darkness and rang the word back at him as he clanked his way slowly down the last few steps.

He could see the faint outline of the doors at the base, light seeping around their edges.

"Let's not be total dicks about this," he said. "We're just going to unbolt and open. We're gonna step over to the rail and do this. OK?" His voice echoed in the dark all around him. "That's the plan. Are you with me, Dad?"

I'm with you, MonkeyNuts. I always have been.

He stepped across the basement floor in total darkness, guided

361

only by the door's outline. He stepped on granules of broken glass that crackled, on something tacky that squelched in the dark, then Leon found himself beside the door.

He knew, the moment his hand grasped the bolt, there could be no stopping. No last-moment jitters or change of heart. No deals with God.

He could hear the soft moaning of the gentle wind outside squeezing its way through the cracks. This world was slowing down, cooling down, going into a hibernation from which it might never wake up.

It's time to leave the party, Leon.

"I know, Dad."

And don't go beating yourself up, Son. It's not like you're checking out early. You fought for as long as you could.

He could the feel the weight of the gun in his anorak, bumping against his ribs.

Let's go, Son.

He reached out for the bolt and found it with the tips of his fingers.

CHAPTER
51

"Hey...Leon?" The voice echoed around in the darkness.

He remained where he stood, stock-still, his fingers on the bolt, his other hand wrapped around the gun's grip.

"Leon?"

The voice was female. If it had been male, he would have let it go and stepped out. He wasn't delusional; he knew he'd been talking to himself for the last two years. He knew Dad was dead and gone, not keeping him company up there in that room.

But this voice was female. "Leon...don't go outside."

It was vaguely familiar. Not Kim though. Kim had had a London accent. Not Cora—she'd had a *northern* accent. Maybe he really *had* gone nuts. He heard the soft scrape of something moving closer to him.

He slid the bolt and pushed the door open. Light flooded in, pushing back the gloom and revealing a figure standing in the middle of the damp and cluttered floor.

"It's me," she said.

The figure was still forming. In the half-light, he could see the glistening nodules of knitting flesh, dangling loops of pink and red tubes pumping raw material into and onto her unfinished frame. Her neck and head, however, had enough skin that he recognized her features.

"Freya?"

"Yes. It's me."

It was her voice. He wasn't yet sure about the waxwork dummy molding itself before his very eyes.

"You...you're the virus?"

"I'm a part of it." She nodded. "Yes."

He was vaguely aware of the cool weight of the gun still in his hand. One swift arm movement, one twitch of his index finger. Not to shoot her, but himself. He knew well enough how ineffective guns were on the virus.

"I can guess what you've come down to do... Please don't."

I'm looking at Freya. She's right there. She's right in front of me. That's her!

Another voice inside his head, equally compelling, was screaming: *That's not Freya! That's not her. That's a viral!*

He jerked the gun out of his jacket and...

"No!" she cried.

...put the barrel to the side of his head.

"DON'T!"

She didn't move forward, didn't try to reach out for the gun. Instead, she held her still-forming hands out—an invitation, not a threatening gesture.

PLAGUE LAND: NO ESCAPE

"Forget our pact!" she cried. The words bounced around the enclosed space while outside the freezing-cold sea slapped lazily against the rocks. "Forget it. We were so wrong!" Her voice was firm. "Death is death, Leon. It's stupid. It's really stupid!" She smiled. "You know, it's for morons with no imagination."

That sounded so like her. He realized he wanted her to sound convincing. Wanted it so badly. His finger fidgeted on the trigger, gentle compressing and releasing it, compressing and releasing, anxious, it seemed, to get on with the plan as previously agreed.

"You go and do that, and there'll be nothing left of you, Leon," she said. "No rebirth. No second chance. You're gone for good."

"That's the point," he replied.

"Then it's a dumb point."

He lowered the gun ever so slightly. "You *are* Freya...aren't you?"

"Uh-huh. I know I don't look so good." She smiled. "Bad hair day."

"What...what happened to you?"

"The very same thing that happened to Grace. To everyone else."

"She's infected too?"

"She was saved. And she saved me."

Second by second, he could see Freya's form developing, her skin knitting, thickening, losing its shiny translucency and acquiring opacity and color. Like a ghostly form emerging from a mist. The ethereal becoming real. He could hear liquids moving in the darkness behind her, drips of goo running down and puddling, the soft crackling of hard-edged resin fragments locking into place.

"I don't want to die," he whispered. "You...you got that, right? You understand?"

"I know."

"But I *will*. Tonight. When it gets dark. I'm finally gonna run out of—"

"We know."

"Fuel. I'll freeze. I'll go to sleep, then I won't ever wake up again." Saying that out loud to her, his voice hitched and he struggled to hold back a sob. "But I…I don't want to g-go that way either. I don't want to die."

"Then take my hand, Leon."

He shook his head. He glanced at the glistening crisscrossing growth tendrils on the floor, throbbing gently as they propelled forward the gobbets of soft tissue inside them. "I…I…really can't…"

"*Don't be frightened, Son.*"

The faint sound of his father's voice didn't shock Leon. He was certain it was Dad inside his head. Dad, the ever-present adviser, the inner provider of pep talks. He glanced out of the open door at the concrete walkway outside—three steps down, then the rusty, old handrail. In just a second of time, he could run and throw himself over that. If he wasn't killed by the drop onto the rocks three yards below, he'd be unconscious within a minute in the freezing water.

Dead within two.

"The gun or jump? Or you can join us. That's what you're thinking about, right, MonkeyNuts?"

A figure emerged from the gloom behind Freya. Like her, it was in the rapidly accelerated process of completing itself. From both arms, from the stomach, the neck, throbbing umbilical tubes of gristly flesh dangled like gas station fuel hoses. The figure was a nightmarish form, but there was enough of its face for Leon to see it was Dad.

PLAGUE LAND: NO ESCAPE

"You've done so well, Son. You managed to outlast everyone."

Freya nodded. "He's right. We've looked far and wide. Every corner of the planet. We really can't find anyone else left. It really looks like it's just you."

"You're the last man left on Earth," his father said. "It's one hell of an achievement, but it's time to come home, Son."

Leon backed away from the sight of both figures, out through the open door into the half-hearted daylight.

"Leon, please? Don't do it," pleaded Freya.

Both figures took hesitant steps forward.

He was outside now. Out in the unprotected cold. He took one more step backward and felt the small of his back bump up against the handrail. He felt the soft breeze chasing around the base of the lighthouse, chilling his hands and face.

In the daylight now, they stood framed in the doorway, dragging the pumping cords of fluid after them. In the full daylight, he could see through their membranous skin, see a faint webbing of bluish arteries, the pulsating of organic machinery simulating the tasks of human organs. He could see the pull and bulge of cord-like sinews, the gristle and gnarled ends of resinous bones.

It was horror made real.

"Leon, I nearly took my own life. Don't make that mistake."

His father and Freya, flayed of most of their skin and shambling like zombies.

"Leon," implored Freya. "Please...I've missed you so much!"

He shook his head. "You...you're *not* Freya. You're *not* Dad!"

"Leon," said Dad. "This isn't how we are—how we look. This

is not who we are anyway. On the inside, we're complete. We're just as you remember us. And everyone you ever knew is in there."

"Not Mom though."

"No." He shook his head slowly, sadly. "Not Mom, I'm afraid."

"What about Grace?"

"I'm here."

The voice came from his left. He turned and saw her. Grace. Standing right there on the walkway, wrapped in a threadbare parka she must have scavenged from the basement. She was just as he remembered her before the fire, completely unscarred. Precocious and pretty. Small. Intense. The hood was pulled up around her face, her skinny, bare, and pale legs and feet poking comically out at the bottom.

"Oh my God," he whimpered.

"It's me, you big dork." She smiled at him. "Please..." She held out a fully formed hand, her skin as pale and as unblemished as it had always been. "Please," she said again, "believe it's me."

Leon could feel warmth trickling down both of his cheeks. Tears, he realized, as they quickly cooled and soaked into the scant few whiskers of an unconvincing beard.

"We've been looking for you everywhere," she said. "Asking everyone, sending the word all around. Finally...we found you alone out here. Just in time."

Alone. Yes.

He'd counted every day, every minute of his solitude. "What... what's going to h-happen to...to me?"

"We want to take you home, Leo. We want to take you home where you belong."

PLAGUE LAND: NO ESCAPE

The gun. Or join. Decision time.

"You know, *They* told me something," said Grace.

"They?"

"The virus. Deep down in their DNA is their history. It's incredibly ancient, Leon. They've been around almost forever. And guess what." She edged a fraction closer to him.

"W-what?"

"They think they might've been here before."

He was getting very cold now. He wondered how Grace could bear to be standing there with the skin of her legs exposed to the freezing wind.

"B-been here?"

"Uh-huh. Something like this may have happened here *before*."

He looked at Freya and Dad. With every passing second, they were becoming more and more humanlike. Freya's extended hand looked complete, looked like the hand he'd held a long time ago. Held and squeezed. She had lips on her face, lips that he'd kissed once.

And only the once.

"We were like *this*"—Freya gestured back into the gloom behind her—"once before. Joining us now, coming down to live in the inner universe, it's not an end to things, Leon. Trust me! It's not death. It's a *transition.* That's all it is!"

Dad nodded. "It's like heaven, Son."

"It's a return," said Grace. Her hand closed the gap between them, one finger resting gently on the back of his. "Come on. Let's go home, Bro."

Leon closed his eyes, letting the ice-cold world fade away.

The voices were still, waiting for him to make the call. And in the calm silence inside his head...

He took in a deep breath and chose...

AFTERWORD

From the speech of Dr. Edward Chan in the Astrobiology Science Conference, San Diego:

IT'S KNOWN AS THE FERMI PARADOX—THE ASSEMBLING OF A bunch of reasonable assumptions about the almost infinite number of stars and exoplanets out there in the universe and coming to the conclusion that we *should* be being bombarded with extraterrestrial 'howdy' messages.

There are only three conceivable explanations for why we *aren't*. First, life on Earth was a unique one-off, a one-in-a-trillion chance encounter of variables. Second, that the assumptions we made are off by a significant factor. Or, third, there's something else at work, some 'filtering' event that's vacuuming up life wherever it finds it.

I'm inclined to believe life here was not unique. I'm also inclined to believe that we've got our science about right when it comes to considering the permissible boundaries within which life can develop. Therefore, I have to consider the third possibility.

It's not beyond the bounds of probability that in the universe's fourteen-billion-year history, some distant civilization, vastly more advanced than ours, came to the same conclusion that we're encountering now—that space is simply far too big a thing to travel across, that the laws of physics and quantum physics uniformly say a clear and resounding no to interstellar travel.

What would an advanced civilization do when faced with such a damning conclusion? Give up? Accept their fate to remain alone forever? I could imagine they might create some kind of device designed to travel, endlessly reproduce, and spread the memory that they once existed. A viral device maybe. Something that might eventually evolve in its own right, rewrite its core programming. Become something more than how it had been when it started out. Perhaps, if RNA truly is a universal constant for life, it might even, one day, bring us the genes of creatures far and wide, and, in turn, gift our DNA to civilizations who would never otherwise have had a chance to meet us.

ACKNOWLEDGMENTS

WRITING THIS SERIES REQUIRED MORE THAN JUST A SICK MIND and a laptop. Behind my name on the cover exists a team whom I shall name and thank now.

Thank you, Debbie Scarrow, for countless rereads and feedback (sometimes necessarily blunt!). Thank you, Venetia Gosling and Lucy Pearse at Macmillan Children's Books, for being my editors; your work has taken this series upward several notches in quality. Thanks to Rachel Vale and James Annal, for fantastic covers and design. And thank you, Veronica Lyons, Samantha Stewart, and Nick de Somogyi, for being the final line of defense and sparing my blushes!

ABOUT THE AUTHOR

ALEX SCARROW USED TO BE A ROCK GUITARIST. AFTER TEN years in various unsuccessful bands he ended up working in the computer games industry as a lead games designer. He now has his own games development company, Grrr Games. He is the author of the bestselling and award-winning TimeRiders series, which has been sold into over thirty foreign territories. *Plague Land: No Escape* is the third and final book in the explosive Plague Land trilogy with Sourcebooks Fire.

Visit his website at alexscarrow.com.

WANT MORE THRILLS? CHECK OUT *H₂O* BY VIRGINIA BERGIN.

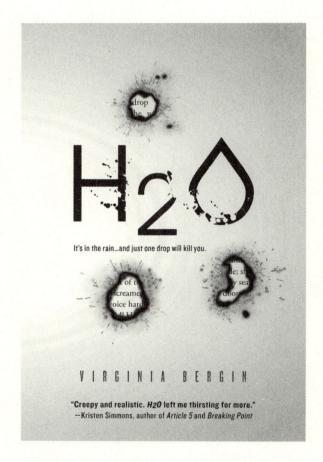

It's in the rain...and one drop will kill you.

#getbooklit

Your hub for the hottest young adult books!

Visit us online and sign up for our newsletter at FIREreads.com

 @sourcebooksfire

 sourcebooksfire

 firereads.tumblr.com